Dear Reader,

Do *you* have a secret fantasy? Everybody does. Maybe it's to be rich and famous and beautiful. Or to start a no-strings affair with a sexy mysterious stranger. Or to have a sizzling second chance with a former sweetheart…. You'll find these dreams—and much more—in Temptation's exciting new yearlong promotion, Secret Fantasies.

Versatile, quirky Lynn Michaels has written another winner with her unusual and compelling version of one of the enduring romantic myths—the vampire. Willow Evans has no idea what she's getting herself into when she inherits her grandmother's Cape Cod house. At least, not until she meets Jonathan Raven….

In the coming months, look for Secret Fantasies books by Kate Hoffmann, Tiffany White and Madeline Harper. Please write and let us know how you enjoy the "fantasy."

Happy Reading!

The Editors

c/o Harlequin Temptation
225 Duncan Mill Road
Don Mills, Ontario
M3B 3K9
Canada

Dear Reader,

If your M&M candies didn't melt in your hand when Frank Langella turned his head and looked straight into the camera in *Dracula*, then, my dear, you and I need to talk.

If your pulse didn't race when Errol Flynn buckled his swash in *Captain Blood*, well, then—never mind.

These are two of my favorite secret fantasies— vampires and pirates—which I really enjoyed mixing in *Nightwing*. I also had a good time poking fun at—and holes in—some of the sillier myths about vampires.

There's something deliciously kinky about a tall, dark and handsome man with a widow's peak and very sharp teeth…something dangerously wicked about a tall, dark and handsome man with a gleam in his eye and a frilly white shirt open to the navel….

Turn the page and find out what. And just to be on the safe side, leave the M&M's in the fridge.

Lynn Michaels

*Y*ou're About to Become a
*P*rivileged
*W*oman.

INTRODUCING
PAGES & PRIVILEGES™.

It's our way of thanking you for buying
our books at your favorite retail store.

— *G*ET ALL THIS *F*REE —
WITH JUST ONE PROOF OF PURCHASE:

◆ Hotel Discounts up to 60% at home and abroad

◆ Travel Service - Guaranteed lowest published
airfares plus 5% cash back on tickets

◆ $25 Travel Voucher

◆ Sensuous Petite Parfumerie collection ($50 value)

◆ Insider Tips Letter with sneak previews of
upcoming books

◆ Mystery Gift (if you enroll before 6/15/95)

*Y*ou'll get a FREE personal card, too.
*It's your passport to all these benefits– and to
even more great gifts & benefits to come!*

There's no club to join. No purchase commitment. No obligation.

As a Privileged Woman,
you'll be entitled to all these Free Benefits.
And Free Gifts, too.

To thank you for buying our books, we've designed an exclusive FREE program called *PAGES & PRIVILEGES*™. You can enroll with just one Proof of Purchase, and get the kind of luxuries that, until now, you could only read about.

BIG HOTEL DISCOUNTS

A privileged woman stays in the finest hotels. And so can you—at up to 60% off! Imagine standing in a hotel check-in line and watching as the guest in front of you pays $150 for the same room that's only costing you $60. Your *Pages & Privileges* discounts are good at Sheraton, Marriott, Best Western, Hyatt and thousands of other fine hotels all over the U.S., Canada and Europe.

FREE DISCOUNT TRAVEL SERVICE

A privileged woman is always jetting to romantic places. When <u>you</u> fly, just make one phone call for the lowest published airfare at time of booking—<u>or double the difference back</u>! PLUS—

you'll get a $25 voucher to use the first time you book a flight AND <u>5% cash back on every ticket you buy thereafter through the travel service</u>!

*F*REE GIFTS!

A privileged woman is always getting wonderful gifts.
Luxuriate in rich fragrances that will stir your senses (and his). This gift-boxed assortment of fine perfumes includes three popular scents, each in a beautiful designer bottle. <u>Truly Lace</u>...This luxurious fragrance unveils your sensuous side. <u>L'Effleur</u>...discover the romance of the Victorian era with this soft floral. <u>Muguet des bois</u>...a single note floral of singular beauty. This $50 value is yours—FREE when you enroll in *Pages & Privileges*! And it's just the beginning of the gifts and benefits that will be coming your way!

$50 VALUE

*F*REE INSIDER TIPS LETTER

A privileged woman is always informed. And you'll be, too, with our free letter full of fascinating information and sneak previews of upcoming books.

*M*ORE GREAT GIFTS & BENEFITS TO COME

A privileged woman always has a lot to look forward to.
And so will you. You get all these wonderful FREE gifts and benefits now with only one purchase...and there are no additional purchases required. However, each additional retail purchase of Harlequin and Silhouette books brings you a step closer to even more great FREE benefits like half-price movie tickets...and even more FREE gifts like these beautiful fragrance gift baskets:

L'Effleur ...This basketful of romance lets you discover L'Effleur from head to toe, heart to home.

Truly Lace ...A basket spun with the sensuous luxuries of Truly Lace, including Dusting Powder in a reusable satin and lace covered box.

*E*NROLL *N*OW!

Complete the Enrollment Form on the back of this card and become a Privileged Woman today!

Enroll Today in *PAGES & PRIVILEGES*™, the program that gives you Great Gifts and Benefits with just one purchase!

Enrollment Form

☐ *Yes!* I WANT TO BE A *PRIVILEGED WOMAN*.

Enclosed is one *PAGES & PRIVILEGES*™ Proof of Purchase from any Harlequin or Silhouette book currently for sale in stores (Proofs of Purchase are found on the back pages of books) and the store cash register receipt. Please enroll me in *PAGES & PRIVILEGES*™. Send my Welcome Kit and FREE Gifts -- and activate my FREE benefits -- immediately.

NAME (please print)

ADDRESS   APT. NO

CITY   STATE   ZIP/POSTAL CODE

PROOF OF PURCHASE

Please allow 6-8 weeks for delivery. Quantities are limited. We reserve the right to substitute items. Enroll before October 31, 1995 and receive one full year of benefits.

NO CLUB!
NO COMMITMENT!
Just one purchase brings you great *Free Gifts* and *Benefits!*
(See inside for details.)

Name of store where this book was purchased_____

Date of purchase_____

Type of store:

☐ Bookstore   ☐ Supermarket   ☐ Drugstore

☐ Dept. or discount store (e.g. K-Mart or Walmart)

☐ Other (specify)_____

Which Harlequin or Silhouette series do you usually read?

_____

Complete and mail with one Proof of Purchase and store receipt to:

U.S.: *PAGES & PRIVILEGES*™, P.O. Box 1960, Danbury, CT 06813-1960

Canada: *PAGES & PRIVILEGES*™, 49-6A The Donway West, P.O. 813, North York, ON M3C 2E8   PRINTED IN U.S.A

Nothing. That was what Willow saw.

Absolutely nothing in the mirror she aimed over her right shoulder at Raven's retreating back.

"Wait a minute," she muttered, angling the glass higher—and still saw nothing in the mirror but Raven's car. Willie didn't get it, not even when she saw the driver's door open by itself. She thought there had to be something wrong with the mirror, so she turned around.

Turned around in time to see Raven glance up and wave at her as he slid behind the wheel of the car and leaned forward to turn the key in the ignition. Willie frowned and waved back and aimed the mirror at the car.

She still couldn't see Raven.

The powerful growl of the departing engine sent a shiver up her spine. What was it she'd thought earlier? That she didn't know much about mirrors? Except that they were expensive to resilver and you couldn't see vampires in them....

Talented and versatile **Lynn Michaels,** who also writes as Paula Christopher, is an award-winning, bestselling author who specializes in unusual but always intriguing stories. Known for her humor and fast pacing, she often jokes that if it weren't for the weird stuff, she'd have nothing to write about. Luckily, she finds weird stuff at every turn.

Lynn, her husband and their two boys make their home in Missouri.

Books by Lynn Michaels

HARLEQUIN TEMPTATION

NIGHTWING
Lynn Michaels

Harlequin Books

TORONTO • NEW YORK • LONDON
AMSTERDAM • PARIS • SYDNEY • HAMBURG
STOCKHOLM • ATHENS • TOKYO • MILAN
MADRID • WARSAW • BUDAPEST • AUCKLAND

With thanks to:
Linda Randall Wisdom, for the "Forever Knight" tapes
Connie Severson, for helping me refine my vision
Nancy Haddock, B.S., M.A., Speech-Language Pathology, for
double-checking my sign language
Malle Vallik, my editor, for going on
vacation at just the right time
Special thanks to
Frank Langella, Errol Flynn and Geraint Wyn Davies,
for their inspiration and very strange dreams

ISBN 0-373-25642-6

NIGHTWING

Copyright © 1995 by Lynne Smith.

Printed in U.S.A.

Prologue

Egypt, August 1878

HIS HORSE, A BLACK ARAB mare whose name he couldn't pronounce, was saddled and waiting, cropping dry grass sprouting on the banks of the wadi. The camp mule hitched to one of the high-sided, two-wheeled carts used to haul supplies lazed in its traces.

The mare was ready, the mule was ready and still Jolil prayed, facing east, kneeling on a sandy prayer rug in the thin shade beneath the palm trees. Shouting at him to hurry would do no good; he'd only pray longer. Eleven months in Egypt had taught Jonathan Raven that much, at least.

He sighed and stepped inside the medical tent to triple-check his store of quinine. The wadi was dry now, but the rains would come again soon, as would the mosquitoes. The sluggish green water the Nile belched into the ditch would blacken with larvae, no matter how many times Raven ordered it skimmed off and buried in the sand. There was no such thing as too much quinine. Not in Egypt in the rainy season.

Even with sunset approaching and one canvas side of the tent thrown back, the hot air trapped inside was almost unbreathable. Raven made a last check of his medical stores and ducked quickly outside. Jolil was still praying.

He sat down to wait on a folding stool. The pink cliffs encircling the Valley of the Kings, the Land of the Dead, burial place of the pharaohs of ancient Egypt, shimmered in waves of heat rising from the desert floor. When the sun sank behind them, the temperature would plummet and the sweat stinging the back of his neck would make him shiver.

It would be a chilly first leg of the three-day trek to Cairo, but the idea was to get there and back alive, not kill themselves and the mare and the mule in the process. Traveling at night was sometimes dangerous, but there was no risk of heat stroke, a major killer of white men stupid enough to cross the desert by day. And there were no snakes.

Raven hated snakes. His old Harvard chum, Teddy Gorham, a junior foreman on this joint Anglo-American dig, hadn't breathed a word about cobras or horned vipers when he'd approached Raven to serve as chief medical officer on this two-year project. Teddy, an assistant curator at the Boston Museum, had spun tales of adventure and treasure and sloe-eyed belly dancers wreathed in nothing but transparent veils. Raven had yet to see a transparent veil. Most of them were black, head-to-foot shrouds, not see-through gauze.

He'd lost count of how many snakes he'd killed and bites he'd treated. One or two on good old Teddy. Minor enough that Raven took perverse pleasure in them, for Teddy wore only ankle-high work boots, eschewing the thick, knee-high leather riding boots Raven took off only when he bathed.

He was beginning to hate boots, too. When he got to Cairo he'd take them off first thing. And he wouldn't put them on again until he and Jolil headed back to Thebes.

If they ever got to Cairo. The wiry little Egyptian's forehead was still pressed to his prayer rug. Raven leaned his elbows on his knees and raked his fingers through his hair. It was too long and too hot, curling well below the unbuttoned collar of his thin Egyptian cotton shirt. In Cairo he'd find a barber who spoke English or French and get a haircut. It was that or buy a ribbon in the Mouski, the bazaar.

He planned to buy an Egyptian shawl and silver bracelets for his mother, a piece of pottery for his brother, Samuel, and ship them home to Stonebridge, Massachusetts in time for Christmas. It would be almost autumn there now. The leaves of the beach plums would already be turning, and the whales would be singing in the moonlight on Nantucket Sound.

Whale song was the reason his whaling-captain grandfather had built the house close to the beach. Raven would hear humpbacks sing again, but not for thirteen more months filled with sand and heat and snakes.

At last Jolil finished his prayers, rolled his rug and rose to his feet. "So, hakim, you are ready?"

"I've been ready for a while, Jolil." Raven set the stool inside the tent and dropped the flap. He'd already slid his carbine into his saddle holster. "For the last half hour."

"You had only to say so." Jolil laid his rug in the mule cart and gave him a wounded look. "I live to serve you."

So long as it didn't interfere with prayers or petty thieving. Most of the natives stole, mostly small artifacts from the dig to sell on the black market. Raven looked the other way and had made it clear to Jolil he would, so long as he kept his hands off his medical supplies. The dark little man who lived to serve him was one of the sneakiest thieves in the camp. Perhaps that was why his prayers were so lengthy.

"Never mind, Jolil. Let's just be on our way."

"Your wish is my command, hakim."

Jolil scrambled into the cart and clucked to the mule. The black mare laid back her ears as Raven gathered her reins and swung himself into the saddle. She snorted and arched her neck as another mule came flying at a gallop over the rise behind the wadi.

Its unshod hooves flung up a wake of dust and sand. The Egyptian on its back was Yusef, Teddy's servant, whose dark eyes were as wide and wild as those of the lathered mule.

"Hakim!" he screamed. *"Yallah! Yallah!"*

Doctor, hurry, hurry. Raven understood that much, and the word *turab*—tomb—but the rest of Yusef's panicked Arabic was lost to him as the mare whinnied and spun away on her hind legs. Jolil hauled the cart mule to a stop, leapt down from the high seat and ran to catch the bridle of Yusef's badly blowing mule.

Raven saw the pulse beating in the hollow of Yusef's throat above the open, sweat-darkened neck of his robe. He was babbling, gesturing wildly in the direction of the dig with one arm and tugging at Jolil with the other.

"What is it, Jolil? What's happened?"

"It is very bad, hakim. Many men hurt. Yusef says there is much blood."

"My kit. Quick. Then bring the cart. We may need it."

Jolil ran into the tent for Raven's canvas medical bag and tossed it to him. He caught it by its strap, looped it over his saddle and gave the mare a sharp kick. She snorted and leapt at a gallop over the rise toward the dig.

The sun was just touching the rim of the cliffs, throwing thick black shadows across the rutted cart track scarring the valley. Gooseflesh rose on the back of Raven's neck. Not from the chill creeping into the air, but the high-pitched wails of the native workmen rushing toward him, waving their arms. One stood in the center of the track flagging him toward the ravine where the diggers had been dumping baskets full of sand and rock hauled away from the entrance of the tomb Teddy had been excavating for the past three weeks.

"Hakim!" he shouted. *"Hena! Yallah! Yallah!"*

Here. Hurry, hurry. Poor bastards, Raven thought. Probably caught in a cave-in while sifting through the debris for small artifacts Teddy and his crew might have missed. Raven glanced behind him and saw Jolil—with Yusef beside him on the seat—bouncing the mule cart over the rise. He heeled the mare off the track toward the ravine.

There were two men on the ground near the graveled rim of the ditch. One was dead, his face and upper body covered with someone's brightly striped outer robe—Yusef's, he thought. Teddy knelt beside the other, his back blocking Raven's view. Two natives were holding the man down; his thin, dark legs were twitching and white with dust.

Raven pulled the mare to a stop, kicked his right foot out of his stirrup, unlooped his bag from the pommel, swung his leg over it and dropped to the ground running. Teddy glanced at him over his shoulder, his sweat-darkened felt hat pushed back on his thick brown hair, his sunburned face oddly pale.

"Johnny! Thank God! Help me!"

Teddy was holding a blood-soaked bandage to the man's throat. Or what was left of it. Most of it was torn away, Raven saw when he lifted Teddy's hand. The brown flesh was ripped and jagged, the exposed carotid artery no longer spraying but seeping and pulsing dully.

There was nothing Raven could do. He knew it before he dropped to his knees on the man's other side. His robe was soaked to the waist with blood, as were Teddy's shirt and the robes of the men holding him down. There was no pulse in the thin, brown wrist Raven gripped. The pupil of the man's right eye was already fixed and dilated when he lifted the lid; the eye rolled forward.

"It's too late, Teddy. He'll be gone in a minute. What in God's name happened?"

"The diggers found a tomb in the ravine, thought they'd loot it on their own and make a fortune on the black market." Teddy sat back on his heels, wiping sweat off his forehead with the back of one shaking, bloody hand. "Seven of them went in but only these two came out. They were attacked. By a jackal, they said. A jackal that walked on two legs."

A shudder racked the man on the ground. His eyes fluttered open, his limbs convulsed once, then stilled. Raven closed his eyes and smoothed the death grin from his face.

"Did you send a search party in after the others?"

"None of the diggers will go."

"Then we'll have to," Raven said. He'd taken an oath to save lives, but he suddenly wished he'd never come to Egypt.

"I know. That's why I waited for you."

Raven stepped over the body and lifted Yusef's robe. The other man had also had his throat ripped out. He lowered the robe and glanced over his shoulder at the mule cart thumping to a halt on the rocky ground behind him.

Teddy rose, called to Yusef and Jolil to bring torches, then asked Raven in a low voice, "What the hell did this, Johnny? Jackals don't walk on two legs."

"They might, Teddy. In the guise of tomb robbers."

"And rip a man's throat out like this?"

"Hardly. But a two-thousand-year-old dagger that's lost its edge might."

"Possible, I suppose. Come see this."

He led Raven down the steep, rocky ravine toward a gaping black hole cut in the opposite flank. The edges were clean, sharp and obviously chiseled. The loose shingle rattling away beneath their boots bounced against a tall stone slab carved with rude hieroglyphs that meant nothing to Raven.

"Here's where they got the jackal." Teddy blew dust off the slab and pointed at an angular figure with the body of a man and the head of a jackal. The open mouth revealed top and bottom fangs bared in a stiff, stylized snarl. "It's Anubis, god of the dead. He's always depicted with the head of a jackal, but this is the first time I've seen him with fangs."

"Seems logical. A jackal is a carnivore." Raven pointed to a row of smaller pictographs below the figure of Anubis. "What's this say?"

"The usual warning, open this tomb and die. And the name of the person interred here." Teddy tugged a small, stiff brush out of his back pocket and swept away more sand. "It's someone named—Nekhat. There's more, but I can't make it out. Looks like these glyphs were done in a real hurry."

Raven heard the shingle rattling behind him and glanced up the slope at Jolil and Yusef stumbling toward them, each carrying two torches. Teddy fished matches out of his pocket, struck them and lit the brands.

He gave one to Raven, one to Jolil and the other to Yusef. The two Egyptians looked nervously at each other.

"I don't want to go in here any more than you do, but if you don't go with us, none of them will ever enter another tomb." Teddy nodded at the knot of workmen milling and muttering on the edge of the ravine. "Just stay close. Johnny, you bring up the rear."

Raven gripped the torch in his left hand, looped the strap of his medical bag over his right shoulder, caught the lintel over the doorway and ducked beneath it behind Jolil. The stone felt oddly cold; the air inside the tomb, trapped in a narrow, empty chamber with a low ceiling and rough-hewn walls, smelled fetid and faintly of rust.

The next chamber was equally bare and unadorned. Teddy stepped closer to a wall, his torch gutting in a breath of air sweeping toward them from the next room. The flame danced over rudely sketched, merely outlined figures.

"This tomb isn't finished, is it?" Raven asked.

"Hardly started," Teddy said, puzzled. He moved forward and called out in Arabic.

No one answered. Raven saw why when he ducked into the next chamber behind Jolil and heard his sharp intake of breath. In the flickering torchlight he saw the walls, splashed and smeared with blood, and the other five men who had entered the tomb, two torn literally limb from limb.

"Jesus, Mary and Joseph," Teddy murmured in a stricken whisper. "There isn't a dagger anywhere in heaven or hell that could do this, Johnny."

Another breath of air sighed toward them from the inky depths of the tomb, eerie enough to bristle every hair on Raven's body. So was the growl that came with it, echoing faintly off the walls and shivering up his back. Jolil stopped murmuring prayers and began to tremble.

"Get out. Get out and run." Raven grabbed him, then Yusef, and shoved them back into the second chamber. He grabbed Teddy and pushed him, stiff with shock, through the doorway. "C'mon, Teddy. *Move.*"

He did and stumbled in the doorway, dropping his torch. The light fell by half and darkness engulfed Raven, swept him up in cold, fierce claws and sank icy fangs into his throat: two below his jaw, two more scraping the cervical bones in the back of his neck.

He felt the punctures, felt his flesh tear and hot, prickling pain shoot down his arms. He managed to lift them, somehow, his medical kit sliding off his shoulder, and flail his torch at the thing gripping him from behind. It bellowed and dropped him, leapt over him and Teddy and then whirled on them once again, shrieking with rage.

Through the haze filming his eyes, Raven saw Teddy roll on his back, torch and sidearm raised. He fired two shots, point-blank, into the chest of what appeared to be a man, a pharaoh come alive in a golden kilt and braided, black wig. It only roared and snarled, flexing bronze muscles in powerful arms. A tall, handsome figure of a man, except for the bared, bloody fangs gleaming in the torchlight.

Teddy fired two more shots, screaming something Raven couldn't hear over the roar in his head. He saw the barrel flash twice more and Jolil and Yusef leap at the thing from behind, their swinging torches spraying trails of sparks through the dark chamber.

The creature spun around and flung out its arms, toppling Jolil and Yusef as it sprang toward the entrance to the tomb. The last clear thing Raven saw was a jewel, a fiery opalescent stone flashing in a heavy gold amulet around the thing's neck, then its shape blurred out of focus, wavered and shifted like smoke onto all fours in the shape of a jackal.

Raven felt blood pooling in the back of his throat, felt an icy, deathly cold seeping through his veins from the punctures in his neck. He tried to swallow, but couldn't. The muscles were frozen. So were his eyelids, wide open and staring at the low, stone ceiling and the pale, ghostly image of himself rising from his body.

Panic seized him. He felt it thudding wildly in his chest, though he knew his heart had stopped beating. He was dead. Oh, God, he was dead. Lying on the floor of the tomb with his throat torn out, gazing up at himself, at the bewildered, disoriented expression on his face.

He watched his mouth open to scream, but he made no sound, watched himself turn away from his body, reeling and staggering out of the tomb behind the thing—dear God, what was it?—that had killed him. Come back, he screamed silently at himself. Come back, come back.

We're not dead.

1

Stonebridge, Massachusetts
Present Day

HE FOUND HIMSELF on the beach again, as he always did when he came back to Cape Cod, to the house near the town of Stonebridge where he'd been born. He came back every now and then, he wasn't sure how often, usually within months but sometimes days of his birthday, July 19.

He was a Cancer, a child of the moon, but this time, he returned in sunlight on a blazing afternoon. The sky was white with heat, the sun a shimmering silver disk melting toward the horizon behind him. He felt it sizzle on his shoulders, felt the scorched sand throb beneath his boot soles.

He sat down facing the sea, his back to the withered salt grass wilting against the flanks of the dunes. He then tipped his head back and looped his arms around his drawn-up knees. The heat was a balm to him after the long, numbing cold.

He was here for a reason, but he couldn't remember what it was. Or where he'd come from. He used to know things like that, lots of things, but they were gone now, just simply not there—the way he was most of the time. He didn't think he was dead. He didn't feel dead, just disconnected. Something had happened to him, but he couldn't remember what. He couldn't even remember his name.

His senses still worked, though he didn't know how. He could see and hear and touch and taste and smell. He could weep, but he shed no tears. He could laugh but he made no sound. He knew one other thing—that it was a blessing he couldn't remember anything else.

He sat gazing at the sea until the tide began to crash on the beach and the swells behind the foam-headed breakers began to darken. He got up then and blinked at the sky, at the sun shooting long silver beams through the purple and gray clouds on the horizon. It was still hot, yet he felt himself shiver. It was nearly sunset. Time to get himself up to the house and hide until morning.

He didn't know what he was hiding from, any more than he knew which one of the paths beaten through the beach grass to follow. He always picked the right one, always found his way through the maze of sandy hills that buffered the land from the sea. When the house came into view he stopped on the crest of the last dune and smiled.

Someone had given its clapboard sides a fresh coat of white paint and changed the color of its shutters from weather-beaten green to bright, cheery blue. There were clay pots of flowers on the flagged terrace, and pink and white and salmon geraniums atop a table with a glass top and a yellow umbrella.

Joy swelled in his chest. This was how the house was supposed to look, how he remembered it, when he could. He ran down the hill through the open French doors in the dining room. Sheer curtains fluttered in the offshore breeze.

It was wonderful inside. The heavy, dark furniture and scratchy woolen carpets were gone. Oak tables and bookcases filled the downstairs rooms. Ceiling fans whirred softly, fluttering the edges of a magazine left open on a chair.

In the kitchen, a jar of yellow poppies wilted in a blue mason jar on a white-tiled table. A pot of chicken flavored with tarragon and swimming with noodles and carrots bubbled on the stove. He put back the burning-hot lid he'd lifted without a pot holder and raced up the stairs laughing, taking two steps at a time.

The bedrooms were beautiful, filled with brass-and-enameled beds covered with handmade quilts. There were only four instead of six. Two were bathrooms now. He rushed into one of the bedrooms, then outside through another set of French doors onto the widow's walk.

The railing was new, waist high and painted white. Last time he was here, the old one had been broken and rotted. He remembered that now, but he didn't remember if the chaise longue padded with yellow cushions had been there or not. Why couldn't he remember?

His joy fading, he went back inside and sat on the foot of a bed made with pink sheets and a double-wedding-ring quilt. The iron spring beneath the mattress didn't squeak. He clasped his hands between his knees and looked at himself in the mirror bolted to the wall above a cherry dresser.

His hair was wind tousled and too long, the ends curling just below the collar of his full-sleeve white shirt. The top buttons were missing, and the gaped front exposed his throat and a fair portion of his chest. Rusty red stains splashed the front of his shirt. Dirt streaked his brown leather vest and buff-colored breeches. Sand caked his knee-high boots.

He didn't like boots. He remembered that now. They were too damned hot, but they protected him from snakes. Only slightly more than he hated boots, he hated snakes, so he wore them. But not here. He never wore them here. He didn't need them. There were crabs and starfish in the tidal pools, but not a single cobra or horned viper within two thousand miles of Stonebridge, Massachusetts.

He crossed his right leg over his left knee, reached for his boot and caught another glimpse of himself in the mirror. Disgraceful. He'd find a barber who spoke English when next he trekked the three days by mule cart to Cairo for supplies. He'd get a haircut. Or buy a ribbon in the bazaar.

A shiver laced through him and his hands froze on the heel and toe of his boot. What the hell was he doing in Egypt? How had he gotten here? It was a three-month trip by clipper ship from Nantucket, but he couldn't remember a boat. He couldn't remember anything but snakes.

And cold. But the desert wasn't cold. It was vicious and merciless and filled with terrors far greater than cobras or sand vipers. He knew that better than anyone, but he couldn't remember how he knew.

He didn't remember the girl who came humming out of the bathroom wrapped in a yellow towel, either, her collarbones dewy and gleaming above the tuck between her breasts, her bare feet leaving wet prints on the pegged-pine floor. He leapt off the bed, catching the white-enameled frame in his hand as he backed hastily away from it. He expected her to scream, but she didn't.

She didn't so much as glance at him standing by the foot of her bed. She just kept humming, a song he didn't know, or one he couldn't remember, as she opened a dresser drawer and wiped a trickle of water from the hollow of her throat with an end of the towel.

Her hair was auburn and damp, pinned to the top of her head in rich, dark red curls. He could just see her full mouth and short, upturned nose in the corner of the mirror. He couldn't see that her eyes were brown until she lifted them as she shut the drawer and turned around.

He expected her to scream then—she was looking right at him—but she didn't. She simply walked *through* him, still dabbing at her throat, still humming. He felt her voice in every atom of his being, felt every hair in every follicle on his body stand on end, and realized with a jolt, and an anguished cry she couldn't hear, that he was dead.

2

THE CHILL THAT SHOT through Willie Evans was as cold as a
November no'theaster. It made her shiver and remember
Granma Boyle's caution against cool baths in summer.

"Warm all year round, no matter what the temperature,"
she'd say in her starched Yankee accent. "Otherwise, you'll
give yourself the ague."

Willie had always thought it was one of Granma's wacky
old wives' tales. She'd never given herself the ague—whatever that was—and she'd been taking cool baths in the summer, in the house her grandmother had named Beaches, for
most of her life.

She preferred showers now, rather than soaks in the claw-
footed tub in the bathroom she'd turned into a combination
bath and laundry room. Best money she'd ever spent, even
though it had taken every dime she'd inherited from Granma
along with Beaches last August, as well as a good chunk of
her trust fund from Grandfather Evans.

Her father had thrown a fit. First that she hadn't sold "the
old wreck," his term for both Beaches and Granma, and second that she'd sunk a bloody blue fortune into the house.
Behind his back, her mother had rolled her eyes.

So did Willie, remembering, as she put on her underwear,
rubbed the chill off her arms and opened the louvered doors
of the walk-in closet she'd happily sacrificed twelve feet of
space for. Her father had thrown a fit about the closet, too,
but he'd done it long-distance, since by mid-January Willie
was firmly entrenched at Beaches.

Three weeks before, on December 24, right after the public relations department Christmas party, *Material Girl*
magazine had handed her a pink slip. When she'd called her

mother in tears, Amelia Boyle Evans had slogged her way across Manhattan's upper west side in a blizzard to comfort her. Two weeks later when her father left for Paris to attend a banking seminar, her mother had pleaded the flu to stay home and help Willie sublet her apartment, pack and get out of town. Not quite in a New York minute, but close.

Whitaker Evans hated Beaches—he said the old wreck gave him the creeps—and he'd come straight from Kennedy to drag his only daughter back to New York. By her hair, if necessary, he'd warned as he'd come through the door. It had been close, but Willie had held firm. She still had her independence and still had Beaches, too. And she was determined to keep both.

The house was her haven and always had been, just as Granma had been a warm-fuzzy extension of her mother, a much-needed second buffer between Willie and her well-intentioned but autocratic father. So was Zen, short for Zenobia Greene, her best friend from college and a certifiable New Age wacko. She'd come up to "get in tune" on the spring solstice and announced that Beaches had good vibes. Willie agreed. She felt safe here, watched over almost, which hadn't made a lick of sense to her father.

Whitaker Evans hadn't been able to budge her out of the house, and Dr. Jonathan Raven wasn't going to, either. He could take the last will and testament of his great-uncle, Horace Raven, from whose estate Granma Boyle had bought Beaches, and shove it sideways. It wasn't Willie's fault the probate clerk dropped the will behind a filing cabinet in 1947 and forgot to fish it out and register it.

She had money enough to keep her fledgling public relations firm afloat and Dr. Raven's claim to Beaches tied up in court for a good long time if it came to that. Willie hoped it wouldn't, hoped her attorney-brother Whit Junior knew what he was talking about and wasn't merely doing Whit Senior's bidding when he'd suggested this evening's meeting to try to work out an equitable settlement.

"If this is business," she'd demanded, "why do I have to invite him to dinner?"

"Because you're a damn good cook and it'll soften him up. Make fried chicken. It's my favorite."

"You're coming?" Willie had been amazed, since Whit shared their father's distaste for Beaches.

"'Course I am. You're my sister and this Raven character could be an ax murderer for all we know."

Willie doubted it, since he was a doctor. She'd agreed to the meeting, even though she hadn't liked the idea of inviting into her house a man who was trying to take it away from her. She still didn't, but she trusted Whit. Loved him, too, and was always glad to see him, which wasn't often, even though he lived in Boston. He was like their father, a workaholic. Willie was a Boyle, and that said it all.

She put on a sundress with tiny yellow flowers printed on sage green cotton, tied the sash below her breasts, unpinned her hair and brushed it out to dry around her shoulders in its usual thick curls. It was too hot to do anything else but slip her feet into yellow sandals.

As she sat down on the bed to buckle them, Willie noticed a gray blur in the bottom left corner of the mirror. She'd paid a pretty penny to have it resilvered, because it was Granma's and used to hang above the dressing table where she'd sat every night and brushed her snow white hair. She retrieved her towel from the pull on the closet door where she'd left it, but by then the smudge was gone.

Must be the light, Willie decided, bending over the dresser to rub a finger across the glass. The long summer twilight filled the bedroom with lavender shadows. She could see her bedside clock and the time in the mirror: six-fifty.

Dr. Raven wouldn't be here until eight-thirty, but Whit would be along any minute. She'd mix the dumplings, put them in the fridge and make the daiquiris. Strawberry, her favorite and Whit's. It was cooling off some, she thought as she headed downstairs. Surely by eight-thirty she'd be able to cook the dumplings without fainting from heat prostration. Or hunger.

When Dr. Raven had called to accept the invitation she'd extended through Whit, he'd chosen the time. She'd wondered about the late hour until he'd said he worked the graveyard shift in the emergency room at Stonebridge General. He usually slept until six and had to be on the floor by eleven.

Sweat popped on Willie's upper lip as she turned the chicken down and tried to decide if she should install central air conditioning. The ceiling fans were usually enough, but on days like this the sun porch she'd converted into an office was like a blast furnace. She weighed the pros and cons while she mixed the dumplings, dumped ice into the blender and answered the yellow wall phone when it rang.

"Don't hold supper for me," Whit said, his voice clipped with annoyance. "My goddamn car shot craps on the turnpike."

"Your brand-new Beemer?" Willie tucked the receiver between her shoulder and jaw, stretching the long cord across the kitchen to the refrigerator. "What happened?"

"The warranty expired. I'm waiting for a tow truck. Do you want to change the meeting with Raven?"

"And cook tarragon chicken again in this heat?" Willie plucked a pint of cleaned and hulled strawberries off a shelf and pushed the door shut with her hip. "No way."

"I thought you were making fried chicken."

"I was until I found Granma's recipe."

"Where? She never wrote down a recipe in her life."

"She lied," Willie said with a grin. "I found it in one of her quilt-pattern notebooks, along with a birthday card you made her in fourth grade and a letter to the editor of *The Stoneridge Chronicle* I don't think she ever mailed."

"Sneaky old woman," Whit said with an affectionate chuckle. "How many of those quilt notebooks did you and Mother find?"

"The official count is twenty-two, but I keep finding more tucked away here and there."

"Keep looking until you find her chocolate cake recipe. You sure you don't want to reschedule?"

"Positive. I want this over with."

"Okay. Your choice. You're the big three-oh now. Just be careful. Call me tomorrow and let me know how it went."

"Yes, Whit." Willie rolled her eyes and dropped strawberries into the blender. "First thing."

"Okay, Will. Love you."

"You, too. Bye."

Willie hung up the phone and turned on the blender, humming "Margaritaville" by Jimmy Buffett. With a daiquiri in one hand and a bowl of salad in the other, she went outside to light the candles in the luminarias, small pastel bags weighted with sand that edged the low terrace wall.

It was nearly dark. The sky was plowed with long furrows of pink cloud, and the sea murmured faintly beyond the dunes. She ate her salad sans dressing with her fingers, watched the windows in her friend Frank Chou's little blue saltbox house begin to glow, and figured she ought to turn on the porch light.

She did, plus a lamp in the living room, the carriage lamps flanking the dining room French doors, and the floodlight above the kitchen sink as she rinsed her bowl. Over the hiss of the water she heard the thrum of a powerful engine, the crunch of tires on the gravel driveway. She grabbed a dish towel and hurried to the front door in time to see Dr. Jonathan Raven stretch out of a red Corvette convertible.

He was much younger than Willie had expected, midthirties, tops, and the handsomest man she'd laid eyes on since Mel Gibson's last movie. His hair was dark and long, curling just below the collar of his white oxford-cloth shirt. The sleeves were rolled and his shirttails were tucked into jeans that were nicely faded and snug in all the best places. In the second before the headlights shut off automatically, she noticed his top three shirt buttons were undone. She also noticed the determination in the set of his jaw and the gleam of covetousness in his narrowed gaze.

None of which showed on his face when Willie flipped the towel over her shoulder and pushed through the screen door. He smiled as he came up the steps and stopped in front of her. He was very tall. Six-two, maybe six-three. He couldn't help his height, or her lack of it. Still, at five foot four, maybe four and a half if she stretched on her toes, Willie could jolly well keep him the hell out of her house.

"Hello, Miss Evans. Nice of you to invite me."

"Thank you for coming, Dr. Raven." She lifted her hand toward the corner where the porch turned around the house. "Hot as it is, I thought we'd have dinner on the terrace."

"Fine. I like the heat." He smiled as she led him down the steps onto the terrace and shot him a what-are-you-nuts look over her shoulder. "Hospitals are cold as morgues."

"And just about as pleasant," Willie replied.

He laughed. He had a great voice, a deep, rich baritone that made Willie's stomach flutter.

"Would you like a drink?"

"Just water, thanks. But please, you go ahead."

When she came back with another daiquiri and ice water with a twist of lemon, he was sitting in one of the padded white iron chairs at the table, elbows on the arms, fingers laced across his midriff. He wore a large, heavy-looking ring on his left hand. Willie thought the stone was an opal, set in silver and flanked by two small diamonds. An interesting ring for a man, she thought, watching it shimmer and his hair gleam blue as a raven's wing in the soft glow of the luminarias.

Very punny, Willie, she thought, smiling as she put the glass down in front of him. He murmured thanks and sipped.

"Your brother hasn't arrived yet?"

"He had to cancel. After I sweated off five pounds making enough tarragon chicken to feed an army."

"Good." He smiled. "More for me."

"Shall I serve now?"

"Finish your drink. I'm not ravenous. Not yet." His smile widened. "I haven't been awake long enough."

A snatch of warm breeze rustled the luminarias. The candle wicks and Jonathan Raven's dark eyes flickered. So did Willie's pulse.

"Let's start with the salad, shall we?"

"If you wish."

Willie wished, all right. She wished she'd held her ground with Whit and nixed this meeting. She'd had men to dinner before. Doctors, lawyers, even a couple of real Indian chiefs, but her hands shook as she spooned the dumplings on top of the chicken. Maybe because this was personal, not business.

She tried to put a professional spin on the meal, serving it in brisk, well-timed stages, making pleasant, impersonal small talk in between courses. It worked well until Raven finished his coffee and key lime pie, leaned back in his chair and said in his rich, lush voice, "You have a beautiful first name. May I call you Willow?"

Willie could think of better choices. Like *darling* or *sweetheart*, but she said, "I'd prefer Miss Evans."

"All right." He laid his napkin next to his plate and laced his fingers across his midriff again. "How much?"

"You don't have enough money to buy Beaches, Dr. Raven."

"You're wrong, Miss Evans. How about two million dollars, for starters?"

"Good heavens." Willie blinked at him, stunned. "The assessed value is only two hundred and thirty thousand."

"It's worth far more than that to me. Shall we say—four million?"

"Beaches is not for sale, Dr. Raven." Willie rose to her feet. "At any price."

He didn't take her hint that dinner and the negotiations were over. He just sat looking at her, his head tilted at a curious angle, a bemused half smile lifting one corner of his mouth. What a mouth. As lush and sexy as his voice.

"Everyone has a price, Miss Evans. Name yours."

"You're not listening, Dr. Raven. I just said—"

Only Willie hadn't a clue what she'd just said. Perplexed, she blinked at her half-finished daiquiri and pushed it away. Another of Granma's cautions was no cold drinks in summer, though she'd swilled iced coffee on the qt when she thought Willie wasn't looking. Especially when she ironed.

"My last offer," Raven said, "was five million."

Think what you could do with all that money, whispered a voice in Willie's head. Move the Evans Agency to Manhattan...lease a whole floor on Madison Avenue...prove to your father you're not a little girl anymore...find a stylist with skill enough to tame that wild Irish mop—

"No fair, Willie!" Frank Chou called out of the darkness beyond the terrace. "I can smell key lime pie a mile away."

The voice in Willie's head snapped off, so suddenly she had to grip the edge of the table to keep her knees from buckling. She blinked at Raven, who was stretching to his feet with a scowl on his face.

"Oops." Frank stepped past the ring of luminarias, a sheepish smile on his face, his hands in the pockets of his cut-offs. "I didn't know you had a guest."

"Dr. Jonathan Raven, Frank Chou," Willie said. I'll get Whit for this, she thought.

"Nice to meet you, Doctor." Frank stepped forward, pulling his right hand out of his pocket.

"A pleasure, Mr. Chou. The key lime pie is excellent." Raven shook his hand, then glanced at Willie. "If you're free tomorrow evening, Miss Evans, I'd like very much to take you to dinner."

It was tempting—Raven was tempting—but he wasn't interested in her. Just in Beaches. He hadn't said so, but he didn't have to. The cool distance he kept said it for him.

"I think you'd better ask my attorney, Dr. Raven," Willie said. "He likes French cuisine, by the way."

"He's not my type, but I'll give him a call." He smiled again, this time with an arched, dark eyebrow. "Thank you for dinner, Miss Evans. Good evening to you both."

He walked across the sandy lawn rather than up the steps and along the porch. Willie watched him go, his white shirt shimmering in the warm summer darkness. She watched until the headlights came on, swooping around in a half circle as Raven backed up the car. When the Corvette purred away down the driveway, Willie rounded on Frank.

"The next time I see Whit, I'm going to smash his cellular phone over his head."

"Won't do any good, Willie. He'll just buy another one."

"Then I'll smash yours over your head. How's that?"

"C'mon, Will, lighten up. We love you."

"Love me, Frank." Willie stacked the dishes on a tray and glared at him. "But don't smother me."

"You mean it?" His dark eyes lit up and he wagged his eyebrows. "At last?"

She laughed. Frank grinned, picked up the tray and carried it into the kitchen. Willie stayed behind to blow out the luminarias, and got enough sand in her eyes to make them water like crazy.

Which is exactly what she thought she was when she looked up and saw a man standing on the porch, gazing down the driveway toward the thin ribbon of road that wound along the beach toward Stonebridge. A man wearing breeches and knee-high boots, a vest and a shirt with full sleeves billowing in the offshore breeze—transparent sleeves she could see through.

Willie's heart leapt and raced in her throat. She shut her eyes, counted to three, wiped the tears away and opened them. There was no one there, just the shadow of the porch swing rocking back and forth and squeaking in the wind.

"No more daiquiris tonight," she said firmly.

Then she ducked into the house, shut off the terrace lights and locked the French doors behind her.

3

RAVEN FELT THE LOCKS click as if he'd turned them with his own fingers. He wanted to throw back his head and howl, but gripped the wheel instead and punched the accelerator.

The red Corvette slithered through an S-curve as neatly and quickly as a snake. Raven hated snakes. He'd bent them to his purpose from time to time, but he always killed them after. Usually hacked them to bits from tail to head. Slowly.

He had to get rid of the meal he'd swallowed. Even cooked, and so minute they'd be hard to detect with the most powerful microscope, the traces of animal blood in the food were enough to send his system raging. He despised puking on the roadside, but there was no choice. He had to halt the blood madness now, while he still could. It was that or wheel the car around and lure Willow—no, *Miss Evans*—from the house, rip out her throat and hand it to her.

The bitch. The silly little carrot-headed bitch.

The warning red tinge was already pulsing at the corners of his vision. He took his foot off the gas, eased the Corvette onto the sandy shoulder and kicked the door open. It sailed through the warm summer night, whistling, and landed, kicking up sand as it bounced end over end, forty yards up the dunes on the other side of the road.

The steering wheel was still in his hands—only he was standing beside the car. He tossed it onto the seat and ran for a small copse of scraggly pines, fell on his knees, hands buried to his wrists in the sand, and emptied his stomach. He scraped sand over the mess like a cat, crawled out of the trees and sprawled on his back on the beach, one arm flung over his eyes. If he'd been able to, he would have wept.

It always took a long time for the residue of the blood madness to fade. He was already late for his shift in ER, but he'd see to it that no one would notice or even remember.

Guilt used to come to him easily. Now he had to reach for it, remind himself he was a doctor, that he'd taken an oath of responsibility. When guilt failed him completely, amorality would consume him, destroy everything he'd once been and yearned to be again before he forgot how. If he'd been able to, he would have prayed, but prayer was forbidden to him.

He could only lower his arm and let the moon bathe his face. The pale, cold light was a balm to him. He was Luna's child now, more than he'd ever been.

A trill of whale song rippled through his senses. It was a blue, breaking the surface and blowing far offshore. Raven could feel him, could almost see the tall, bandy-legged old man who used to bring him here to listen to the whales sing. The memory was faint, as all his memories were, and growing fainter with each passing full moon.

Raven sat up, looped his arms around his knees and saw the lynx crouched nearby, watching him through slitted eyes. He raised his left hand and the cat arched beneath his palm, its rough fur bristling. The moonstone on Raven's finger swirled with pale, opalescent color.

In India once, his despair had drawn a Bengal tiger. He'd spent the night in the jungle hunting with the great cat. He'd used the skills he'd learned from the tiger to stalk and take the moonstone from Nekhat, from the amulet he wore around his neck. Once he'd dealt with Miss Willow Evans, he'd stalk Nekhat again. And this time he'd send him back to Hell where he belonged.

The lynx rubbed its jowls against his leg, peeling back its lip and exposing its curved fangs. They shimmered in the feeble light of the first-quarter half-moon. So did the ankh, the ancient Egyptian symbol for eternal life, carved into the moonstone on Raven's finger.

He asked the lynx if it had seen his Shade. The cat sat on its haunches, flicked its ears and began to purr. Raven listened. At sunset the lynx had risen to hunt, had tracked the shadow of a man whose scent matched his, making his way through the dunes toward the house.

Raven felt his senses quicken, much as the lynx's own would when he sensed prey. This was the closest he'd come to his Shade in the 117 years since he'd lain on the floor of Nekhat's tomb and watched it rise from his body.

He'd been tracking his Shade since 1898, since the Vatican scholar he'd held for a time as a Thrall had brought him an illuminated manuscript from the twelfth century. It was a copy of a papyrus once cataloged in the library at Alexandria. In it he'd found the Riddle of Rejoining.

The monk who had translated the scroll from the original Aramaic had substituted the word *soul* for *shade*, but the meaning was the same. Raven preferred Shade, for he wasn't sure he believed in a God who allowed an abomination like Nekhat—or himself—to live.

He'd realized that what he'd seen rising from his body was his soul, the essence of his humanity, and for the first time he'd felt hope—of regaining his mortality, of ending his tortured existence. From there, it had taken him two years of fevered study to decipher the rest of the Riddle, to determine the items needed to perform the Ritual of Rejoining, the where and the when and the how.

The first step was gaining the moonstone, the second capturing his Shade. He'd thought he'd sensed its presence when he was on the terrace, but his awareness of it had been faint. As the moon waxed toward fullness, so would his Shade, gaining the focus and strength to resist Raven and the power of the moonstone to bind it to him until the time of the Ritual.

It was imperative that he catch the Shade now, while it was too weak to fight him. From the long years he'd spent tracking it and learning the pattern it followed, Raven knew the Shade was most vulnerable when it Cycled here in Stonebridge, where long ago he and Raven had been one. And happy. Now the Shade was terrified of him. He didn't blame it. He was terrified of himself.

He supposed it was ironic that a mortal had made herself an obstacle in his path. He'd almost gotten rid of Willow

Evans tonight, and would have if the Chinese man hadn't interrupted. Much as he loathed the idea of taking her in Thrall, of enslaving her to his will, it would be necessary for the sake of expedience. She was wary now, so it would be more difficult. And it would take time he didn't have—another irony, for his Shade had come late.

It should have arrived nearly a week ago with the new moon. Raven had spent the past six nights sweeping the beach and the dunes with his senses in search of it. He knew from the Riddle that the pattern of the Shade's Cycle never varied, yet it had. A worrisome wrinkle.

Raven stretched to his feet. The lynx wound around his ankles, purring and inviting him to hunt. It was tempting, and simple to shift his shape, safe then to ingest animal blood, so long as he spent the day in stasis and gave his system time to metabolize it. But it also hastened the descent into bestiality, so Raven declined, softening the refusal by dropping to his heels to cup the cat's head and use his own rough tongue to lick its ears.

The lynx purred more deeply and returned the favor. The sandpaper scrape along his temples and his eyebrows raised no shivers and stirred no senses, for Raven had none. Not by mortal definitions. He was aware of it, but that was all.

When they parted, the lynx slipped away into the dunes to hunt. Raven walked back up the beach to the road, stretching his awareness into the night. He could feel every heart that pulsed in Stonebridge and a goodly area beyond, could tell the age and condition of the muscle. The sensitivity was often useful in the ER, though that was not its purpose.

If he were to hunt in his present form, he would isolate those already marked for death, much as a lion stalks the old or infirm and cuts them from the herd. Most of those like Raven hunted in the same fashion, preferring an easy kill. But not all. Nekhat was one who did not.

He hunted and fed in binges, when the mood or the hunger struck, in rampages of blood and terror. His feeding patterns were an aberration, a horror even to those like him. Raven had spent years studying Nekhat, carefully and from a distance. He possessed the scientific skills and knowledge and had little else with which to occupy himself between the Cycles of his Shade. He'd even returned to Egypt to research, though he'd ventured no farther than the Cairo Museum.

He'd spent three mortal years there in deep, nonstop study, inhaling the dust of millennia from crumbling papyrus scrolls in arid storage rooms, for he did not require sleep, and needed stasis only when he ingested animal blood. He'd left Cairo knowing all there was to know of Nekhat and the abomination of his creation, how the ancients had managed to trap Nekhat and seal him in the tomb.

By the time Raven reached the ruined red Corvette, he was mostly himself again—calm and controlled, without feeling and as cold as the moon. He picked up the cellular phone and called a tow truck, then Stonebridge General to report he'd had car trouble but would be there soon. It was the mortal thing to do. Then he ripped the stereo CD player out of the dash, drew back his arm and hurled it into the sea.

Next he retrieved the car door, erasing the marks it had left in the sand with a glance. He puzzled over what to do with it for a moment, then tossed it onto the shoulder behind the car, folded his arms and leaned against the rear fender. He left the steering wheel on the seat.

While he waited, he stretched his awareness one last time, far beyond the confines of Stonebridge. Nekhat still lay in stasis, not on this continent but near enough that when he rose Raven would know. The uneasy ripple in his senses, stirred by the tardiness of his Shade, edged away.

When the tow truck approached, the beams of its headlights swirling in the fog beginning to wisp around his ankles, Raven leaned off the car. He put a bewildered smile on his face as Jake Smith, who owned the only tow service in Stonebridge, swung out of the cab. He was a big, beefy man with a strong, booming heart despite the roll of fat overhanging his belt and the cigar clamped in his teeth.

"What the hell happened, Doc?" Jake lifted his grease-stained Boston Red Sox baseball cap, scratched his head and walked slowly around the Vette.

"Beats me, Jake." Raven shook his head and ran a hand through his hair. "I stopped to walk on the beach and this is what I found when I came back."

"What you doin' clear out here this time o' night?"

"Willow Evans invited me to dinner. I was on my way back to town, on my way to work, actually."

Jake chuckled and grinned around his cigar. "Don't tell me you was mad enough to do this yourself."

"Hardly." Raven laughed. "I was mad enough to kick the tires a couple times and go for a walk to cool off."

"Cute little gal, Willie, but provokin', sometimes. Just like her Granma. Betsy Boyle was a real pistol." Jake took a flashlight out of his back pocket and shone it into the car. "Took your CD player, Doc. But, jeez." He picked up the steering wheel and shook his head. "How the hell'd they do this and tear off the door?"

"I can hardly wait," Raven said mournfully, "to call my insurance agent."

"Mebbe it was aliens." Jake winked and put the wheel in the back seat. "I seen on TV where some goofballs out in California claim they come and took 'em outta their beds."

"What will they think of next?"

"Damned if I know, but I been haulin' folks outta ditches and snowdrifts for near twenty year and I ain't never seen anything like this." Jake walked behind the car, grunting as he bent, heaved the door over and ran the flashlight over it. "Looka here, Doc. Had to use a crowbar or somethin', but there ain't a scratch or a dent noplace."

Oops. "Pull the other leg," Raven said. The light's poor, he thought to Jake. You're mistaken. Just put the door in the car and forget about it.

"I'll show you when we git to the garage." He rose with the door in his arms and laid it in the back seat. "Got anything you need in here, get it out while I winch it up."

While Jake swung the truck around and backed it up to the Corvette, Raven leaned into the back seat. With one hand he retrieved his bag, slipping the phone inside it, and his white lab coat. With the other he dented the door, near the hinges where it would look pried, and dragged scratches in the vivid red finish with his nails.

"Yep," Jake said, swinging out of the truck again to attach the winch. "I definitely think it was aliens."

"How about fairies?" Raven called over the whine of the cable as he opened the passenger door. "Or werewolves?"

Jake laughed. Raven swung into the cab, ripe with the smell of cigar smoke, laid his bag on the floor and draped his lab coat over his knees.

What's the world coming to, he wondered as he peeled red paint out from under his fingernails, when aliens are more believable than vampires?

4

BY EIGHT-THIRTY FRIDAY MORNING, when Willie finished her third cup of coffee, it was seventy-eight degrees and the humidity was 82 percent. She gave up, shut off her Macintosh computer and called Jim Eggleson at Eggleson Heating and Cooling.

"You know Beaches as well as you know me, Jim," she said. "Bring whatever you think'll work best and hook it up."

"I thought ahead when you bought the new furnace. Duct work's already in. Me and the boys'll be there directly."

"Terrific. I'll give you lunch."

"Got any key lime pie left? Jake said y'baked one."

"When did Jake get to be clairvoyant?"

"That Dr. Raven's car quit on him after he left your place last night. Jake towed him in, a course."

A course. Willie thought briefly, but not wistfully, of Manhattan and its anonymity.

"If it ain't poisoned," Eggleson went on, "me and the boys'll be glad to polish off that pie."

"It's not poisoned." Willie laughed. "It's yours."

She hung up, and the phone rang. She answered it and Whit said, "You forgot to call me."

"Your office doesn't open for half an hour."

"I've been here since seven. What happened with Raven?"

"Promise you won't tell Dad?"

"Did he make a pass?"

She should be so lucky, Willie thought. "He offered me five million dollars for Beaches."

"Good God!" Whit exclaimed, then groaned. "You said no, didn't you?"

"Of course I said no."

"Willie, Willie—"

"Why do you suppose Beaches is worth that much to him?"

"Beats me. Maybe I should dig a little deeper into Dr. Raven. An offer that size means he knows as well as I do his uncle's will gives him a feeble at best claim to the house."

"So why investigate him?"

"Beaches is pretty isolated and right on the water. Maybe he's a drug dealer or something."

"He's a doctor."

"That doesn't mean he isn't a crook. It just means he's been to medical school. You wouldn't happen to know where?"

"Hardly. Jake Smith might. He's the resident clairvoyant in Stonebridge."

"Good idea. Poke around town. See who knows what. I'll run his social, but I'll only get facts and dates. You can put flesh on the bones."

"So you can strip it off again?"

"Do you want Raven to leave you alone?"

"All right, all right. Hey, Whit. What's the difference between a dead lawyer in the middle of the road and a dead snake in the middle of the road?"

"I don't know."

"There's skid marks in front of the snake."

Whit laughed, said, "Call me later" and hung up.

So did Willie. How odd that both Whit and Raven had had car trouble last night. But maybe not. Radiators overheated and hoses broke all the time in heat waves like this.

Willie iced the rest of the coffee and drank it on the terrace while she put away the luminarias. The sense of peace she'd always felt at Beaches settled over her like warm, strong hands on her shoulders. The sea hissed, "You're safe, you're safe," beyond the dunes, and made Willie smile.

Whit said its unending murmur drove him nuts and kept him awake nights. He used to wake up crying when they were kids, certain he'd seen something in his room. Monsters in the closet, Granma said with a wink. Willie winked back but kept her mouth shut about her pirate, the imaginary friend she'd dreamed up for the game of buccaneers she and Whit played on the beach.

Some days, when the sun hit the water just right, she could almost see him. A tall man in breeches and knee boots, with long dark hair and a white shirt with sleeves that billowed like sails in the wind. Just like the man she thought she'd seen on the porch last night.

Whoa. Willie put her glass down with a clunk and rubbed a shiver of gooseflesh on her arms. Was that weird, or what? She hadn't thought about her pirate in years, not since she and Zen had found the Andrew Wyeth print *Giant* in a gallery in Soho on their lunch hour. It showed six kids on a beach watching a giant spun out of clouds and surf stride across the sky with a club on his shoulder. She'd bought it and hung it in her office at *Material Girl*. On bad days it worked better than tranquilizers.

She'd tried to tell Whit how it made her feel: safe and watched over, the way she felt at Beaches. He hadn't understood, but Zen had. She'd tell Zen about the man on the porch the next time she called, but she wouldn't tell Whit. The boy who'd seen monsters in the closet always told her she had too much imagination for her own good. Go figure.

Willie thought briefly of asking Frank to go with her to Stonebridge, but decided against it. There was enough talk about them already. Unfounded talk, since they'd known each other since they were fifteen, but Willie didn't want to stir up gossip. It might get back to Raven, who just might be interested in more than Beaches.

And maybe the national debt was just a subtraction error. But a girl could dream. Willie hummed "Some Day My Prince Will Come" while she pulled out of the garage in the yellow Jeep Wrangler she'd bought used when she'd moved to Beaches.

Her father had *really* thrown a fit about her plans for the garage, so of course she'd built it. Whatever Whit Senior wanted her to do, Willie did the opposite. Which sent her Raven fantasy up in flames, since her father still dreamed that someday she'd marry a rich doctor. What girl in her right mind wouldn't love to, but Willie would rather eat cranberries, which she loathed, than admit it to her father.

She ought to at least admit to herself that her libido was stuck in overdrive, that it had been since she'd watched Dr. Jonathan Raven stretch out of his red Corvette. The thought of watching him do that every night when he came home to his darling, devoted little wife—namely, her—made Willie's pulse thud in places she didn't even know she had a pulse. He was a doctor, so he'd know all those secret little pulse points, and he'd make them trip-hammer when he kissed her hello and asked her what was for dinner. He would never ask about dessert; they'd both known what that would be.

"Down, girl," Willie told herself sternly. "You are absolutely nuts to even *think* he's interested in you. The only thing he wants is Beaches. Period."

But maybe that was why she wanted him, because he didn't want her. She hadn't spent her life being contrary and dating oddballs because it drove her father up a wall for nothing. And that was exactly what she had to show for it—nothing but a string of dead-end relationships. A relatively short string compared to those of most of her friends. And her current love life was as dull and boring and alarmingly predictable as the rest of her life.

Which suited Willie just fine. Daydreams were fun, but she wasn't a boy-crazy teenager anymore. At least, Willie didn't think so until the florist van from Petunia's Posies crunched up the driveway ahead of Jim Eggleson's blue pickup. Then, God help her, she almost squealed as she hurried to the door to meet Petunia's husband, Bob, bearing a white vase full of long-stemmed yellow roses.

"You wouldn't believe what Pet offered me," he said, "but I wouldn't let her read the card. You owe me, Willie."

"Lemme guess, Bob. Key lime pie?"

"That oughta square us."

While Bob wolfed pie in the kitchen, and Jim and the boys unloaded a compressor from the pickup, Willie carried the flowers into her office. She put them on her desk, sat down and opened the card, her hands shaking with excitement.

"Thank you for a lovely dinner. Please reconsider my invitation. Your brother really isn't my type." It was signed Raven, with a P.S. that read "Promise I won't offer you money or even mention the h-o-u-s-e," followed by his phone number.

If only he hadn't mentioned Beaches, Willie might have fallen for it. Instead, his note convinced her that he was no more interested in her than the man in the moon. The flowers were a nice touch, though; she was sure Bob had told him yellow roses were her favorite. ·

Her father would probably tell Raven to shove his roses, which meant she should pick up the phone and say yes. But there was something not quite right about Raven, something missing. She didn't know what, but she trusted her intuition to tell her eventually. She put the card in a drawer, picked up her purse and mail and turned on the answering machine.

She saw Bob out, hollered down the basement stairs to Jim and the boys that she'd be back for lunch and headed for Stonebridge. She might as well have stayed at Beaches handing screwdrivers to Jim and the boys. She learned only two new things about Raven: his address and the fact that every single woman in town was trying to trip him and beat him to the ground.

Even Hester Pavao at the post office knew no more about him than Willie did—only that he'd moved to town two months ago, and in the county clerk's office when he'd found out about his uncle's will he'd thrown a fit Whit Senior would have envied.

"Don't talk much when he comes in," Hester told her. "Minds his business and nobody else's."

Equally unhelpful were the check-out girls at Pac 'N Save. All they did was pump Willie while they rang up her groceries, since everyone in Stonebridge knew she'd had Raven over for dinner.

Clouds began to gather and darken on her drive back to Beaches. So did Willie's mood. Just her luck the weather would break *after* she sprang for central air conditioning.

She didn't see the cat, a black, tan and gray calico, until she almost hit it, as it came pouncing out of the salt grass edging the road in pursuit of a field mouse. Willie slammed on the brakes, hard enough to make them screech. The cat froze, cringing in terror. So did Willie, her heart pounding in her throat. She was afraid to get out and look. But she had to, and she did, holding her breath and one hand over her mouth as she dropped to her heels and peered under the Jeep.

The cat blinked up at her beneath the bumper, its gold eyes huge, its tail bristling. Willie sobbed with relief and sagged against the hot fender. The cat meowed and rubbed her shins. It was hardly more than a kitten, its fur dirty and gritty with sand and matted with burrs. It purred and arched its back when Willie reached out to it. She felt every vertebra in its spine, and her throat swelled with memory.

Granma had always kept cats at Beaches. She'd had four when she died last August, but they'd all run away within days of her death, just slipped away into the dunes and never came back. This scrawny, half-starved little calico was the image of Betsy Boyle's favorite old tom, Patches.

"Do you know my father?" Willie scooped up the cat and tucked it in the curve of her elbow. "He says I'm the first certifiable sucker ever born in the Evans family."

The cat said "Brruup," and closed its teeth gently on the tip of Willie's finger.

"I see you've met him. Good. Then you won't be surprised when he throws a fit about you."

Willie drove home with the cat curled in her lap, its eyes half-closed and its ears twitching. Jim and the boys, his two middle-aged sons, Jeff and Jim Junior, broke for lunch and carried her groceries into the house.

The cat was a female—Jim Junior checked—and hopped from lap to lap mooching tarragon chicken until Willie opened a can of tuna and filled a bowl with water. The cat ate and drank, then collapsed in a sunbeam slanting across the dining room floor. Willie named her Calico, Callie for short.

"Y'oughta have a dog rather'n a cat," Jim told her as he carried his empty pie plate and coffee cup to the sink. "A nice big dog with a real loud bark."

So long as she had her father she didn't need a watchdog, Willie thought, but just smiled at Jim. He and the boys went back to work and she headed for the beach with a beat-up old baking pan. Callie went with her, slithering in and out of the salt grass and digging alongside Willie when she knelt to fill the pan with sand.

She raced ahead on the way back to the house and meowed to be let in when Willie came up the porch steps. In the laundry room she stepped into the pan and christened it when Willie put it down. She climbed out shaking her paws, rubbed Willie's shins and blinked up at her, purring.

"You know what to do with sand," Willie said, scooping her up. "Now let's see how you do with water."

It was possible to bathe cats, Willie knew, so long as the stars were aligned just so in the heavens. She gathered towels and soap, put Callie on the drain-board and turned on the water. The cat batted and played and swooped and dived until she soaked herself. All Willie had to do was soap her hands, rub Callie down and let her play again, with a few strategic handfuls splashed here and there, until she'd rinsed herself.

The phone rang twice while Willie sat toweling the cat dry in her grandmother's rocking chair. She wanted to leap up and grab it, just in case it was Raven, but steeled herself and let the machine answer. When Callie jumped down to finish on her own, Willie hung up the towel and checked the messages.

Neither one was from Raven. One was a client, the other was Zen. Willie called her first, in her office at *Material Girl*, where she was still art director.

"I've been thinking about you all day," Zen said, her voice as soothing as camomile tea. "What's up?"

Willie smiled. Zen always knew when something was up. Sometimes she even knew what.

"Dr. Raven came to dinner last night, and guess what?"

"He's old, ugly and filthy rich."

"Nope. He's young, *gorgeous* and filthy rich."

"That was my second guess. How young and how gorgeous?"

Willie told her. Zen made a wolf whistle.

"He offered me five million dollars for Beaches and this morning he sent me flowers. Yellow roses."

"I see. So you think he's only interested in the house."

"Wouldn't you?"

"I might if I'd dated one loser too many just to get even with my father for being arrogant and overbearing and trying to run my life. What else is going on?"

"Who said there was?"

"I did. What is it?"

"Remember my imaginary friend the pirate? I could swear I saw him on the front porch last night."

"Maybe you did."

Only Zen or Shirley MacLaine would think such a thing.

"He isn't real, Zen. I made him up."

"Are you sure? Spirits are often drawn to places, you know. Sometimes people."

"He's not a spirit. He's a figment of my imagination."

"If you say so. Just don't be surprised if you see him again. I have a hunch you might."

"How about Dr. Raven? Got any hunches about him?"

"I've got a hunch you'd *give* him Beaches if he blew in your ear."

"That obvious, huh? Even long distance?"

"Especially long distance." Zen laughed. "I can hear your heart throbbing in your voice."

Willie laughed, too, sheepishly, promised to call Zen in a week or so and phoned the client, who happened to be Frank. He was thirty, like Willie, and already semifamous for his ceramics and Chinese porcelains.

"Is this business or buddy stuff?" Willie asked him.

"What are you in the mood for?"

"Moo goo gai pan."

"Shrimp or pork?"

"Shrimp. No, pork. No, shrimp."

"Have you found Betsy's recipe for chop suey yet?"

"No," Willie lied. In truth, she'd forgotten.

"I know there's lots of notebooks. Want me to look?"

Willie wished she hadn't told Frank she'd found the tarragon chicken recipe. Finding the card made by eight-year-old Whit had made her cry. Besides the letter to the newspaper, she'd found a funny, exasperated note Betsy had written about her father. If there were any more like that, she wanted to be the one to find them.

"I'll keep looking," she told Frank. "Promise."

"Okay. I'd just like to know how she got the flavor right without MSG. How 'bout seven-thirty for the moo goo gai pan? I just fired up the kiln."

"Fine. My place." She smiled and stroked Callie's fur as she leapt into her lap. "I've got a surprise for you."

"If it's black peekaboo lace I'll be right over."

"It isn't."

"Then I'll see you at seven-thirty."

Jim and the boys finished at three. Willie wrote the check and walked them out to the truck. It was blistering, the wind kicking sand up around her ankles. Only a few clouds were still hanging around, their undersides bruised and shot with silver where the sun broke through.

"It'll take the house a spell to cool down," Jim said as he climbed in behind the wheel. "Thanks for lunch, Willie."

"My pleasure." She waved goodbye and went back to her office, where she lifted Callie off her chair and into her lap, fired up the Mac and started on a press release for a mystery-writer client with a new book.

Outside the window the compressor thrummed, slowly pushing the mercury in her desktop thermometer-barometer below eighty. Cool and relaxed for the first time since the onset of the heat spell and the arrival of the first letter from Dr. Raven's attorney, Willie lost herself in her work.

She meant to stop about six and shower and change before Frank showed up with the moo goo gai pan, but it was almost quarter past seven when her glance caught the desk clock. Uh-oh. She'd have to hurry. Frank was notoriously on time.

Callie glided upstairs beside her, jumped on the bed and went to sleep. She was gone when Willie came out of the bathroom in a towel, probably off to explore her new territory. Humming "I'm Forever Blowing Bubbles," Willie dug clean underwear out of a drawer and shut it. She glanced up in the mirror as she started to turn around—and froze.

The man in riding breeches and knee boots, the vest and white shirt with sleeves like sails, the man she'd only thought she'd seen on the front porch last night, stood beside her bed watching her.

Oh, my God, Zen was right, Willie thought dazedly, it's my pirate. *And he looks exactly like Dr. Jonathan Raven.*

5

IT WAS NOT her imagination. He stood leaning on one foot with his head cocked, as if he was peering at her around a door. Any girl who'd ever caught her brother spying on her knew the look. And any woman who'd ever sat across a table from Jonathan Raven, even on a hot, candle-lit summer night, would know those luminous dark eyes.

What Willie didn't know was how he'd found out about her pirate, how he'd managed the projection on the porch last night and how he'd gotten into her house. She only knew he wasn't going to get away with scaring her out of it.

"All right, Dr. Raven." Willie spun herself around on one foot. "I don't know what you think—"

There was no one beside the bed, yet there was *something* beside the bed. A silvery shimmer in the air that swept her with vertigo. Her head spun and the room with it, which was far more frightening than having a man in her bedroom. It had been so long since that had happened—

The shimmer moved and so did Willie, without thinking or screaming. She didn't run, she flew—clutching the towel around her—out of her bedroom, along the hall and down the stairs, until her still wet right foot shot out from under her on the uncarpeted steps.

She bounced down the last two and landed, hard, on her tailbone on the dining room floor. Needles of pain flashed up her spine and her right shin; she'd somehow managed to wrench the hell out of her ankle, which Callie gripped with her claws. The cat suddenly let go of her ankle and leapt into Willie's lap, her fur bristling and her eyes huge.

"It's not black lace," Frank said, "but it'll do."

Willie swept the cat off, whipped her head around and saw
Frank standing in the kitchen doorway, holding a covered
wok with blue-checked hot pads. "Knock it off, Chou, and
help me up. I sprained my ankle."

"I wondered why you were sitting on the floor in a towel."
Frank put the wok on the table and knelt beside her. "You
didn't answer when I knocked, so I let myself in."

Thank God, Willie thought, holding on to Frank with one
hand and her towel with the other as he eased her up, her
weight on her left foot. Callie meowed and rubbed Frank's
bare, dark-haired ankles above his brown leather boat shoes.

Frank nodded at the cat. "Is this the surprise?"

"One of them. Her name's Callie." Willie sucked air between her teeth and gave up trying to put weight on her right
foot. "I had Jim Eggleson over today. Can you tell?"

"I wondered why the place was shut up and cold as a mau-
soleum. How'd you sprain your ankle?"

"I slipped running down the stairs."

"Dare I hope," he said, his eyes gleaming with mischief,
"that you were running to meet me at the door?"

"In your dreams. I'd just gotten out of the shower and I
saw —"

Willie stopped herself. What had she seen? A man in the
mirror, who wasn't there when she turned around? The same
man she'd seen on the porch last night, who wasn't there
when she blinked? How would that sound to Frank? Or better yet, to Whit, when Frank called him. Which he would as
surely as Willie would be limping for the next couple of days.

"The time," she said. "I saw the time and realized I hadn't
put the rice on. So I came running downstairs."

"Sounds like you. Want me to help you upstairs so you can
get dressed?"

"*No.*" Her sharp refusal drew a raised eyebrow from Frank.
"I mean—I've got some clothes in the laundry room I haven't
put away yet."

"Good. Get dressed and I'll make the rice."

On Frank's arm, Willie hopped across the kitchen into the
laundry room. Callie slithered in just before she shut the

door, stepped into her pan and used it while Willie dug through the dryer and a basket of folded clothes. Sometimes it paid not to finish the laundry.

It took her ten minutes to put on underwear, gray sweat shorts and a blue pocket T-shirt, her ankle throbbing all the way up to her knee. Willie dropped the lid on the toilet, sat down to catch her breath and watched Callie fling sand all over the white-tiled floor. She didn't want to think about what she'd seen—or hadn't seen—in her bedroom, but snatches of the face in the mirror and the shimmer beside her bed kept flashing through her brain.

What had she seen, *really*? Her imaginary friend the pirate? A ghost? A trick of the light? Maybe what she'd subconsciously wanted to see—Raven in her bedroom. Willie couldn't decide, but whatever it was, the memory made her shiver as she eased herself up, opened the door and hopped into the kitchen.

By the time they finished their moo goo gai pan and rice, Willie's ankle was three times its normal size, pulsing with pain and beginning to bruise beneath the ice bag Frank had put on it.

"I think you oughta have an X ray, Will," he said.

"Me, too. My purse and my keys are in the office."

Frank drove. Willie propped her ankle on the door frame to keep it elevated, her foot hanging out what would have been the window if the shell had been on. She hopped through the emergency entrance of Stonebridge General, Frank's arm around her waist, hers around his shoulders, at nine-twenty. Since Raven didn't go on duty until eleven, Willie figured she was safe.

But it was Raven who raked aside the green curtain enclosing the cubicle the admitting nurse had put her in. Seeing him sent a jolt of surprise and pure sexual what-a-hunk awareness through Willie that made her ankle throb even more and her heart start to pound.

He had a stethoscope looped around his neck rather than a tie. The collar of his green oxford-cloth shirt was unbuttoned, giving her a pulse-thudding peek at lots of dark chest hair. He looked up from the clipboard with her chart on it, and smiled at her, an amused curve on his provocative, oh-so-sexy mouth.

"Hello again, Miss Evans."

"What are you doing here?" Willie blurted out.

"I could ask you the same question, but it's obvious." He put the clipboard down on the gurney and removed the ice pack the nurse had put on her ankle. "We're shorthanded so I came in early. How'd you do this?"

She'd already told the nurse, who had written it down, but she repeated the story she'd told Frank, looking pointedly away while Raven probed her swollen ankle. His fingertips were warm, his touch surprisingly gentle. And arousing. Willie tried to steel herself against it, but she was only human, a sucker for foot rubs, and Raven's dark eyes were just as luminous in the harsh glare of the hospital lights as they'd been in the soft glow of the luminarias.

They were the same eyes she'd glimpsed in the mirror, in the face of the man standing beside her bed. The man who looked enough like Raven to be his twin. The man who hadn't been there when she'd turned around.

She was lying. Her pounding heart and trip-hammering pulse told Raven so. It stirred and excited him. He gave himself a moment to savor her excitement, the mad race of her blood, then quelled the urge and brushed his mind against hers.

She'd seen his Shade. In the mirror in her bedroom, but it was gone when she'd turned around. She'd seen the temporal disturbance it made; that's what had frightened her and sent her running down the stairs.

"Ouch." Willie flinched as Raven's fingers tightened on her ankle.

"Sorry." He took his hand away and smiled. "I don't think it's broken, but we'll take an X ray and make sure."

He already knew it was just a bad sprain, not a break, but he made it sound good. He picked up his clipboard and left the cubicle, drawing the curtain shut behind him. He saw two more patients while Willow Evans was in X ray, viewed the film when it came back from radiology and took it into the cubicle with him to show her the results on the wall-mounted viewer.

"As you can see, there's no fracture, the bones are whole. You double-sprained the ankle, turned it both ways when you fell, which stretched and severely wrenched the ligaments."

"A double whammy," she said simply.

"Exactly. Keep it elevated and use contrast baths—cold, hot, then cold again." He took a prescription pad and a ballpoint pen out of his white lab coat pocket and wrote instructions.

Then he cupped his hand gently over her ankle. While he told her about tendons and ligaments, he touched her mind, slipping past the conscious level to her autonomic nervous system. *All is well here.* He spoke to the nerves and ganglia that innervated her blood vessels, to the blood itself pooling around the injury. *Return to your proper path.*

"Naturally, stay off it for a couple of days," he added, though he knew she wouldn't need to, that in the morning she'd be amazed at her quick recovery. "I can prescribe something for pain, if you'd like."

"Thank you, no. I don't do drugs, only regular-strength Tylenol."

"If you change your mind, call me. Here or at home. You have my number." Raven picked up the clipboard and signed off on her chart. "I'll stop by tomorrow evening and have another look."

"That isn't necessary. I know my way here."

"I'm a doctor, Miss Evans. You're my patient." He looked at her when he was finished writing. "Don't take it personally."

She flushed and glanced at her hands knotted in her lap. She'd chewed a hangnail on her thumb. A wafer-thin line of blood seeped along the cuticle. Raven's mouth watered.

"Thank you, by the way," she said, "for the roses."

It galled her to say it; he could hear it in her voice, sense it in her thoughts. She didn't want to owe him anything or be beholden to him. It amused him almost as much as her physical attraction to him repulsed him.

"Enjoy them, Miss Evans. I'll see you tomorrow evening."

He was gone, the curtain yanked shut behind him before Willie could open her mouth. She ground her teeth in frustration as a nurse pushed her in a wheelchair with a squeaky rubber tire down the hall to the waiting room. Frank looked up and put down the month-old issue of *Time* he was reading, and went to get the Jeep.

"Want me to stay over?" he asked as he helped her hop into the house, through the dining room French doors where there were no steps.

"No," Willie said, and meant it. She'd never been afraid to stay alone at Beaches, and she wasn't going to let whatever she'd seen in her bedroom—or *thought* she'd seen—frighten her. Not again. Once was enough. "Just help me do this contrast-bath thing."

It took an hour, first with a bucket of cold water, then hot, then cold again. Frank made tea, nuked them each another plateful of moo goo gai pan, then washed the wok, loaded the dishwasher and turned it on. While Willie changed into a pair of blue cotton pajamas, crinkled from lying in the dryer for two days, Frank went upstairs for her toothbrush, a quilt and three pillows. When Willie was settled on the couch, he doubled one pillow under her foot, tucked two behind her head, covered her and sat down on the coffee table.

"I kicked the thermostat up," he said. "Don't want you turning into a Popsicle overnight. Want the lamp on?"

"No. Just leave the light on over the stove in case I have to go to the bathroom."

"Okay. See you in the morning." He leaned over, kissed the top of her head and turned off the lamp on the table next to the couch. "I'll make you breakfast."

When the locks clicked behind him, Willie sighed and shut her eyes. Her ankle wasn't throbbing anymore, just pulsing dully. Callie jumped on her stomach, startling her for a moment. Then she smiled, scratched the cat's ears, yawned and let her eyes drift shut.

The dishwasher droned and the refrigerator gurgled. A loose shutter and the French doors rattled in a gust of wind. The porch swing squeaked. Common everynight noises in an old house. Callie was a warm deadweight—half purring, half snoring—on top of her. The sea murmured faintly, fitfully, beyond the dunes. With her left hand cupped around the cat's round, full stomach, Willie fell asleep—too tired to think anymore, too exhausted, she hoped, to dream.

Neither Willie nor Callie stirred when the man in knee boots and breeches, the brown leather vest and billowy-sleeved white shirt sat down on the coffee table to watch them sleep.

6

HIS NAME WAS JONATHAN, but he had another name, one he couldn't remember. He wished he could. He wanted to tell Willie he was sorry he'd frightened her, that he'd tried to catch her when she'd tripped but she'd fallen right through his hands.

He held them out in front of him and spread his fingers. He couldn't understand it, or remember how he'd suffered the hook-shaped scar below the knuckle of his right index finger. He'd been touching things in the house all day, picking them up, examining them and putting them back, but Willie had slipped through his fingers like smoke.

He laid his right palm on the arm of the sofa, behind the pillows tucked beneath her head. He could feel the nubby texture of the upholstery, a rose brocade chain-stitched with pale green vines and tiny yellow flowers. He raised his hand, fingers half-curled, brushed her cheek and felt—nothing. He tried again, pressing harder, saw his knuckles sink into her cheekbone, and jerked his hand away, startled. She stirred in her sleep, murmured and turned her head away on the pillows.

Apparently he could touch and feel things, but not people, not flesh, since he had none of his own. The creature Willie called Raven had flesh, the body that had once been his.

He got up from the table and walked to the French doors in the dining room, being careful to avoid the furniture. He'd realized he wasn't dead when he'd staggered—still reeling with the shock of believing he was after Willie had walked through him—facefirst into her bedroom wall. He'd knocked himself senseless and had lain on the floor, grief stricken and bewildered, until Raven had come.

The house had turned cold and rigid with terror around him. He'd heard Raven speak with his voice, flat and lifeless in his dead mouth. All his instincts had screamed at him to hide, until he'd heard Willie answer. Then he'd run downstairs, shouting at her not to let him in, shrieking at Raven to go away and leave her alone, leave him alone, to go back to hell where he'd come from.

He'd never done that before. He'd always run from Raven whenever he came. And Raven always came. Wherever he went, wherever he found himself, Raven came looking for him. He remembered that, too, but he couldn't remember why.

He stood at the French doors looking out at the terrace through the white curtains, at the moon-silvered top of the wall, the backs of the chairs and table legs, the dew jeweling on the table's pebbled glass top. He'd stood here last night watching himself eat and drink and laugh and talk. He'd wept with the bitterness of it, and he'd raged when Raven had tried to use his terrible powers to make Willie give him the house.

Her friend the Chinese man had made Raven angry—very, *very* angry—and that frightened him. He'd seen Raven's temper, though he couldn't remember when. He thought it was in Egypt, a long time ago, but he wasn't sure.

He had to find a way to warn Willie and Frank. Perhaps he could use the mirror. He hadn't realized Willie could see him in it, or that he made a reflection, until she'd turned around and called him Dr. Raven.

He remembered he was a doctor, but he wasn't Raven. The thing that had his body was Raven. Nor was he Jonathan, though he knew he was named for an old man he couldn't remember, Jonathan William Edward Raven. His family and friends had called him something other than Jonathan; he just couldn't remember what.

His mother had shown him his name in the family Bible. He couldn't remember her face or how old he'd been at the time. He could only remember her soft voice, her lily-of-the-valley scent, the soft stroke of her fingers in his hair, and a dusty beam of sunlight glinting on the gold-edged pages of the thick, heavy Bible spread across her lap.

Last night he'd remembered she was dead, that she'd died a long time ago. He remembered visiting her grave in the Stonebridge churchyard, remembered throwing his arms around her headstone and howling with grief when he'd seen her name etched in the stone, eroded by time and weather: Mary Rachel Elizabeth Kincaid Raven, Cherished Wife And Beloved Mother, Born March 17, 1824, Called Home To Heaven January 9, 1879.

His mother had died of shock and grief five months after he'd been murdered in Egypt. He'd died in August of 1878, only he wasn't dead. He knew that now, though he had no idea how. Raven was the one who was dead. He knew that, too, and it terrified him.

He heard Willie murmur in her sleep again, heard the quilts rustle around her. He crossed the dining room and stood behind the couch looking at her, saw her brow furrow in the pale moonlight pooling through the window facing the porch.

Last night he'd remembered Willie, too. Not as the grown woman she was now, but as the bright little girl she'd been with orange freckles and copper pigtails. She'd come in the summer when he did, with her brother, Whit, a surly boy with red-gold hair but no freckles. They would stay with the old woman who used to live in the house. Their grandmother. He remembered her, too, and realized she was dead now. He'd wept for her and for his mother, but mostly he'd wept for himself as he'd wandered the house remembering.

He used to trail Willie and Whit along the beach while they played pirates, paddled in the shallows, chased crabs along the dunes with sticks and hunted starfish in the tidal pools. He'd take off his boots, his socks and his vest and roll up his sleeves. He'd race across the beach with them and splash in the waves, savoring the feel of the wind in his hair and the wet sand squishing between his toes.

He'd kissed Willie once when a starfish stung her, gently on the tip of her pert little nose. He'd tasted sand and the salt in her tears, smiled as she'd sniffled and rubbed what must have felt like a tickle to her, then held his breath when she'd cocked her head to one side and squinted up at him. Could she see him? *Did* she see him? He'd held himself perfectly still as she'd raised her nail-bitten, sand-caked fingers toward his face, but she'd patted the air a good six inches to the left of him.

The old woman had seen him before she'd gone away to the hospital in Boston to have the cataracts taken off her eyes. She'd had lovely eyes, green as the sea on a still, cloudy day, until the lenses had thickened and turned her eyes filmy and dim. He'd come in the winter, several times, he thought, when the sea was gray and heavy and the shutters were fastened against the cold.

He'd come once at Christmas, when the tree was up and twinkling with lights in the living room, when the house smelled of holly and bayberry and cinnamon. The old woman was in the kitchen making jelly from cranberries she'd picked herself before the bog had frozen over. She'd seen him in a corner watching her, smiled and wiped on her apron the thick magnifying glass she needed to read the labels on jars and cans, and said, "Well, there you are, Johnny. I wondered if you'd gone for good this time. Come taste the jelly and tell me if it needs more sugar."

Johnny. That was his name. That was what his mother and the old woman named Betsy had called him. Johnny. Oh, God. Thank God, thank God. He felt almost whole knowing his name.

He remembered tasting the jelly. He hadn't swallowed it because he couldn't. The old woman, Betsy, had held up a spoonful. He'd touched his upper lip to the still-warm jelly and smacked his lips, silently, of course, for he could make no sound. Betsy had laughed, pleased, and talked to him while she filled blue half-pint jars with thick, red jelly.

She'd told him Whit was in law school and Willie was in college. On the dean's list, she added proudly, and dating a boy her father didn't like. Betsy told him Willie always dated boys her father didn't like, that she'd told Whit Senior Willie did it *because* he didn't like them. But did the jackass listen to her and keep his mouth shut? Hell, no.

The jackass had come while he was there—a big, handsome man with a ruddy face. He and his wife and Willie and Whit had come to spend Christmas with Betsy. He didn't like Betsy and he didn't like the house. Johnny had followed him everywhere, making him start nervously and look behind him. He and Betsy had laughed about it afterward.

He couldn't remember his own grandmother, but he remembered Willie's. He remembered, too, how much he'd loved her. So much that he'd wept when Betsy came back from Boston and couldn't see him anymore. She'd tried to find him, kept talking to him and looking for him in shadowy corners and on moonlit nights on the beach. He'd tried everything he could think of to make Betsy see him; he'd stood in bright lights and waved his arms, but he hadn't known about mirrors then and neither had Betsy.

He missed her so much his throat clenched as he sank to his knees—his forearms folded on the back of the couch, his chin on his wrists—and gazed at Willie. She made a soft little snort in her sleep that made him smile, rolled her head away on the pillow and flung one arm over her head.

The movement caused the front of her pajama top to gape, giving him a moon-silvered glimpse of soft, sweet curves. He ached to touch her, to feel flesh warmed by a beating heart. She looked so lovely and so vulnerable. And no match for Raven.

He could leave if he wanted. He wasn't tied to this place. For the time he spent here, his will was his own. He knew that, though he didn't know how. He'd fled Raven before, though he couldn't remember where he'd gone or when. He could only remember that Raven had pursued him and that Raven had been angry. Very, *very* angry.

If he thought Raven would follow him without wreaking vengeance first on Willie, he'd run as far and as fast as he could from Stonebridge. But Raven's temper was too capricious, too swift and too terrible to even think about doing that.

It was best if he stayed. Better yet if he found a way to warn Willie. He had no idea how, but he'd think of something. In the meantime, he'd protect her from Raven.

Somehow. Some way. God willing.

7

WILLIE THOUGHT SHE WAS still dreaming when she woke up rubbing her nose, but she wasn't a little girl crying on the beach because a starfish had stung her. She was sprawled on the couch in the living room, a calico tail twitching in her face, her neck scrunched beneath the purring weight on her head. The oldest wake-up-and-feed-me cat trick in the book.

"Get off, goofy," she mumbled, giving Callie a poke.

The cat stretched onto Willie's chest, giving her a faceful of bony little behind. Willie swept her onto the floor and struggled up on her elbows, blinking and spitting cat hair.

Bright morning sun flooded the porch and slanted through the windows in broad, dusty beams across the floor. Willie yawned, scratched her head and saw that her left foot was on the floor and her right was still propped on the doubled-up pillow.

She pushed herself all the way up, wincing in anticipation, but felt only a twinge of stiffness as she lifted her ankle off the pillow. It took most of her weight when she swung it to the floor and stood.

"Look, Ma, no hands," she said, flinging her arms out.

Callie sat on the coffee table looking at her nonplussed, then jumped down and trotted ahead of Willie as she made her way into the kitchen. Getting there and into the bathroom wasn't half bad. There was no pain, only weakness in her ankle, and the swelling was nearly gone. The bone was sore, and so was her fanny—Willie felt the bruises there—but on the whole she felt great. Raven was some kind of doctor.

The microwave said it was 7:32. Callie said feed me, meowing petulantly around Willie's legs when she came out of the bathroom. Willie gave her half a can of tuna with fresh water, made coffee and headed for the stairs.

Here was the real test, of her nerves as well as her ankle. Willie took a deep breath, wrapped her hand around the banister and started upstairs. She made it without two-footing a single step or seeing anything that wasn't supposed to be there. On purpose, she took a long time brushing her hair at the mirror, but no apparitions appeared in the glass.

Willie wasn't sure if she was relieved or disappointed. Whatever she'd seen was gone now, but not forgotten. It was time to investigate. Beaches first, Dr. Jonathan Raven second, and third, if necessary, her sanity.

She hadn't gone ballistic when the first certified letter from Raven's attorney in Boston had arrived; she'd called Whit, then she'd gone straight to the county clerk's office, where Nancy Crocker had told her about Horace Raven and his will.

"Near as I can figure," she'd said, "Dr. Raven's from the branch of the family who moved down Boston way when the whaling gave out. Might have been another doctor in the family, but I b'lieve it was quite a while ago."

Willie hadn't dug any further, but she was going to now. First in a bottom drawer for the ankle brace left over from her tennis-playing days in college. She put it on with white Reeboks to give her ankle maximum support. Then she put on khaki shorts and a tropical-print blouse. Next she went down on her hands and knees and looked under the bed and behind the furniture.

She searched the closet and the baseboards for wires, mirrors, cameras—anything Raven could have used to project a hologram. Then she searched the rest of the house, even the circuit box, though she was sure if Jim and the boys had found anything funny in the wiring they would have told her. She found nothing. Which was exactly what she'd expected.

On her way to the kitchen, Willie shut off the air conditioner and opened the French doors. Probably not bright economically, but living in New York had given her a bellyful of artificial environments. Willie liked fresh air, even muggy, you'll-be-sorry-later fresh air.

While she drank her first cup of coffee, she fried link sausages in a cast-iron skillet and wondered about the man in the knee boots and breeches. If she hadn't imagined him, if he wasn't her pirate or a hologram, then what was he? And what was the silvery shimmer she'd seen beside her bed?

Willie frowned, mixed pancakes and poured the first batch. She was just wondering if maybe she should have her eyes checked when Frank came through the French doors.

"How come you're not flat on your back where I left you?"

"'Cause my ankle feels great." Willie turned away from the counter. "So great I'm making you breakfast."

"Lemme see."

Willie kicked off her shoe, peeled off her sock and the brace and stuck out her foot. Frank cupped her heel in his hand and turned her foot gently from side to side. She felt only a twinge, and gave Frank a see-I-told-you-so smile as he glanced up at her with a raised eyebrow.

"You s'pose Raven's a witch doctor?" he asked.

He was kidding, but Willie wondered, even though she laughed as she put the brace and her sock and shoe back on. She was not hysterical; she'd never been hysterical. She'd seen something in the mirror. She just couldn't explain it. Not yet.

While Willie flipped the pancakes onto a plate with the sausages and covered it with a towel, Frank warmed the syrup, then followed her onto the terrace with plates and silverware. An already-hot wind snapped the yellow umbrella he opened to protect the pancakes from the gulls.

They came every morning from the beach to horn in on the grackles and blue jays that pecked out their breakfast on the back lawn beneath Granma's fruit trees. While Frank and Willie ate, Callie stalked the birds, her ears flat and her tail twitching. The birds ignored her.

"The feathers are gonna fly here in a minute," Frank predicted in a low voice.

"Not a chance. The gulls will run her off."

"Y'know, Will, Callie looks a lot like ol' Patches. Now, there was a gull killer. Sic 'em, Callie." Frank leaned forward in his chair, elbows bent on his knees. "They shit on my car every time I wash it."

"That's what birds do, Frank. Don't encourage her." Willie stacked the sticky plates and picked up her coffee. "If she gets one, I'll just have to take it away from her."

"It's instinct, Will. Let her hunt."

"I'll let her hunt. I just won't let her strew bones and feathers all over the house."

"Killjoy."

Callie dug in her back claws and launched her attack on a fat gull grooming its wing feathers, just as a huge black crow came swooping in for a landing. The jays, gulls and grackles took off in a flurry. So did Callie, streaking back to the terrace to hide under Willie's chair.

"Some gull killer you are," Frank said, leaning over the arm of his chair to frown at the cat.

Callie blinked up at him and meowed, her ears flat and her tail bristling. The crow gave a raucous caw and flapped up into the peach tree. The flock came back, brazen gulls and grackles first, then the blue jays.

"That's the biggest crow I've ever seen," Willie said, watching the huge black bird fold its wings on one of the lower branches and cock its head at her.

"It's not a crow. It's a raven."

"How can you tell?"

"It's bigger, blacker and bold as hell."

"Sounds like another Raven I know," Willie quipped.

"Biting the hand that heals you, Will."

"Not without just cause."

Frank helped her carry the dishes inside and rinse them. Through the window above the sink, Willie could see the raven still perched in the peach tree watching the other birds. She told Frank about Dr. Raven's offer to stop by and check her ankle and asked him what he thought of it.

"Why do you do this?" Frank asked. "Why do you ask me this kind of stuff?"

"Because you're my friend." Willie squeezed out the dish sponge and shut off the water. "I value your opinion."

"How come you never pay any attention to it?"

"'Cause you're always wrong."

"Then I repeat my original question. Why do you ask me?"

"If it's such a big deal, Frank, never mind." Her voice sharper than she intended, Willie turned quickly away to wipe up grease spatters, but not quickly enough.

"Did something happen you're not telling me?"

"No," she lied. "I just wondered what you thought."

"Okay. I'll tell you what I think. I think Raven's very interested in you."

"Of course he is. I've got Beaches and he wants it."

"I think he wants more than Beaches, Will."

"Oh, Frank, c'mon." Willie rolled her eyes at him over her shoulder. "Think with something other than your gonads."

"See? It happens every time. I tell you what I think and you tell me I'm crazy."

"I'm sorry I asked."

"Do you want me to drop by tonight?"

"No. I can handle Raven."

"If you change your mind, call me. See you later."

Frank left. Willie tossed the sponge into the sink, went to the French doors and watched him go, his stiff-legged stride screaming bent male ego. She'd never known Frank to be so touchy. Maybe the heat was getting to him. Maybe she should have kept the air conditioner on. Or her mouth shut.

She knew the perfect way to make it up to him. Coq au vin and lemon meringue pie for Sunday dinner. She needed lemons, mushrooms and burgundy, as well as cat food, litter and a cat box with a lid for Callie. Standing at the counter by the window, she made a list. At the top of it she wrote *"Find out about the guy in the riding boots and breeches."*

The big question was how. Willie considered it, clicking the pencil she'd found in the junk drawer against her teeth. The raven cawed in the peach tree. She glanced up, saw its gleaming blue-black head cocked at the window. One shiny onyx eye blinked at her, then it flew away.

"Go shit on Frank's car," she muttered, and glanced down at her list.

Now why had she written *how* with two question marks? She knew how—the Stonebridge Historical Society Museum. If she couldn't find the guy in the boots and breeches there, she wouldn't find him anywhere. Except in her mirror, maybe. Willie tucked the list in her purse, turned on the air conditioner and locked the house behind her.

The digital time and temperature board outside East Cape Savings and Loan said it was eighty-two degrees and 10:12 a.m. as Willie crossed the street and climbed the steps of the Stonebridge Historical Society Museum. It was housed in one of the oldest shingled saltboxes on the Cape. The curator, Lucy Pulver, dressed in a colonial gown with an apron and a lace-trimmed cap, smiled when Willie asked what she had on the Raven family and where she'd find it.

"Front parlor," she said, nodding at the low, square doorway to the left of the entry hall.

The slanted floor creaked as Willie stepped into the room. A wooden settle sat in front of the fireplace. Cane-backed chairs and spindly tables holding oil-wick lamps and candlesticks were scattered across a faded rag-braided rug.

Over the mantel hung a framed portrait of Horace Raven. A gold plaque beneath it said he was a patron of the Stonebridge Arts Council. He'd died of pneumonia in 1947 while touring castles in England. It didn't say that on the plaque; Nancy Crocker had told her. He had Raven's dark eyes behind horn-rimmed glasses, a grim expression and a receding hairline. Give his great-nephew thirty years, Willie thought, and he'd be a dead ringer for old Uncle Horace.

There were other photographs inside a display case built along the wall opposite the windows. Willie turned on the shaded fluorescent tube above the glass top, leaned her elbow on the wooden edge and bent forward to study them.

Most of the photos were grainy and faded with age. Still, she had no trouble recognizing the dark eyes she'd first seen by the glow of the luminarias on the terrace. He stood smiling in a sepia-tinged photograph on the steps of a house, his right elbow bent on the banister, his left arm slung around the shoulders of a man a good head shorter than he was, with bristly muttonchops. There were two brief lines typed on a slip of white paper pinned beneath the picture.

Jonathan Raven and Theodore Gorham, the first two Harvard graduates from Stonebridge. Photo taken June, 1877. Both men murdered in Egypt, at Thebes in the Valley of the Kings, August, 1878.

"Oh, my God," Willie murmured, a slow chill crawling up her back.

His hair was shorter, he wore a tweed suit and brocade waistcoat, a high collar and elaborately tied cravat, but it was him. The man she'd seen in her mirror. He not only looked enough like Dr. Jonathan Raven to be his twin, he had the same name.

Only he'd been killed—no, *murdered*—117 years ago.

8

WILLIE STOOD, STUNNED and staring at the photograph until her purse slid off her shoulder and hit the floor with a thunk. Startled, she swooped it up by its strap, her heart pounding, and glanced at the doorway. Lucy Pulver stood there, her head cocked curiously to one side.

"You okay, Willie? You look a little pale."

"I'm fine. Just surprised," Willie admitted. "I didn't expect to find another Jonathan Raven here. Especially one who looks enough like Dr. Raven to *be* Dr. Raven."

"You did?" Lucy cocked a dubious eyebrow. "Where?"

"Right here." Willie tapped her finger on the case.

Lucy took her glasses out of her apron pocket, put them on and peered at the photograph. "Oh, this one," she said with a shrug. "There's a resemblance, I suppose."

"Clean your glasses, Lucy, and look again."

"I've seen this picture a hundred times, Willie. Every day when I polish the case. You're seeing things."

I know that, Willie wanted to shout. Instead she asked, "Isn't it kind of gruesome to tell people he was murdered?"

"Heck, no. The tourists love it. The stocks and the dunking chair on the common are our biggest attractions."

"Do you know how he died?"

"Of course I do. That's why I'm curator." Lucy winked and tucked her glasses back in her apron. "Real sad story. Johnny Raven and Teddy Gorham were born and raised in Stonebridge. Went to Harvard together, then off to Egypt with the Boston Museum when they started findin' all the mummies and such. Teddy was a curator, too. Now, this Dr. Raven—"

"Whoa." Willie flung up one hand. "*Which* Dr. Raven?"

Lucy tapped the glass. "This Dr. Raven."

Willie blinked, another chill crawling through her. "*He* was a doctor, too?"

"Runs in the family. So does the name Jonathan. This one—" Lucy tapped the glass again "—was medical officer for the expedition. He was killed by grave robbers, Teddy by Nile pirates. They saw Raven's coffin on the boat crossing the river, figured it was a pharaoh and attacked. That's when Johnny's mother, Rachel, lost her mind, when she found out the boat was sunk and she wasn't gonna get her boy's body back to bury. He was killed in August. She died in January. Froze herself to death out there at Beaches, rockin' on the porch in a no'theaster with nothin' but a shawl on, mutterin' 'He isn't dead, he isn't dead,' over and over till she couldn't mutter no more. Got so bad the other boy run off. Just before Christmas, as I recall."

"Other boy?" Willie blinked again. "What other boy?"

"Her youngest. Named Samuel. Terrible winter that year. Early frost killed most of the crops. Fodder was so scarce the deer came right into town. Brought the wolves right behind 'em. We had wolves around here, then. Some say we still got bobcats. Anyway, Stonebridge lost near a dozen folk that winter, 'tween the cold and the wolves and—"

"Some other time, Lucy. Thanks for your help."

Willie flung her purse over her shoulder and raced out of the museum. Her hands didn't stop shaking until she'd clamped them around the Jeep's steering wheel, closed her eyes and leaned her forehead against it. The hard vinyl circle was hot, almost sizzling, but it helped chase the chill that had swept through her as she'd listened to Lucy.

Granma Boyle had died at Beaches, too, peacefully in her sleep. She hadn't rocked herself to death in a gale, hadn't driven her only surviving child away with her madness.

The story Lucy had told her wasn't sad. It was weird and creepy. Straight out of Edgar Allan Poe, Willie thought as she raised her head and saw the raven perched on a low branch of the elm tree growing in front of the Jeep. The bird was watching her as Lucy had, its head tilted to one side.

There were ravens everywhere. Willie knew that now, realized she'd been mistaking them for crows until Frank had pointed out the differences. If you've seen one raven, Willie told herself, you've seen 'em all—with the possible exception of Dr. Jonathan Raven and his lookalike ancestor. Yet she couldn't quell the certainty she felt, or the shiver it gave her to know that the raven peering at her from the elm was the same one she'd seen in the peach tree.

The odds against it were astronomical, but so were the odds that Beaches was haunted. Yet it had to be. It was the only logical explanation for what she'd seen in her mirror—which had to be the ghost of the first Dr. Raven, dressed in riding boots and breeches. If you could call such things logical.

Or coincidental. But that was what it had to be. Pure coincidence that the ghost of Johnny Raven, murdered in Egypt in 1878, had shown up in her mirror at the same time his descendant with the same name, the same face—and the same profession, no less—had shown up in her life.

As for the raven peering at her from the elm tree, it was just a bird. A noisy, nosy, car-crapping bird. No more the same one she'd seen in the peach tree than she was the same Willie Evans who'd snuck out of New York to avoid her father's I-know-what's-best-for-you bullying.

"Bye-bye, birdie." Willie started the engine and gunned it, startling the raven out of the tree with a squawk.

Watching it flap away gave her an idea. Lucy said she was seeing things. Willie didn't think so—not the way Lucy meant. But there was a simple way to find out. Not cheap, but simple.

The glimpse she'd had of Johnny Raven on the porch was so fleeting she'd thought it might have been too many daiquiris. She *knew* she'd seen him in her mirror, though she didn't know how it was possible. She knew mirrors were expensive to resilver and you can't see vampires in them because they don't cast reflections. How a ghost did she hadn't a clue.

But if she could catch him again in one of the two dozen mirrors she bought on her way home—along with the stuff for Callie and the ingredients for Sunday dinner—she could at least prove to herself that she *was* seeing things. She might even make paranormal history. If she didn't scare herself silly.

It took Willie the rest of the afternoon to set up her ghost traps, rearranging the mirrors she already had with the ones she had bought—at six different shops in Stonebridge so she wouldn't raise eyebrows. Or questions. She didn't stop for lunch, just munched Oreos and drank a glass of milk while she set up one large mirror in every room of the house and aimed smaller ones at them from the corners.

She thought about calling Zen, but decided the last thing she needed, let alone wanted, was the parapsychological research club Zen belonged to crawling all over Beaches with cameras and microphones. Nor did she want to look like a fool if the ghost of Johnny Raven turned out to be nothing more than her overactive imagination. Or underused libido.

The mirrors worked well, except for a few blind spots she figured she could cover with the gold compact mirror she tucked in her pocket. When Callie came into the dining room to lie in a sunbeam, she froze and arched her back at the five images of herself hissing back. Willie knelt and scratched the cat's ears until she started purring, then she opened the curtains to give her more sun, and went out to get the mail—deliberately, with only a moment's flicker in her pulse rate, via the front door and the porch where Rachel Raven had frozen to death.

It hadn't fazed Willie to redo Betsy's bedroom and make it her own. She had only happy memories of bouncing Granma awake in her lumpy old four-poster, and of rocking away purple evenings in the porch swing listening to the whales sing and high tides boom on the beach. No ghost and his crazy mother were going to take those away from her.

It was almost five-thirty, the sun a blistering orange ball sinking below the dunes. A gusty wind sent sand and gravel dust into Willie's eyes as she walked down the driveway to the road and the rural mailbox. On the way back she picked up

The Stonebridge Chronicle from the lawn, unrolled it, tucked the mail under her arm and read the front page.

The unseasonable heat wave blazing into its sixth week was big news. The lead story claimed income from tourism was up 40 percent from last year, always good news in Cape towns like Stonebridge. The latest unemployment statistics from Washington rated smaller headlines. So did world news: peace talks here, economic negotiations there, an outbreak of sudden and bloody civil war in a tiny Central American country Willie had never heard of and couldn't pronounce, and cattle mutilations in the Yucatan peninsula of Mexico.

Tomorrow's *Boston Globe,* which she took on Sunday for the comics, would probably tell her the former was the work of the CIA and the latter the work of aliens. Why ETs would grind up cows in pastures at midnight Willie couldn't figure. If they were smart enough to find their way to earth, surely they were smart enough to find their way to McDonald's.

She turned left on the porch toward the terrace to check her geraniums. They were bone dry. She put one pot on the table to weight down the paper and the mail, took her watering can out of the bin and headed for the kitchen sink.

She heard a crash and a yowl from upstairs as she came through the French doors, put the can down on the dining room table and bounded up the steps. In the bedroom next to hers she found Callie peering out from under the bed, and her grandmother's sewing cabinet, which she used as a nightstand, overturned on the woven cotton rug in the middle of the room.

Willie had put it there with one of the shaving mirrors she'd bought at Pac 'N Save on top, angled and aimed at the one over the dresser. She dropped to her knees, picked up the flimsy plastic mirror and saw it was unbroken.

"Lucky for you," she said to Callie as the cat crept out from under the bed. "Or you'd have seven years of bad luck."

The drawer fell out as Willie righted the cabinet, spilling buttons, thimbles, a tape measure and one of her grandmother's quilt-pattern notebooks with a blue dotted-swiss cover. Willie let Callie bat a thimble around while she replaced spools of thread on the brass brackets built inside the flip-top lid to hold them.

Then she put the drawer back and took the thimble away from the cat. Callie fought her for it and snagged a claw on one of the strips of bright material laid between the pages of the notebook. Willie gently disentangled her and refocused the mirror. Then she opened the book and flipped through it, hoping to find the chop suey recipe for Frank.

The quilt pattern her grandmother had sketched was "Drunkard's Path," a crazy up-and-down zigzag that made Willie smile. Maybe she'd try this one. The pattern was goofy enough that her mistakes wouldn't show. Willie got to her feet smiling, turned the page and froze. Below the drawing of a quilt block and some notes on fabrics, her grandmother had written in pencil and her age-crabbed script.

Johnny came today. Saw him at dusk walking up from the beach. First time I've seen him outside. He looked sad and lost until I called to him. Then he smiled and seemed to remember where he was. Hasn't a clue where he's been. Never does, poor thing.

Oh, God. Willie clapped the book against her pounding heart and stared at her wide-eyed reflection in the dresser mirror. Granma had seen Johnny Raven's ghost, too, and knew his name. So did Lucy, but Lucy was supposed to. She was a curator. Like Teddy, his friend who'd been killed by pirates. How had Betsy found out his name? Did ghosts talk?

Willie peeled the book off her chest and flipped quickly through the rest of it. She found a recipe for quince jelly, a grocery list, a reminder not to forget to send "the jackass" a birthday card, but no more notes about Johnny.

She wanted to scream, but went flying out of the bedroom instead. It took her an hour to find eighteen more notebooks, the mirrors mocking her harried, room-by-room pawing through drawers and bookshelves. There were lots more someplace, but Willie didn't take the time to find them. She raced the ones she had into her office and dumped them on her desk, knocking over the mirror trimmed with glued-on seashells she'd made Granma in Girl Scouts. A few shells fell off, but the glass didn't break. Willie stood the mirror up, dropped into her chair, booted up the Mac and opened a new file she named JOHNNY.

Sunset was in full purple-and-mauve swirl outside the office windows, but the glow from the monitor gave Willie light enough to read. It took her half an hour of fevered skimming to find another entry. It was written in pencil and smeared, as if Granma had rubbed her hand over it while she wrote.

Johnny sat on the porch with me after supper. He can't talk, so we just rocked in the swing and listened to the surf. We heard whales, too, and Johnny cried. Didn't shed one tear, still I thought his heart was going to break.

"How did you find out his name, Granma?" Willie asked. "And why didn't you tell me you were leaving me a ghost along with Beaches?"

If Johnny Raven could rock in a porch swing and cry, even without tears, why couldn't he talk? Willie frowned and picked up a notebook with a purple paisley cover. What she knew about ghosts she knew from books and movies. Hardly scientific, but if Jacob Marley could talk to Scrooge in *A Christmas Carol*, how come Johnny Raven was mute?

Willie frowned and opened the purple notebook. The patterns and notes Betsy had written here were mostly in ink. Her handwriting looked stronger and clearer, too. She must've started this one after her lens replacement surgery, Willie thought, a chill creeping up her back as she turned a page and found an entry written in green ballpoint, dated July 12, barely six weeks before Betsy died. It was the only dated entry Willie had found so far. She tried to ignore the pang it gave her, but her eyes filled with tears as she read.

Yesterday I found a sand dollar on the kitchen table, in a pool of sand still warm from the beach. Today I found poppies, red ones—my favorite—in the old blue mason jar. Presents from Johnny, I know it. It's July, and he always comes for his birthday. I haven't forgotten him, even though I haven't been able to see him since I had the damn cataracts taken off. Makes me feel good to know he hasn't forgotten me, either. Makes me wonder, too, if I'll be here when he comes next summer.

"Oh , Granma," Willie said around the lump in her throat. She wiped tears off her lashes with her fingertips and re-read the passage. Her eyes filled again, but this time she smiled and murmured, "Thank you, Johnny," just as she glanced up and saw him in the seashell mirror.

9

HE SAT on the white wicker trunk against the wall by the door, elbows bent on the knees of his riding breeches, a faint, expectant smile curving one side of his mouth—that oh-so-sexy mouth she'd last seen in the emergency room of Stonebridge General—as if he'd been waiting for her to look up and notice him.

He didn't seem at all threatening. Still, Willie felt every hair on her body stand on end. It was one thing to set traps for a ghost, but something else to actually catch one. Now that she had, she didn't know what to do. Except meet his dark eyes in the mirror and repeat, "Thank you, Johnny."

He raised his right hand, palm upturned, and swept it in a graceful arc toward his body. *"You're welcome,"* he said in American Sign Language.

Gooseflesh shot through Willie. Someplace around here there was a sign language dictionary she'd found her grandmother studying when she'd come to visit during spring break her junior year at Cornell. "You're never too old to learn a language," she'd said, but now Willie knew the real reason.

The rest of the few simple phrases Betsy had taught her flew out of Willie's head as she spun out of her chair. But all she could see was a silvery shimmer in the air above the trunk. Just like the one she'd seen beside her bed.

Last night she would've sworn it had no shape, but now it looked like a reverse image on a negative, of a man about six foot two, maybe three, with very broad shoulders. It gave her the creeps and a nasty shock of vertigo. She turned her head quickly toward the pedestal mirror she'd put in the corner, saw Johnny Raven on his feet and moving toward the door.

"No, please!" Willie flung one hand toward him in the mirror. "Don't go!"

He stopped and looked back at her, catching her gaze in the seashell glass. He knows about the mirrors, Willie realized with a jolt that sat her down, hard, in her chair.

"I'm okay now," she lied. "You just startled me."

He gave her a wry, no-kidding smile. Willie stared at him, wondering what to say. He looked as real as she was—as long as she kept her eyes on the mirror—so real she could see sweat stains on his brown leather vest, sand caked on his boots and grass stains on his breeches. And he looked so much like Jonathan Raven that her heart skipped. Not with fright, but with pure female awareness that, alive or dead, this Raven was as stunningly handsome as the other. And why not? They looked like identical twins.

"I'm Willie," she said. "Betsy's granddaughter."

He nodded *I know* and sat down again. Over the top of the mirror Willie saw fireflies hovering in the leaves of the oak tree in the side yard. The shadows beneath the tree deepened toward dusk. She wanted to turn on her desk lamp, but didn't; she was afraid Johnny would vanish in bright light.

"Can you see me without looking in the mirror?" she asked, and he nodded. "How come I can't see you?"

He shrugged and spread his hands. In any language the gesture meant *I don't know.*

"You can hear me, but you can't speak, right?"

He nodded, then shook his head. Yes and no.

"How did you learn sign language?"

He pressed his hands together, then let them fall open.

"A book?" Willie asked, and he nodded. "You can read?"

He nodded, his luminous dark eyes gleaming with amusement in the mirror. Dumb question, Willie supposed, since he'd gone to Harvard. Over a century ago, when Cambridge was a half day's ride on horseback from Boston.

"Wish I knew where Granma's sign language dictionary is."

Johnny leapt to his feet, made a wait-here gesture like that of a traffic cop, and ducked out of the room—through the doorway, thank God, not the wall. Willie was pretty sure Jacob Marley's ghost had walked through walls. So why did Johnny Raven observe the spatial laws of physics?

Don't think about it, she told herself, or you'll run out of here screaming and never come back. And wouldn't that just delight the hell out of Dr. Jonathan Raven?

She didn't see how Johnny could be in cahoots with Raven to scare her out of Beaches, but she didn't like the fact that the possibility had occurred to her. Was there something wrong with this picture or was she nuts? If Johnny Raven was dead, how could he see and hear and read? Why was he visible only in mirrors? Was he really a ghost? And if he wasn't, what the hell was he?

She almost asked him when he came back with the blue-and-white soft-covered dictionary she remembered, but didn't. She wasn't afraid to hear the answer; she was terrified. Johnny held the book up to her in the mirror, one dark brow raised.

"That's it," Willie said.

He smiled, leaned over her and put the book on the desk. The sleeve of his shirt fell away in soft folds from his well-muscled arm. This close up, she could see splattered, rusty stains on the yoked front inside his vest and buttons torn off the open throat. She remembered he'd been killed by grave robbers, realized the stains were blood and shivered. His wrist, long fingers and the back of his hand were sinewy and sun browned. She could even see a sprinkle of dark hair on his knuckles and a small hook-shaped scar near the second knuckle of his index finger.

In the mirror, anyway. In her peripheral vision there was only a smeared, silvery flicker. The sign language dictionary seemed to be floating onto her desk.

Willie closed her eyes until the urge to toss the Oreos she'd had for lunch passed. When she opened them, she saw Johnny in the mirror, sitting on the trunk again. He made the sign for book, then put his hands together, index fingers touching. He drew them apart, pointed them at his mouth and moved them back and forth, rapidly and eagerly, toward his lips and then away. Willie hadn't a clue what he was saying.

"Slow down," she said, opening the dictionary as she picked it up. "And say it again."

He repeated the signs while Willie glanced from his image in the mirror to the alphabetized drawings illustrating the most common words and phrases and back again. He said it six times before she thought she had it figured out.

"Open the book," she said tentatively, "and let's talk?"

He nodded yes, yes, and raised his right arm, thumb curled below his fist. He flexed his wrist up and down and pointed at his right hand with his left index finger.

"Does that mean yes?"

A smile so radiant it all but lit the room spread across his handsome face. Whatever he is, he's lonely, Willie realized, her heart catching with sympathy. His smile and his joy were so human, so touching and so infectious that when he leapt to his feet and flung out his arms, she did, too.

"By George, I think she's got it!" Willie crowed, tossing the book in the air and spinning toward him on one foot.

Instead of Johnny's glowing smile, her gaze collided with the shimmer. Dizziness swept through her, so sharply and so suddenly she reeled and stumbled. In the pedestal mirror she saw Johnny grab her forearms, yet she kept falling.

She managed, somehow, to get her hands up and catch herself on the desk. She hung over it, breathless and blinking in the seashell mirror, the compact in her pocket digging into her thigh. Johnny stood behind her gazing at his hands, a distressed, I-don't-get-it frown on his face.

Neither did Willie. "If you can pick up a book," she asked him, "how come you can't grasp my arm?"

He looked at her and shook his head. He started to sign something, but his hand froze and his head whipped toward the doorway. It took Willie a good ten seconds of straining her ears to hear the throaty purr of a big engine. The same powerful growl she'd heard from Raven's Corvette.

Johnny's eyes narrowed and his jaw clenched. Hear, my foot, Willie thought, he's got ears like a bat. He flung her another wait-here gesture and raced out of the room.

Willie pushed herself off the desk and followed, stopping in the dining room doorway when she saw Johnny in the closest mirror. He stood at the French doors, palms pressed against the panes she'd exposed when she'd opened the sheers. Purple spears of twilight shot past him, edging his shoulders with lavender and pooling shadows on the hardwood floor.

"It's Dr. Raven, isn't it?"

Johnny whirled around, shaking his head and beating his right fist against his chest.

"I know," she said, "but it's his name, too."

He shook his head again and thumped his chest. When a car door slammed in the driveway, he flung his arms across the French doors and shook his head violently. Willie didn't need a dictionary to figure out what he meant.

"Don't worry," she said. "I have no intention of letting that man into my house."

Johnny turned his head and looked at her in the mirror, a wary, you-wouldn't-kid-me-would-you arch in one eyebrow.

"No way, José. Raven wants Beaches, but he isn't going to get it. No matter how many house calls he makes to check my sprained ankle."

Johnny shook his head and made a sign, fingers steepled like a roof. Willie figured it meant house, that he was trying to tell her Raven didn't want Beaches.

"You and Frank should talk," she said.

The disorienting shimmer that was Johnny outside a mirror swirled suddenly in front of her as she turned toward the front door. Quickly Willie flung her head to one side.

"Don't do that, it makes me dizzy," she said. "I'll get rid of Raven and then we'll talk some more, okay?"

She didn't give him a chance to jump in front of her again, just wheeled and raced for the terrace, grabbing the watering can from the dining room table as she flipped on the carriage lights and ducked outside. She saw Raven's Corvette in the driveway. The top was down, the engine was still pinging and all around the shiny red fenders gravel dust swirled.

The front doorbell pealed as she shut the French doors. The compact in her pocket bit into her thigh again as she bent over the storage bin and took out a trowel. She put the mirror on the table with the watering can, eased the bin shut and turned toward the steps as Raven came around the corner of the porch, saw her and smiled.

She'd thought she could handle this, thought she was prepared for Raven's striking good looks and resemblance to Johnny. She was wrong. Seeing him in the flesh, even in fading daylight and thirty feet away, shot her heart up her throat.

Raven felt it throbbing there, wildly, and his own senses quickened in response. He kept smiling, even as he brushed her thoughts and found his Shade there.

"Good evening, Miss Evans," he said, dipping deeper into her mind as he came down the steps. "I'm pleased to see you up and around."

"My ankle feels fine," Willie said, even though it was throbbing along with her heart. "I was out back weeding the flower beds when I heard your car."

She was a horrible liar. Most mortals were. She'd been in her office with his Shade. She called him Johnny. The name struck a faint chord of memory in Raven. His Shade had shown himself to Willow Evans in a mirror. Raven hadn't known such a thing was possible, hadn't realized that his Shade had either awareness or an existence of its own.

"Do you weed by touch, Miss Evans? It's nearly dark."

"It wasn't when I started."

He came down the steps, one corner of his mouth quirked with amusement. It was so much like the wry, no-kidding smile Johnny had given her that Willie's breath caught and a slow chill crawled up her back. Not just because of the eeriness of the resemblance between man and—well, whatever Johnny was—but the realization that Johnny knew Raven, and judging by his reaction to his arrival, didn't like him. Not one bit.

Why? Willie wondered. How did Johnny know him? Was there some kind of connection between them? Was it Beaches? Is that why Raven wanted it?

He stopped and tilted his head at her. He wore jeans and another oxford-cloth shirt open at the collar. Either white or pale blue, Willie wasn't sure. He stood close enough that the just-risen half-moon seemed to ride on his right shoulder, so near that she could almost count the dark hairs curling in the gaped front of his shirt.

"You look distressed. Have I come at a bad time?"

"Not at all," Willie said quickly. Too quickly, she realized when he arched an eyebrow at her. "I'm just hot."

And getting hotter by the second standing this close to Raven. Willie backed up a step. Still, it was impossible to tell where the steamy summer night ended and the sultry, sexy aura Raven emitted began. She barely knew this man, didn't trust him any farther than she could see him, yet when she noticed a tiny fleck of shaving cream on his left earlobe she wanted to wipe it off. With her tongue.

"Would you like a glass of ice tea?" she asked, hoping it would cool her fevered senses.

"Yes. Thank you."

"I'll get it." She waved him toward the table and turned away. "Please have a seat."

"Won't you invite me in?"

Willie glanced back at him. The amused smile was still on his face, but the covetousness she'd first seen in his dark eyes glittered there again. It worked better than ice tea. Better even than a cold shower.

"I thought you liked the heat," she said.

"I'd also like to see what you've done with the house."

"Since Beaches will never be yours, what I've done with it is none of your business," Willie replied coolly, tossing the trowel aside as she wheeled inside.

When the door slammed behind her, hard enough to rattle the panes in the French door, Raven smiled—until he sat down and his gaze fell on *The Stonebridge Chronicle* tucked under a pot of geraniums.

The glow from the carriage lights didn't quite reach the table, but his night vision surpassed that of the lynx he could sense prowling the dunes. He had no trouble reading the

"World News In Brief" column, and at last understood the
unease that had been gnawing at him all day. He glanced,
frowning, at the house and willed Willow Evans to hurry.

 Nekhat had risen.

10

WITH A QUICK FLICK of her wrists, Willie raked the sheers across the French doors, whirled and sagged against them. She half expected Johnny to leap out at her again, but the mirrors held nothing but shadows.

"Johnny?" she called. "Where are you?"

There was no sudden, in-your-face shimmer and nothing in the mirrors but her own wide-eyed reflection. Even in the dusk-darkened dining room she could see the pallor of her skin and the pulse hammering in her throat.

Maybe he'd gone off to have a snit. Well, fine. She planned to have one of her own, a jim-dandy, just as soon as she got rid of Raven. The kick in the pants was she didn't *want* to get rid of him. She wanted to spend the night gazing into his luminous dark eyes and licking shaving cream off his ears. God help her.

"Raven wants Beaches, and you want his body," she said to herself in the mirror. "You know what that means, don't you? It's been too damn long since you've had a date."

Not to mention a reality check. Was the living, breathing, sexy-as-sin and rich young doctor waiting for her on the terrace *really* a ringer for his ancestor, Johnny Raven? Had she *really* spent almost an hour talking to a dead guy in a mirror? If she hadn't, then she was looney tunes. And that was all, folks.

Only Willie didn't feel crazy. Stressed? Yes. Hot and bothered? Oh, honey. Thrown for a loop and off her pins? You betcha. Maybe even caught in a time warp for all she knew. She'd wussed out on that one, but she wouldn't again. She'd ask Johnny point-blank just exactly who or what he was the second Raven left. Right after she took one of the tranquilizers she hadn't even thought about since *Material Girl* fired her.

It was that or take a hike, and she'd be damned if she'd let Raven or Johnny scare her out of Beaches. It was enough that she'd been scared out of her wits. Twice.

Willie rubbed a hand over her face and made for the kitchen. Her fingers were clammy, but her cheeks felt hot and flushed, despite the sudden chill that made every hair on her body stand as she passed through the kitchen doorway.

She'd felt the same sensation two days ago when she'd stepped out of the shower, when she'd seen the smudge in the mirror that wasn't there when she'd wiped the glass. She reached into her pocket for the compact, remembered she'd left it on the terrace and spun around on one foot.

"Where are you, Johnny?" Willie demanded, but there was no answering flicker, either in the air or the dining room mirrors. "I'm going to give Dr. Raven a glass of ice tea, then you and I are going to talk. Pull up a comfortable mirror and wait for me."

She needed a shower—she *wanted* to slip into something more comfortable—but settled for splashing cool water on her face and the back of her neck. Then she loaded a tray with glasses full of ice, a pitcher of tea, slices of lemon and sprigs of mint.

The sun was gone below the dunes, except for a few last spears shooting through a bank of dark purple clouds. The latter were pushing across the headland from the sea on a muggy, gusty wind. Hallelujah, Willie thought, turning the tray sideways through the French doors, maybe it'll rain.

She didn't quite get the doors latched, and felt them blow partway open behind her. She meant to go back and shut them, but forgot all about them when Raven rose to help her and his fingers closed over hers on the tray.

Just for a second. Just long enough to take the tray away from her. Just long enough to make her forget all about the doors.

"Thank you," Willie said, sinking into the chair he'd turned to face his at the table.

Raven smiled. Already her brown eyes were beginning to glitter. By the time he finished examining her ankle she'd be his completely. He had no desire for her body or her blood, only her mind. Using her attraction to him was the quickest way to take her in Thrall, bind his Shade to him and be gone before Nekhat realized the moonstone was missing.

"You're welcome." Raven put the tray on the table and filled the glasses, saw her breath catch as he passed her one with a slice of lemon.

"How did you know I take lemon?"

"Lucky guess." Raven dropped a sprig of mint in his, clinked his glass against hers and sat down.

The heavy silver ring on his finger gleamed in the carriage lights. It looked old and very valuable with the diamonds flanking the center stone. Willie wondered if the ring was something else that ran in the family.

"That's a lovely stone," she said. "Is it an opal?"

"No." Raven put his glass down. "It's a moonstone."

It was still cool on his finger. So were the smaller stones Willow Evans thought were diamonds. They were zircons— rare, clear ones, faceted to absorb and express energy, ward stones Raven had included in the mounting to protect and shield the moonstone from Nekhat.

For a time, at least. How long, he didn't know.

"Supposedly," he told her, "a moonstone has the power to reunite lovers who have parted in anger."

She flushed and looked away. Raven felt her heart flutter, closed his eyes and savored the moment.

"I'm sorry," she said. "I didn't mean to snap at you. I'm a little sensitive about Beaches."

"I apologize. I didn't intend to put you on the defensive. I was curious, that's all. As you are about my ring."

"I've never seen a moonstone before."

"It's a variety of feldspar, a mineral component of igneous rock," he began, to distract her while he lifted his senses into the squall line spreading across the darkening sky.

Only a vampire could hear the rumble of thunder in the wind over the rustle of the trees and the boom of the tide. And along the oncoming edge of the storm, Raven sensed a claw of unease and distant disquiet. Something had disturbed Nekhat's rest, prodded him from his lair weeks earlier than Raven had expected. Anything strong enough to rouse Nekhat intrigued him, but he dared not pursue it and draw attention to himself.

Instead, while he told Willow Evans about moonstones, he focused a narrow beam of his awareness toward the house. He expected to find his Shade cowering in the farthest reaches of the attic, but it met him just inside the left-ajar doors, repelling him with a blast of rage and hatred.

Its terror of him, the dynamo that powered its fury, was nothing new. What caught Raven off guard was its strength this early in its Cycle. What stunned him was the protectiveness he sensed and could almost see, the silvery shimmer of caring and concern it wrapped around Willow Evans.

Raven could name the emotions, recognize their color and warm vanilla flavor on his senses, but could only vaguely remember experiencing them. Still, it was enough to remind him of what he'd once been and sought to be again, to clench his throat around a howl of rage and the urge he felt to tear Willow Evans to bloody shreds, seize his Shade and be gone.

How had she done this? How had she insinuated herself with his Shade? How had she achieved what he, with all his powers, had never been able to accomplish?

He knew how, and the irony of it galled him. They were the same, his Shade and Willow Evans. They were human creatures of conscience and morality, and he was not. He was the antithesis of their humanity, the nameless fear that jolted them awake, hearts pounding, in the dead of night, the embodied terror of their darkest nightmares. He was monster, beast, vampire.

Soulless but not stupid. Raven withdrew into himself and loosed the tendrils of control he'd begun to weave in Willow Evans's mind. She was hardly aware of it, blinked only once, reflexively, but his Shade relaxed. Slightly. It was still wary, the palpable beat of its anger warning him away.

Raven considered calling its bluff, wondered if his Shade was noble enough to sacrifice itself to save Willow Evans. If so, he would gain time against Nekhat. If not, he would lose what ground Willow Evans had inadvertently gained him.

It should be days yet before his Shade was this strong. So said the Riddle, but what if the Riddle was wrong—as it was about the timing of his Shade's arrival—or he'd misinterpreted? Not only that passage, but the power of the moonstone to bind the Shade against its will?

"And so, since the earliest times," he said to Willow Evans, as he weighed his options, "the moonstone has been associated with lunar magic. The ancients called it the traveler's stone because of the protection they believed the stone gave to those who traveled by night—particularly on the water when the moon was full."

"Fascinating." Willow Evans slid her elbow onto the table and leaned her chin on her hand. "How do you know so much about moonstones?"

If his Shade could reveal itself to her, then so could he, Raven decided. It was the path of least risk. If the Riddle was wrong and he could not bind the Shade against its will, then he would need its cooperation. For the second he wielded the moonstone, Nekhat would know precisely where it was, and he would come for it. With a vengeance.

"I'm a Cancer," he told her. "A moon child. My birthday is in July."

So was Johnny's. Her grandmother had written it in the purple notebook. A shiver crawled up Willie's back but she managed to keep her smile and her voice matter-of-fact.

"Really? What date? I have a friend born in July."

"The nineteenth." Raven went down on one knee in front of Willie. "Let's have a look at your ankle."

Warning, erogenous zone ahead, her brain flashed as Raven cupped her foot in his hand and began untying her shoe. She tried but couldn't budge it out of his grasp.

"You needn't bother," she said. "My ankle feels fine."

"I'm the doctor. I'll be the judge." He scooped off her Reebok, laid it aside and tugged off her sock. "Ah, a brace. Very sensible. Doctors like sensible patients."

How about insensible ones? Willie wondered, feeling herself tottering on the verge of losing control at the brush of his fingertips on her flesh as he peeled off the brace. His long dark hair gleamed blue-black in the carriage lamps. His lips, oh, those lips, pursed consideringly as he flexed her foot carefully from side to side.

Last night she hadn't trusted herself to watch him examine her ankle. Now she couldn't take her eyes off his fingers gently probing the barely sore bone. She felt as if she was melting inside and out, until she saw the hook-shaped scar near the second knuckle of his right index finger—the same scar she'd seen on Johnny's right hand.

Raven felt her flash of horror, the flood of gooseflesh that prickled her skin all the way down to her ankle cupped in his palm. It was something to do with his hands, some similarity she'd seen between his and those of his Shade, but he couldn't make out what over the scream he felt tearing through her mind.

"Did that hurt?" he asked, looking up at her.

"No—I mean, yes," Willie blurted out, pushing the terrifying impossibility of the scar out of her mind. "I mean—"

"Never mind. All done. Your ankle should be fine by morning." Raven handed her the brace and her sock and smiled. "If I promise not to mention the house, will you have dinner with me tomorrow? It's my night off."

She wanted to say yes, but she was afraid. Her panic and sudden fear of him made her heart thud and her blood race. Raven felt himself quicken as he watched her put on her sock and shoe, felt his perceptions sharpen like those of any animal on the hunt. The lynx prowling the dunes sensed it, flared its nostrils in the wind and screamed.

Its wild, feral cry startled Willow Evans out of her chair. She spun, wide-eyed, toward the beach and the dunes. Raven rose behind her, cupped her arms in his hands and felt her quiver—with alarm and reaction to his touch.

"What was *that?*"

"A lynx, I think. I nearly hit what looked like one on the road the other night."

"A bobcat?" She turned in his hands and blinked at him. "I thought the Puritans shot them all two hundred years ago."

"Apparently they missed at least two."

She smiled and rubbed her arms. "That was the weirdest thing I've ever heard in my life."

So far, Raven thought. He felt gooseflesh rise on her skin as he eased her toward him. "You have a beautiful name, Miss Evans. May I call you Willow?"

"I'd rather you call me Willie," she said, glancing up at him. "Willow makes me sound like a tree."

"But such a lovely, graceful tree. So hauntingly melancholy. Like Ophelia, born to weep."

The image made Willie shiver; Raven's nearness made her weak. His grip on her arms was gentle, the brush of his chest against her breasts warm and seductive. The minty waft of his breath fluttered a chill across the nape of her neck as he bent his head over hers and murmured, "So lovely."

A thrill coursed through Willie as she realized Raven meant to kiss her. She knew she shouldn't let him, not until she'd figured out why he and Johnny had identical scars. But she *wanted* Raven to kiss her, more than she'd ever wanted anything in her life. Enough to tell herself that maybe the scar was just coincidence, enough to lift her face to his and stare, mesmerized, at his oh-so-sexy lips parting over hers.

The wind died and the trees stopped tossing. In the steady, unbroken light she could see that his teeth were very white, and that his incisors, both top and bottom, were very long and pointed.

"Oh, my, Grandpa," she murmured, a breathy catch in her voice, "what sharp teeth you have."

"All the better to eat you with, my dear."

What images that stirred in Willie's head. X-rated and wild, of twisted satin and tangled limbs. Hers and Raven's. A soft moan escaped her as his mouth slanted over hers. She parted her lips and edged her tongue toward his.

Raven managed not to shudder with revulsion, simply broke the kiss and said, "Let's leave something for tomorrow night, shall we?"

"You mean for dessert?"

"If you wish."

Willie was way past wishing, had left wanting in the dust. She ached, she throbbed, she needed. Heaven help her.

"Too late for that," Raven murmured, catching her earlobe in his teeth. He felt her stiffen and draw away, raised his head and smiled at her startled, wary expression.

"What did you say?"

"I said don't be late. I'll pick you up at eight forty-five. Bring a scarf for your hair. I like the top down."

"Eight forty-five," she repeated, forgetting all about the coq au vin and lemon meringue pie she'd intended to make for Frank. "I'll be ready."

"Until then. Don't forget your mail." He nudged the watering can aside, lifted the pot of geraniums, tucked the envelopes inside the newspaper and handed her the compact. "Or your mirror."

"Oh—yes. Thank you." She tucked the mail and the paper under one arm, and held the compact between her palms, her head tipped to one side. "Good night."

It was enough that he'd placed the mirror in her hands. He saw it in her eyes, in the brief flicker of her gaze from his face to the compact and back again, in the curious, I-wonder tilt of her chin.

"Good night, Willow." Raven nodded and headed for the car, knowing she wouldn't be able to help herself now, that she'd look in the mirror even if it killed her.

Hopefully, it wouldn't. And then, because he knew what she'd see, he smiled.

11

NOTHING. That was what Willie saw. Absolutely nothing in the mirror she aimed over her right shoulder at Raven's retreating back.

"Wait a minute," she muttered, tipping the glass higher.

She tipped it lower, angled it to the left, then the right, and still saw nothing in the mirror but the Corvette. Willie didn't get it, not even when she saw the driver's door open by itself. She thought there had to be something wrong with the mirror, so she turned around.

In time to see Raven glance up and wave at her as he slid behind the wheel and leaned forward to turn the key in the ignition. Willie frowned and waved back, turned and aimed the mirror at the Corvette. She still couldn't see Raven, yet the engine started.

The powerful growl sent a shiver up her spine. What was it she'd thought earlier? That she didn't know much about mirrors? Only that they were expensive to resilver and you couldn't see vampires in them because they didn't cast reflections.

"Oh, God," Willie moaned, the compact slipping out of her suddenly boneless fingers.

It landed with a clunk and a tinkle of breaking glass on the flagstones. She dropped to her heels and picked it up, so suddenly her head spun, so violently she had to grab the table to keep from fainting. She clung to the pebbled-glass edge, forehead pressed against her wrist, eyes shut, heart hammering. She could still feel Raven's mouth on hers—and bile in her throat.

Dear God. What had she kissed? Not a man. But what? Raven couldn't be a vampire. He just couldn't. There were no such things as vampires. No such things as ghosts, either, yet she'd spent an hour talking to one in a mirror.

Willie wanted to run away screaming but forced herself to stand and open the compact. The glass was only cracked. One more jolt and it would shatter. So would Willie, but she forced herself to look in the mirror one last time. Just to make sure, just as the headlights came on all by themselves.

She winced at the glare, saw the Corvette turn around and steer itself up the driveway. Yet when she spun on one foot, she saw Raven's hair ruffling in the wind, the pale cotton shirt shimmering in the dark.

A terrified mew escaped Willie. She threw the compact one way, the mail and the newspaper the other and flew inside. She locked the French doors behind her, the front door, too, and raced through the house locking all the windows—even the ones in the attic and the basement. It was a terrified, knee-jerk reaction, and nothing short of a miracle that she didn't fall and break her neck on the stairs.

But maybe that's what Raven intended. Maybe that's why he'd put the mirror in her hand and the idea in her head. Did he want Beaches badly enough to kill her to get it? Was it a warning that if she didn't give up, he'd get rid of her his own way?

The possibility inched an icy chill up her back. Seeing Johnny in the seashell mirror, standing with his arms spread across her office doorway, the billowy sleeves of his white shirt falling in soft folds like angel's wings, sat her down on the edge of her chair.

She didn't know where he'd come from, or how she'd ended up here. She didn't remember turning on the lights, either, but her desk lamp and the white enamel torchiere in the corner blazed. Johnny looked just as solid in the bright light as he had in near darkness.

The sad, I-tried-to-warn-you expression on his face wrenched her still-queasy stomach. Now she knew what he'd been trying to tell her earlier.

"Raven doesn't want Beaches, does he?" she said to him in the mirror. "He wants *you*."

Johnny nodded, slowly and gravely.

Willie wasn't sure she wanted to know, but asked, "Why?"

He shook his head, *I don't know.*

"What d'you mean, you don't know?"

Johnny touched his right thumb to his forehead, then on top of his left thumb and drew a clockwise circle with his closed fist over his heart. Willie started to reach for the dictionary, then remembered she'd thrown it in the air.

"Wait a minute." She saw it under the desk, fished it out and opened it. "Say it again."

He did, three times, before Willie deciphered the signs.

"You don't *remember?*" she said incredulously into the mirror. "You're *sorry?*"

Johnny nodded, spread his hands and lifted his shoulders.

"Let me get this straight." Willie felt an iron band of panic and frustration tightening around her chest. She drew a deep breath, but it didn't help. "You remember sign language, but you can't remember why Raven is after you?"

Johnny nodded, watching her cautiously in the mirror, his head tipped to one side.

"Bullshit!" Willie slammed the dictionary against the desk so hard she knocked over the brass thermometer. *"You have to remember!"*

He shook his head, struck his left index finger with his right, twice, and repeated the circle over his heart.

"Don't tell me sorry! Remember!" Willie shrieked at him. "Start with remembering how to talk! If a goddamn vampire can talk, so can you!"

Johnny's hands were moving rapidly, but froze. He blinked at her in the seashell mirror, his lips parting slowly and his eyes widening. Willie saw the sudden, sharp rise of his chest and his hands fly up to cover his face. He lowered them slowly, a stunned and horrified expression on his face.

Either he didn't know what Raven was or he really had forgotten. Either way, she wished she hadn't said it, or at least hadn't screamed it at him.

He raised his right hand to his forehead and signed, "I remember," his hand shaking visibly in the mirror. Lightning flickered outside the office windows as he signed it again and wheeled away from her. He paced toward the pedestal mirror, swung back and repeated, "I remember. I remember." Then he dropped onto the trunk, bent his elbows on his knees, raked his fingers through his hair and clenched his head.

"Maybe I'm wrong," Willie said, hoping to God she was. "Maybe I'm just hysterical. Maybe the mirror—"

Johnny threw back his head, still clenching it as if it hurt, and screamed. He made no sound, but Willie read his pain and anguish in the twist of his mouth, the distended veins and tendons in his throat.

She wanted to put her arms around him and comfort him, but she couldn't. All she could do was press her fingertips sympathetically to the mirror. He jerked away, as if he'd felt her touch through the glass, leapt to his feet and bolted out of the room.

"Johnny, wait!" Willie spun her chair away from the desk and pelted after him. *"John-ny!"*

He wasn't in the dining room. Or the living room, the kitchen, or any other room in the house. Willie didn't see his telltale shimmer, either, yet she could almost feel him dodging away from her, away from the mirrors.

"Talk to me, Johnny," she called as she raced from room to room. "Tell me what you remember. Maybe we can figure out a way to make Raven go away. Please, Johnny. If nothing else, just tell me your birth date."

She ran through the house pleading with him until her ankle started to ache and thunder began to rumble behind the lightning flashing against the windows—dull, angry thunder that crashed over the house like breakers at high tide.

Willie gave up and limped back to her office. She set the thermometer up and dropped into her chair. Her grandmother's notebooks were strewn across the desk. On the monitor, her "Star Trek" screen-save program was busily constructing the Tholian web around the *Enterprise*. She felt as hemmed in as the starship, caught in something so alien it was beyond comprehension. Not to mention belief.

Willie tapped a key and the cursor appeared, blinking at the top of the empty file she'd named JOHNNY. She hadn't transcribed a single one of Betsy's notes, and now she couldn't. Not with rain pelting the windows and thunder rattling the shutters.

Willie didn't save the file, just shut off the Mac and crawled under the desk to unplug it as she always did during thunderstorms. She was flat on her back wrenching the surge protector out of the outlet when she saw Callie, who curled her tail around her paws and blinked.

"Some mother I am." Willie sighed and stroked a hand down her back. "I forgot all about you. You okay?"

"Brruup," Callie said, and began to purr.

It dawned on Willie that she hadn't seen the cat since Johnny had shown up, that last night Callie had done the same thing, disappeared before Willie had seen Johnny in her bedroom mirror. Cats knew things, her grandmother had claimed. Like when it was best to make themselves scarce.

"Too bad I'm not a cat," Willie murmured to Callie. Her hand was trembling, but just a little, as she petted Callie, listened to her purr and the rain drum on the windows.

Sure beat tranquilizers all to hell, hiding here under the desk. Little dusty. Might be a spider or two, but spiders didn't scare her. Ghosts and vampires did. Maybe she'd just stay here until Johnny and Raven went away.

Fat chance. With eternity to kill, it wasn't likely either one of them would get tired of waiting. She had to do something, but couldn't make herself move. It seemed like a dream, or maybe a nightmare, that she'd kissed a vampire. It almost seemed as if it had happened to somebody else.

If Willie worked at it she could probably convince herself of just that. She didn't own a sweatshirt that said Call Me Cleopatra, Queen of Denial for nothing. She was no slouch at avoidance, either. She'd spent her life ducking and bucking her father's autocratic rule, and six years and who knew how many tranquilizers denying that her job at *Material Girl* was driving her crazy.

She'd been a black belt in passive-aggressive behavior until Granma Boyle had willed her Beaches. She'd been standing up for herself and what she wanted ever since. If she cut and ran, to her parents in New York, to Whit in Boston, even to Frank four hundred yards down the beach, would she ever have the guts to break free again?

What could she tell them, anyway? What on earth could she say? "Gee, Dad, now I know why you've never felt comfortable at Beaches. It's haunted!" What would Whit or Frank do if she called them up and said, "Guess what, guys? Raven isn't a drug runner or a witch doctor. He's a vampire!"

They'd drop a net on her, that's what. No one would believe her. Everyone would think she was crazy. At last Willie understood why Granma Boyle had never told anyone about Johnny's visits to Beaches.

She wasn't crazy. But she wasn't Buffy the vampire slayer, either. Nor did she want to be. She wanted Raven to go away before he broke her heart. Or she broke it herself thinking about what could have been. If only he wasn't a vampire.

She wanted to help Johnny, too, though she couldn't say why. Other than that he seemed to be a kinder, gentler version of Raven. She wanted to help him find the stairway to heaven, the light at the end of the tunnel—whatever he needed to stop wandering around like a lost soul.

Willie had a bad feeling that the only way to help herself and Johnny was to find out what Raven wanted from him. And why. Which she couldn't do hiding under the desk.

Thank God she'd bought garlic for the coq au vin. She'd tie a clove of it on the chain with the little gold cross Granma had given her for confirmation. If she could trust the Boris Karloff movies she'd seen, the double whammy ought to send Raven screaming into the night. The image made Willie smile and her heart ache.

"But first we get some sleep," she said to Callie, feeling suddenly bone weary—a sure sign of stress—as she crawled out from under the desk.

The crashing and booming had stopped, but rain still pelted the windows. Willie tucked Callie in her arm, turned

off the lights and the AC and headed upstairs. A foghorn
moaned, and the lynx screamed. Its eerie cry spun Willie
around on the landing. Callie growled, her tail bristling and
brushing the gooseflesh spreading up Willie's arms. Willie
soothed her and scratched her ears. She wasn't afraid of the
dark, just the things that lived and hunted in it.

The lynx screamed again, reminding Willie that Lucy Pulver had told her there were still bobcats in Stonebridge. Lucy
had said something about wolves, too. Willie shivered,
murmuring prayers, and raced up the steps two at a time,
unaware of the silvery shimmer that was Johnny outside a
mirror stepping out of the shadows at the foot of the stairs.

12

WHEN HE HEARD the bedroom door bang shut behind Willie, Johnny wheeled toward the front porch. He'd had enough of shrinking and cowering, a bellyful of Raven and his tricks.

The lynx screamed a third time, much closer to the house. Raven had done this before, taken some poor animal in Thrall to do his bidding. It would be, Johnny swore, the last time.

He undid the locks and flung open the front door. If Willie hadn't latched the screen, too, he would have pushed through it into a fate worse than Raven, for the creature circling the house was not of his making.

Johnny knew it was a lynx, and he also knew of Raven's fondness for cats, but the rest of the creature's signature was unknown to him. It stank of death and decay, of millennia-long entombment, hot and rusty sand.

A flickering memory stirred, of long, bronzed muscles and icy, numbing pain. Then the lynx slunk into view, bringing with it the reek of rotting vegetation, and the smell of something else—something fresh and wet, but not rain. It confused Johnny and shattered the memory, which drifted away like smoke, in the shape of a jackal with bared fangs. He shivered, drew back into the shadows, watched the lynx and felt a pang of sympathy for it.

It crept closer, moving stiffly, jerkily, not of its own volition, toward the porch steps. Its pelt glittered with rain, its tufted ears twitched. Johnny could smell its terror beneath the stench. As much as it feared man, it feared the thing that held it in Thrall more.

The lynx was searching but not hunting. It lifted its nose and sniffed as it skimmed up the steps, lowered its head and flared its nostrils. Johnny drew deeper into the shadows, but the lynx paid him no mind. It swung away, following a scent along the porch.

Johnny eased the door shut, turned the locks and raced to the French doors. From there he watched the lynx prowl the terrace and rise on its short, powerful hind legs. It sniffed the chair Raven had sat in and the table, one paw resting on the pebbled edge, its claws gleaming in the faint sheen of the moon.

Memory flickered again. Johnny had seen claws like that before. No, he'd been clutched mercilessly in claws like that, but he couldn't remember where or when. He tried, but couldn't hold the image. It slipped away yet again, like the fog beginning to curl around the white iron table legs.

The lynx dropped to all fours and stood, head down and panting, its flanks heaving, its breathing shallow and artificially quickened. Johnny wished he had his carbine. It would be a kindness to kill it. If the Thralldom didn't do it in, its life span would be significantly lengthened, its metabolism skewed, its mind warped.

How did he know that? A shiver crawled up the back of his neck. He'd seen this before. Seen someone pull a carbine from a saddle holster and shoot . . . not a lynx, but a jackal. Several of them prowling the fringe of a firelit desert camp. A man with bristly muttonchops who seemed familiar, but whose face he couldn't see, whose name he couldn't recall.

He couldn't remember, yet he had to remember. For Willie's sake. God, let me remember, Johnny prayed, closing his eyes and focusing on the flames leaping in his memory.

He saw rocks ringing the fire, a brown hand grab and swing a flaming brand. He heard horses scream and mules bray, saw them tethered close by—a black Arab mare, a sorrel gelding and two dusty brown mules, their eyes white and rolling with terror.

He heard the bark of the jackals, the snap of their jaws, the groan of wood cracking under stress. He looked for the source and found it, a long, narrow box protruding from the back of a high, two-wheeled cart resting on its braces in deep, firelit shadow beneath a palm tree.

The cart was shuddering and rocking. Three men, two of them small and brown and wearing bright robes, the third the man with the carbine and muttonchops, were shouting and backing toward the fire. The jackals were closing in, their eyes glowing red in the half dark, their fangs gleaming.

The barrel of the carbine flashed; the crack of its discharge rang on the still desert night. A jackal fell, yelping, but its fellows leapt over it, intent on the men—until the cart turned over on one wheel and the box tumbled out with a thump. It was a coffin. The jackals wheeled toward it, whining and scraping their bellies in the sand.

The lid flew off and the sides splintered. The natives fell on their knees, praying, and the man with the carbine stared openmouthed with horror at the figure inside wrestling to be free of its shroud. Canvas ripped, a pale human hand emerged and closed on the shattered side of the coffin.

In the lick of the flames Johnny saw a hook-shaped scar on the index finger and wanted to scream. He wanted to shut the memory off and run from it, but forced himself to look, for Willie's sake, until Raven shrugged free of the shroud and sat up inside the splintered coffin. His face was gaunt and colorless, his eyes as red as those of the jackals as he turned his head, saw the men and smiled.

The lynx screamed. Johnny started and opened his eyes. They were blurred with tears. He dragged a sleeve across his face and saw the lynx shake itself, leap into the air and whirl around biting at its bobbed tail. A glittering finger of mist swirled up from the spot where the cat had been, melted into the fog and disappeared. The lynx snarled and bounded away into the darkness.

Johnny unlocked the French doors, took a tentative step outside and a deep breath. The stench was gone, and with it the creature who'd Enthralled the lynx. There was only the smell of wet sand and dank earth in his nostrils. He picked up the sodden mail and the compact Willie had thrown, went back inside, locked the doors and, leaning a fist and his forehead against them, cursed himself.

He should have left Stonebridge and drawn Raven away while he'd had the chance, but he'd been selfish and craven. Now a monster far worse than Raven had come, searching for him and the ring he wore. Johnny knew that much, but he didn't know how. Nor did he know who or what the creature was and why it wanted the stone.

He felt a tug at his senses and glanced up at the half-moon gliding behind a skiff of ragged, racing clouds. Two small stars winked nearby, like the clear stones flanking the jewel in Raven's ring. Already his time here was shortening. He knew by Luna's phase, felt in every atom of his being the first icy fingers of cold, black nothingness reaching out to drag him back. It terrified him more than Raven did, even more than remembering his grandfather's funeral.

He'd been no more than seven or eight, his brother, Samuel, a plump, lace-skirted toddler sleeping and blowing milk bubbles on his mother's black bombazine lap. He remembered playing with the ends of her heavy veil while he'd sat on the hard, unyielding pew in the Stonebridge Congregational Church listening to the drone of the minister's nasal voice.

He remembered walking behind her, behind the plain wooden casket borne by his father and his father's five brothers into the graveyard next to the church. It was winter, he couldn't recall the month, and cold enough to make Samuel cry.

He'd clung to his mother's skirts as she'd shushed Samuel and the coffin was lowered on creaking ropes. The edge of the grave was ragged and soft, from the work of the grave digger's pickax and the thaw freshening the wind. He'd felt the ground crumble beneath his feet and tried to scramble away, but his mother clamped a hand on his shoulder and held him fast at her side.

He couldn't tell her he was falling, for his throat was clenched shut with terror. He'd watched his father fling a spadeful of dirt on his grandfather's coffin, heard it rain like pebbles on the wood, and the minister's somber voice intone, "We commend into your keeping, O Lord, the soul of

Jonathan William Edward Raven," just as the ground gave way beneath him and he'd tumbled headlong into the grave.

He remembered his mother's scream, but nothing else except ripping his right index finger open on a coffin nail. He looked at his hands, felt pain flash in his memory, saw blood well and drip on his grandfather's coffin from the hook-shaped scar.

The same scar Raven bore. He knew now that he and Raven had once been one, but something had happened. Some abominable, horrible thing too terrible to remember had separated them and made Raven a vampire, a monster outside the laws of God and man. He didn't know what that thing had been and wasn't sure it mattered. Or if it ever had. He was tired of hiding and being afraid. It was best to bare his throat to Raven and end it. Best for both of them. Best for Willie.

He waited by the doors a while longer, made sure the lynx and the thing that had sent it were gone, then threw the mail and the compact in the trash can in the pantry and went upstairs. Willie was asleep, huddled on her side beneath the double-wedding-ring quilt with a pillow over her head. The cat was curled in the small of her back.

She'd left a lamp burning on the table between the bed and the half-open window, beside the brass wall mirror she'd angled to match the dresser mirror. The curtain fluttered in a damp breath of wind and overturned a small amber plastic vial on the table. Johnny picked it up and read the label. Tranquilizers. He didn't blame her.

He turned off the lamp and watched moonglow backlit by lightning spill through the window and the uncurtained doors leading onto the widow's walk. Thunder rumbled faintly; the trees outside the window rustled and bumped against the roof.

The cat raised its head, laid back its ears and growled. Willie rolled out from under the pillow onto her back and made a fretful noise in her throat. The cat hissed and shot off the bed, its tail bristling, and disappeared.

Johnny mouthed the words, "Good night, Willie," and raised his left hand to the mirror. He intended merely to touch her reflection, as she'd touched his in the seashell mirror. Instead, he saw his hand reach *through* the glass, and he jerked his arm back, stunned.

Was this an illusion, some trick of his deprived senses, or could he really touch her? Johnny raised his hand again and inched his index finger toward the mirror. He saw it slice through the glass and immediately felt the tingle of contact with the fine, soft hair on Willie's right forearm and a dizzying whirl of sensation.

Oh, God. He could *feel* the satin smoothness of her skin, the pebbled rise of gooseflesh tracking the graze of his fingertip down her forearm. His senses soared and filled with wonder.

Willie murmured and rolled away from him, away from the mirror. Johnny closed his hand around her wrist in the glass and held her, felt the flex of her muscles, the bone in her wrist, the slow throb of her pulse. At last, oh, God, at last, flesh warmed by a beating heart.

He tried to touch her outside the mirror, but his fingers passed through her as they had twice before. He could see and feel her wrist clasped loosely in his left hand, so long as he watched in the mirror. If he looked directly at Willie his head spun and the room with it.

He didn't try again. He had no idea how this was possible, how silvered glass could bridge the chasm of time and space between them, nor did he care. It was enough to sit beside her on the bed, stroke the oh-so-soft skin of her inner wrist and feel alive.

Until she murmured something he couldn't hear and rolled toward him so that her left knee, bent beneath the covers, touched his right leg. In the mirror he watched her straighten and felt her leg slide against his—felt it in every atom of his being. He felt the friction of the quilt against the taut cotton of his breeches, felt every stitch in every seam.

Willie flung the quilt back and sighed. He felt the soft waft of her breath on his right hand braced between them, a shiver of awareness and sudden, unexpected arousal. How it was possible without the body Raven had taken from him, he didn't know, but it was as real as Willie's wrist circled in his fingers in the mirror, as lush and wondrous as the shadow of her breast through the blue cotton top of her pajamas.

Heaven and hell, only real in the mirror. But sweet, oh, so sweet! The ache made his senses throb, made him shift on the bed and lift his hand from her wrist to her breast. He closed his eyes and savored the soft, full swell of her, stroked his thumb across her nipple and felt it peak. She murmured and sighed.

Johnny raised his hand from the mattress, cupped her hip tightly against his, caressed her breast and rolled her against him in slow, sinuous circles in the mirror, reveling in the curves and hollows of her body.

She made a soft, purring noise in her throat and flung her left arm over her head. Johnny glanced in the mirror, saw that she was still asleep, saw the gaped front of her pajama top. He slid his fingers past the top button, felt the heat of her skin, the rough pebble of her nipple like sandpaper on his senses, raking sweet, raw shivers through him.

Willie moaned and curled herself around him. He opened his fingers to take more of her, felt the button pop and free his hand, filling it with the full weight of her breast.

It was glorious. Not only to feel again, but to know he could make Willie feel, too. He kneaded her breast tenderly, brushed her nipple and ached to suck it deep into his mouth. She shivered and murmured restlessly.

He slid his hand inside her pajama bottoms, cupped her and rocked her against him, felt her quiver and writhe against him. When she stiffened and her breath caught, he rolled her away from him, went up on his right knee and made sure he could still see her in the mirror. Then he raked her pajamas out of his way and caressed her, molding her against the palm of his hand.

"Ohh, Raven," she murmured in her sleep. "Ohh, Johnny."

She arched against him, whimpered and relaxed, her fluttering eyelashes spiking shadows across her cheeks. Johnny tugged and tucked her back into her pajamas as best he could, raised his hand and breathed deeply. He felt his nostrils flare as the scent of her filled his senses. Then he spread his arms on either side of her and saw her smile, a sliver of moonlight glimmering on the curve of her nose.

He wanted to kiss her, but wasn't so eager to go with Raven that he'd risk sticking his head through a mirror. It was enough that he'd given her pleasure, that he'd been allowed to love Willie. His own sweet little Willow.

Oh, how he loved her. He always had. When she was a child he'd loved her frizzy braids and freckled nose, her imagination and sense of wonder at the world and everything in it.

That love had blossomed little by little, summer by summer, as he'd watched her grow from a girl to a woman. He remembered her first bikini, the fit Betsy had thrown when she'd worn it, the thrill that had shot through him watching her shimmy into it. He remembered the Christmas he'd been here and she'd come with her parents, remembered listening to her talk on the phone to her boyfriend from college and shaking with jealous, impotent rage.

Oh, God. Why had he touched her, made love to her? He couldn't leave her, not now, not again. But he would, he always did. He knew that, remembered the cold and the terror and the wrenching agony of leaving Willie and forgetting her, of remembering her again and how much he loved her, just in time to leave her again and forget her, and then remember her and how much he loved her.

Again and again and again....

13

IT WAS EITHER THE BEST dream or the worst nightmare of her life. Willie didn't know which, nor did she know how she'd slept through it or how she'd lost a button on her pajamas.

She sat on the flank of a dune overlooking the beach, arms looped around her legs, chin on the knees of her blue jeans, the button between her fingers. She didn't remember it being loose, but maybe she just hadn't noticed. Or maybe she'd slept on her stomach and broken the threads.

But she didn't think so. She was pretty sure Raven had been in her bedroom last night. She couldn't think about him making love to her. Not and stay sane. She couldn't imagine why he'd want to, either, even though he'd kissed her.

Maybe that was why she hadn't wakened. Maybe he'd done some hoodoo vampire thing to her mind, or she'd been too scared to wake up. Or maybe too drugged. Maybe that was why she'd dreamed about the starfish again.

She'd taken enough psychology courses in college to know the human mind never forgets anything. Every experience, every incident of your life is stored someplace in your brain. Still, she couldn't figure out the significance of the dream, why her subconscious had led her twice in as many nights back to that morning on the beach when she'd been nine years old and she'd been stung by the starfish. What was she supposed to see that she couldn't remember when she was awake?

Willie hadn't a clue. She rubbed her nose as she had in the dream and wondered how Raven had gotten into the house. Johnny couldn't pass through walls, but maybe Raven could. Which didn't bear thinking about. Not before breakfast.

The morning tide had long come and gone, reclaiming most of the debris the storm had blown ashore. Willie had cleaned up some of it before she'd sat down to puzzle over the missing button and the starfish dream, and watch the sun burn through the fog bank on the horizon.

That was a good long while ago, yet the clouds still hung low and gray, spitting a chilly wind in her face that frizzed her hair and made her shiver. She wasn't cold, but her jeans were wet. She got to her feet, shoved the button into her pocket and picked up the red plastic bucket and shovel left over from her childhood.

She always brought them with her after a storm to rescue starfish. She'd saved half a dozen this morning and felt good about that, but she didn't feel good about returning to Beaches. Her body had been violated, and so had her sanctuary. If she wasn't safe at Beaches, she wasn't safe anywhere, and that *really* pissed her off.

A good-size breaker crashed up the beach, drawing her attention from her white canvas espadrilles, which she was shaking sand out of, to the rolling green sea, still disquieted by the storm. Willie loved coming to the beach after a big storm, seeing how the wind and surf had reshaped the dunes. It was a lesson in humility, a reminder that there were forces in the universe beyond even her father's control. Like vampires.

She reached inside the navy sweatshirt she'd pulled over a white turtleneck and closed her fingers around the little gold cross she'd dug out of her jewelry box. About five seconds after she'd wakened, she'd realized what had happened wasn't a dream and raced to the mirror looking for punctures. She hadn't found any and had almost fainted with relief.

She'd been trying since to build a case for Raven not being a vampire. But what she had so far wasn't much more than pure and simple this-can't-be-happening disbelief. She'd considered the psychological disorder she'd read about that made people think they were vampires, and the blood disease that imitated the symptoms and gave its victims a strong aversion to sunlight, but every theory she came up with fell apart when she came to Raven putting the mirror in her hand.

If he wasn't a vampire, if he hadn't known what she'd see when she looked in it, why had he given it to her? Why did he want her to know he was a vampire? Was it a warning, as she'd first thought, or something else?

Willie had too many questions and not enough evidence. She needed answers and she needed proof. Not to mention the guts to go after them. She'd put on the cross because it made her feel safe, and had come to the beach to hatch a plan and give herself a pep talk. Well, she'd hatched a plan. It was time to go eat something and set it in motion. She put on her shoes, picked up her bucket and headed for home.

Johnny stood watching her on the crest of the dune, bare feet spread and arms folded, the sleeves of his shirt snapping in the brisk, offshore wind. Willie didn't hear it, just slogged past within three feet of him, through wet sand and soggy beach grass, a frown wrinkling her brow, her cheeks reddened by the chill.

He wanted to tell her it was him, not Raven, who'd been in her bed last night. He'd been in her room when she'd wakened, had seen the horrified look on her face as she'd rushed to the mirror. He ached to tell her and to touch her again, to prove it to her, but he couldn't.

He could only watch her walk past and just miss stepping on his boots. If she'd been closer, would she have tripped over them? He wished he had a voice, wished he could shout at her to look at him, that he was real, that he loved her, but he couldn't. He could only pick up his boots and follow her.

As he was every Sunday morning in the summer, Frank was on the terrace—in jeans and a windbreaker, the *Boston Globe* in his lap and his ankles crossed on the table. He put the paper and his coffee cup down beside the watering can and the pot of geraniums she'd left there last night.

"Ahoy. It's the shore patrol. Your comics are untouched, Commodore, just the way you like 'em."

"Did you drink all the coffee?" Willie put her bucket in the storage bin and saw the trowel she'd left beside it.

"Yeah, but I made fresh. What's for brunch?"

"Sea rations," she said, dropping the trowel into the bin.

"Ho, ho, ho, and a bottle of rum."

"Oatmeal and toast."

"I was hoping for eggs Benedict."

"Then hope your way to Denny's."

Willie had forgotten about the mirrors until she stepped into the house ahead of Frank. She held her breath waiting for him to ask, but he didn't, just followed her into the kitchen and said, "Wild night, huh?"

"You can say that again."

"The storm blew a couple of branches off the fruit trees. I broke them up and bundled them."

"Thanks." Willie took out a saucepan and lid, a measuring cup and salt, ducked into the pantry for the oatmeal and saw in the trash the mail and the compact she'd thrown to the four winds. Maybe Frank had picked it all up. She wondered, but instead asked him, "How about the oak in the side yard?"

"Dropped a few leaves and some dead twigs. I'll rake after breakfast."

"I'll do it." Willie gave him a bright smile as she came out of the pantry. "I like to rake."

Frank cocked his head at her. "Since when?"

"Since it's been too hot to do anything but run like hell for the car and turn on the air conditioner."

"Okay." Frank shrugged and went outside for his cup.

Willie sighed with relief, mixed the oatmeal and set it to cook on the front burner of the stove. She had about as much chance of sneaking off to Raven's house with Frank raking the side yard as Raven did of buying or scaring her out of Beaches.

"So, Will," Frank said as he came back into the kitchen, "what's with the mirrors?"

She had to hand it to him. He managed to make the question sound as mundane as oatmeal. And almost as sticky.

"Well, Frank, it's like this." Willie took the pan off the burner and put the lid on. "Beaches is haunted and the mirrors are ghost traps. And I'm pretty sure I was ravished by a vampire last night."

He stood in the doorway looking at her, his head tipped at a dubious angle and one eyebrow notched. Willie gave him a toothy smile.

"I walked right into that one, didn't I?" he said just as Johnny stepped into the dining room mirrors behind him.

Willie's heart shot up into her throat. She felt every touch, every caress Raven had stroked on her body last night, felt her knees go weak and her breath catch. She'd been afraid of this, of what she'd feel seeing Johnny, the phantom image of Raven. He was a good head and a half taller than Frank. His arms were folded and his face was a thundercloud. She'd never seen a pissed-off ghost before, and hoped Frank wouldn't turn around and see one, either.

Willie yanked her gaze away from Johnny and wagged her eyebrows at Frank. "Gotcha," she said, turning toward the toaster. "Would you hand me the butter?"

"Sure. So what are the mirrors for, really?"

"The cat," Willie lied, glancing over her shoulder as she peeled four slices of wheat bread out of a loaf. "Callie loves to chase herself in them."

Frank looked at her funny, but didn't say anything, just handed her the butter out of the fridge. Johnny was still glowering at her. Why was he angry? What had she done?

"You okay, Will?" Frank laid his hands on her shoulders. "You look like you've just seen a ghost."

Willie laughed. What else could she do?

"I'm fine, Frank. Just tired. The thunder kept waking me up." She put her hands on his shoulders and walked him backward to the table. "Sit down and eat."

By the time Willie buttered the toast, put milk and sugar and orange marmalade on the table, Johnny was gone. Still, her oatmeal went down like library paste. She and Frank split the last piece of toast, then carried the dishes to the sink. She rinsed and he put them in the dishwasher.

"I don't know why you bother," he said. "The dishes are clean when you load them."

"At least *I*," Willie said archly, "have never dug half a bowl of spaghetti out of the bottom of *my* dishwasher."

"It wasn't spaghetti. It was macaroni." Frank winked at her. "And it was perfectly cooked."

"Yuk." Willie laughed and passed him a fistful of spoons and butter knives just as Callie launched herself between them at the open window above the sink.

Willie yelped, startled. The silverware went flying and clattered onto the floor. Frank picked it up, straightened and made a face at Callie. She sat on the sill, her tail twitching, her eyes riveted on the birds feeding on the lawn.

"Oh, look," he said. "It's the great calico gull killer."

Callie gave him a drop-dead feline glare and turned back to the window. So did Willie, her heart skidding against her ribs when she saw the lone raven perched in the peach tree, its head cocked as it watched the other birds, gulls and grackles mostly, peck at the worms and grubs the storm had brought to the surface.

"So," Frank said. "How'd it go with Raven last night?"

"Fine." Willie bent her head, scrubbing the wooden spoon furiously with the dish brush. "Pronounced my ankle healed and left just before the storm hit."

"He put any moves on you?"

"Nary a one," Willie lied, since she'd already decided she wasn't going to dinner or anyplace else with Raven. Tonight or any other night.

"Not even 'Hey, baby, come on up to the lab and see what's on the slab'?"

The wooden spoon leapt out of Willie's fingers. Callie meowed irritably and jumped off the windowsill.

"Raven's not that kind of doctor," Willie snapped. "And I'm in no mood to play *The Rocky Horror Picture Show.*"

Not so long as she was living it. Willie fished the spoon out of the disposer and slapped it into Frank's hand.

"You're strung out is what you are. I thought you weren't going to take any more of those pills."

"I took *one*, Frank, so I could sleep through the storm."
Willie snatched the phone off its receiver and thrust it at him.
"Go ahead. Call Whit and tell him I'm on drugs again."

"Cheap shot, Will." Frank took the phone away from her
and hung it up. "We'll talk about this later when you come
down off the ceiling."

He put a kiss between her eyebrows and left. Willie stood
at the sink gripping the stainless steel edge, watching the
raven bob up and down in the wind, which was swaying the
branches of the peach tree.

"Go away!" she shouted.

The flock leapt into the air in a flurry of wings and startled
squawks. Willie ran, straight and unseeing, through the hand
Johnny raised as she raced by him and out the French doors.
He felt a flash of her panic, then a wrenching stab of envy as
Frank turned around when she called his name and she threw
herself into his arms.

"I'm sorry, I'm sorry." Willie buried her face in Frank's
shoulder, felt his arms close around her and wanted to cry.
He wasn't tall and hot and sexy like Raven, but he was real.
He was alive and warm and he was her friend.

"What's going on, Will? And don't tell me nothing. I know
you better."

"I'll tell you later." And she would, Willie decided, backing out of his embrace. "I'll call you, okay?"

"Okay." Frank put another kiss between her eyebrows.

Willie hugged herself and watched him walk away, then ran
back inside for her purse and her car keys. She saw the yellow Post-It note stuck to the monitor as she came through the
office door, peeled it off and read the single neat line of copperplate script: "I was born in this house on 19 July 1843."

The same day as Raven. He and Johnny had the same
birthday, the same profession, the same name, the same face,
the same scar. It stretched credibility too far, even for a gul-
lible soul like Willie.

"First reading, now writing," she said, spinning away from
the desk. "What's next, Johnny? Arithmetic?"

Willie waited, but the mirrors remained empty. Ready to scream, she tossed the note aside and slammed out of the house. Rain speckled the terrace; a stiff, salty wind tossed the trees lining the driveway. Willie opened the garage, dropped a hammer, a couple of screwdrivers and a flashlight into her purse and snapped the shell on the Jeep.

She had no idea what all the similarities between Johnny and Raven meant, but she had a sneaking, frustrating suspicion the answer was right in front of her, that she simply couldn't see it for looking at it.

Willie almost didn't see the raven perched on the terrace wall, either, until she'd pulled the Jeep out of the garage. Her breath caught, and her fingers stopped in midreach for the seat belt. The raven hopped sideways and cawed at her, then flapped away into the lowering gray sky.

"Damn bird," she muttered, stomping on the gas hard enough to spin the tires and spit gravel halfway up the driveway.

Rain and fog blew across the road in gusty sheets. Willie switched on the lights and the wipers. If she believed in omens like the weather, she'd go home and hide under the bed, but she wasn't sure what she believed in. Except her own sanity and that Raven, for some reason, wanted her alive. She didn't know why but she was determined to find out—even if she had to beat it out of him with the clove of garlic she'd tied with a thread to her cross.

Raven lived in one of the stately old Cape houses built along a crookneck inlet of the sound, in an area that was mostly moorland, flat and featureless, its few trees stunted by salt and twisted by wind.

Not quite a horror-movie landscape, but close enough to make Willie think twice about hiding under the bed—until she crossed the bridge spanning the inlet and the rain stopped, the fog lifted and watery sunshine gleamed through thin silver patches of cloud. Mist still hung over the marshes, but she had no trouble finding the address Hester Pavao had given her in the post office.

Finding the courage to get out of the Jeep was something else. Willie parked in the driveway and sat listening to her heart pound in her ears. She should have left a note just in case she was wrong about Raven and she disappeared without a trace. And she should have changed her underwear, like her mother always said, just in case she didn't.

She tried but couldn't read the sticker on the Corvette's back bumper, gave up and got out of the Jeep. The bumper sticker said I'm A + . What's Your Type?

Vampire humor, Willie supposed. She turned up the curved brick walk, wiping her clammy hands on her jeans. There were white miniblinds, all closed, on the windows; a dead-bolt lock, a bell and a knocker on the front door.

She rang and banged as hard as she could for a good ten minutes. It was enough to wake the dead, but not a vampire. As the last chime of the doorbell faded, so did Willie's faint hope that she wouldn't have to break in to the house.

Maybe she'd try the car first. She might get lucky and find something incriminating—say, a black cape or a road map of Transylvania. Willie turned away from the door, digging the flashlight out of her purse, and froze.

The raven sat on the yard light watching her.

14

VISIONS OF Alfred Hitchcock's *The Birds* danced in Willie's head. She squinted nervously at the sky, then ventured gingerly onto the walkway. The raven swooped onto the bricks and hopped toward her. She scrambled back onto the porch and stayed there until it flew to the roof of the Corvette, cawed at her and flapped away around the corner of the house.

Willie didn't follow, even though she had a hunch that was what the raven wanted. Sure enough, it came back within a ten count, swooped onto the Corvette, spread its wings, ruffled its feathers and cawed again.

"All right, all right, I'm coming," she said, gripping her purse with both hands to keep them from shaking.

The raven took off again. Willie followed, peering cautiously around the back of the house when she reached it. The raven perched on the rail of a deck overlooking the inlet. Mist swirled above the still, pewter surface.

Something rattled above Willie's head: an open window on the second floor. The raised blind banged the glass. But that wasn't what the raven wanted her to notice. It flew across the deck and raked its talons at the handle of a sliding-glass door covered by a half-open vertical blind. Then it flew back to the rail and cawed at her.

Willie had a nasty feeling she knew where this was going, but she opened the unlocked door anyway, then backed as far away from it as she could. The raven flew past her into the house. Swallowing hard and saying a prayer for her very mortal and very frightened soul, Willie stepped inside.

She closed the door and leaned against it, rattling the blind slats and blinking to adjust her eyes to the shaded half-light.

She was in the dining room. The kitchen was to her left; the living room and the raven, perched on the seat of a wing chair, dead ahead. A light-colored shirt and a pair of jeans were tossed over the back of the chair.

"Now what?" she asked the bird shakily.

The raven spread its wings—and spread its wings and spread its wings. Each time it seemed to grow larger, until Willie realized the bird *was* growing larger. And changing shape, shifting and wavering in and out of focus. One second it was a bird, the next it was—*Raven!*

Willie clapped her hands over her mouth to keep from screaming, and wished she had two more she could clap over her eyes. She closed them instead, her throat choked with horror, until a firm voice said, "Look at me."

She didn't want to, but she did, and saw the feathers retreating from the face. The beak elongated into a nose, then there came a chin and the mouth she'd kissed last night. The wings were arms now, the talons toes. He was nude. Naked as a jaybird. Raven laughed, his voice still raucous, and crossed his dark-haired legs.

Willie's face was on fire and her hands, still clamped over her mouth, were like ice. She closed her eyes again. Rather, Raven let her close them. She felt it, almost like a finger lifting off a button inside her head.

"You can open your eyes, Willow," he said. She heard denim rustle, a zipper close. "I'm decent now."

"You're obscene."

"I'm a vampire. Which you already suspected or you wouldn't be here."

Willie wanted to be ten thousand miles away from here. Mostly she wanted to cry, but she'd be damned if she would, damned if she'd let Raven know he'd scared her half to death and broken her heart. She opened her eyes.

Raven was shrugging into a shirt, a white one made of soft cotton with long, full sleeves. He buttoned it from the bottom to his chest—his well-muscled chest, thick with dark hair. Willie realized he always did that, that he never fastened a shirt around his throat.

"You gave me the mirror. *You* put the idea in my head. Why?"

"I need your help."

"Sorry. I gave at the blood bank."

"I don't need that kind of help."

He came toward her, his shirt untucked, his feet bare. Willie gripped her purse strap and held her ground as Raven came around behind her to close the window blind, then rounded the oak table and took the lid off a ceramic jar squatting beside a red leather notebook. She'd seen pictures of others like it, recognized the faded hieroglyphs on the curved sides and realized it was a canopic jar, an Egyptian funerary urn.

"My God. You're *him,*" Willie said on a sharp intake of breath. "The Jonathan Raven who was murdered in Egypt, in the Valley of the Kings in 1878."

"I'm half of him." Raven withdrew his moonstone ring from the jar. "The other half you know as Johnny."

"Don't you mean *better* half?"

"I mean mortal," he said, slipping the ring on his finger. "I was attacked by a vampire who'd been sealed in a tomb for nearly two thousand years. Unfortunately, he didn't kill me. He merely—separated me, split me in two."

Oh, sure, Willie thought, happens all the time. "Excuse me?" she said. "What does that mean exactly?"

"It means I became a vampire and the part of me you know as Johnny became my disembodied spirit. My soul, if you believe in such things. I prefer to call him my Shade."

No wonder Johnny seemed like a kinder, gentler version of Raven. No wonder she'd felt all along there was something not quite right about Raven, something missing. The answer had, indeed, been right under her nose. And she wouldn't have guessed it in a million years.

"I thought you were Johnny reincarnated," she said.

"An interesting notion," Raven replied, and turned toward the kitchen. Thin bars of sunlight slanted across the floor through the half-open blind on the window above the sink. He walked through them, unscathed, and opened the fridge.

"You give at the blood bank," he said. "I take."

The shelves held nothing but blood in clear plastic bags. In the bright glare of the frosted bulb they gleamed like slabs of liver. Willie felt her gorge rise, and swallowed.

"Don't they miss that stuff?"

"Blood has a finite life span. These bags were scheduled to be destroyed. I merely helped myself. No one misses a pint or two now and then." He shut the door and shrugged. "It's a little stale but it sustains me."

A light-headed rush surged through Willie. Her ears rang and the corners of the room started to wobble.

"Sit down and put your head between your knees," Raven said. "It'll pass."

Willie dropped her purse on the floor, dragged a chair away from the table and did. When she straightened, Raven stood in front of her with a crystal snifter in one hand.

"It's brandy." Willie took it and sipped, her teeth chattering against the rim of the snifter. "You're perfectly safe with me, Willow. Fresh and sweet as your blood might be, I have other plans for you."

Willie shivered in spite of the fire seeping through her and glanced up at Raven. "What about Johnny?"

"I want him back. I want to be mortal again. Before I forget how."

Her eyes widened with surprise, then narrowed with suspicion. "What do you mean, forget?"

"I have—only a few memories."

They were faint and growing fainter, mere wisps of recollections, so vague they almost seemed like dreams. The one that welled up from Willow Evans's mind caught him by surprise with its vividness. Apparently he wasn't the only one with memories.

"I was not," he told her, "in your bedroom last night."

"Then who—" she began, but glanced quickly away, a flush traveling up her throat.

Johnny, not Raven; a dream, not a nightmare. She should have known. Should have realized when she'd seen him in the dining room mirror. Oh, Johnny, I'm sorry, she wailed silently. Oh, God, get me out of here alive.

"Why are you telling me all this?"

"I want you to tell Johnny." Raven pulled out a chair and sat down, resting his left arm on the table.

"Why don't you tell him yourself?"

"He's terrified of me." Raven turned his gaze toward the leather notebook. It slid across the table on its cracked and sun-faded cover and stopped in front of Willie. "Give him this. It's one of my diaries. It contains the Riddle of Rejoining. It'll help convince him."

"You keep *diaries*?" Willie couldn't believe it.

"I'm a doctor. If nothing else, my present state is scientifically fascinating."

"What is your present state? Clinically speaking."

"As a mortal would say, dead as a doornail. Or a mackerel. And if the fates smile on us, the grunge look."

"But you look so—alive."

"Most of what you see and react to, say, the warmth of my body, is a projection. Vampires are very good at projection. We can make you believe almost anything. Even that we're every bit as alive as you."

"You know what's going on in my head, don't you?" Her smile faded. Raven could feel her heart banging, her pulse skip and race. "You can make me do things. Like the other day. *You* sent me to see Lucy."

"I suggested it. I can't force you to do anything. I can encourage you, but I can't control you."

Her heart rate and her pulse slowed. She took a sip of brandy and eyed him warily. "Does that mean you can't force me to help you if I don't want to?"

Raven nodded, lying to her. If she refused he'd take her in Thrall. And his chances with Nekhat.

"Let's get one thing straight. You can't have Beaches."

"The house is mine, Willow. It always has been."

"The hell it is. My grandmother bought it from—" Willie stopped, stunned, and blinked at him. Hadn't she thought in the museum that in thirty years Raven would look just like his great-uncle? "Horace Raven. That was you, too."

"I have to appear to die every so often. Otherwise, eyebrows are raised. And questions I obviously can't answer."

She drained her brandy in one gulp, choked and pushed the snifter away, her hands trembling.

"I don't care if Beaches is yours, you'll have to kill me to get it."

Her bravado was amusing, all the more because he knew it was bravado. Raven laughed and slapped the table, startling her. She reached inside her sweatshirt and plucked out a gold cross and a clove of garlic on a thin gold chain.

"Willow." Raven looked at her askance, tsked and raised an eyebrow. "Really."

Willie never saw him move. One minute the cross was around her neck, the next it was in Raven's hand. She clutched the front of her sweatshirt reflexively, watched him raise his hand and the cross turn and flash in the cracks of pale sun filtering through the blind behind her.

"Lovely." He broke the thread, tossed the garlic clove into the air, caught it in his teeth and crunched it.

He was playing with her, as a cat would toy with a mouse. Oh, God, why had she come? Because she hadn't believed it, that was why, hadn't believed he wasn't what he appeared to be: a tall, handsome and rich young doctor. Now she knew better. Still, he made her pulse thud, stirred her senses and made her yearn for things she shouldn't want. Not with a monster.

For a horrifying second Willie thought he was going to eat her cross, too, but he simply held it out to her by its chain. She snatched it back, careful not to touch him, and closed it in her fist.

"I cannot enter consecrated ground," he told her, "but I do not wither or spontaneously combust at the sight or the touch of a crucifix. Garlic does no more to me than it does to you. It gives me heartburn and bad breath."

"But you're dead," she blurted out, her eyes widening with panic. "You're a monster, a—a thing."

"A vampire, yes." He nodded and smiled a faint, sad smile. His mouth still seemed terribly sexy.

Willie shuddered and looked away. Raven took the snifter back to the kitchen to refill it. The bar pattern on the floor had brightened considerably and crawled closer to the refrigerator. Raven avoided it.

Willie swiveled in her chair and pushed one of the blind slats aside. Cheery yellow sunshine poured into her lap. The sky was so blue it hurt her eyes.

"Don't do that," Raven said sharply.

Willie let the slat fall and looked at him over her shoulder. He stood in the doorway, blinking and pinching the bridge of his nose with his left hand. The snifter in his right hand trembled.

"You would go up in flames in sunlight, wouldn't you?"

He waited until the slat stopped swinging, then came back to the table and put the snifter down. "I'm vulnerable to sunlight only in this form."

Willie had already figured that out. Raven was still blinking, though she couldn't see any change in his eyes. They were as dark and luminous as always. With no discernible pupil or iris. Willie hadn't noticed that before, not even in the emergency room.

"You're very observant." Raven sat down and rested, his left elbow on the table. His hand trembled. "Most mortals never notice my eyes. I can make those who do forget, so I don't bother with the projection. It's difficult to sustain and very draining."

Willie wished he wouldn't use that word. "Do you need to lie down for a few minutes? In your—uh—coffin?"

"I don't need sleep." Raven smiled, amusement glimmering in his dark, strange eyes. "When I do rest," he explained, "I don't lie in a coffin. I still have horrors of being nailed into one."

"Johnny's eyes are just like yours."

"I wasn't aware of that, but I'm not surprised. He is, to a degree, a reflection of me."

"Maybe that's why I can only see him in a mirror."

"Perhaps." Raven shrugged, an expectant half smile on his face.

He was waiting for her answer. Willie was scared but she wasn't stupid. He hadn't told her everything and she knew it. She did know who Johnny was, and why Raven hadn't killed her. Not yet, anyway. He probably would if she refused to help him. The thought ought to have terrified her, yet she felt oddly calm as she looked at Raven.

"Why are you bothering with me? Why don't you kill me?"

"When I discovered the Riddle of Rejoining and the possibility of regaining my mortality, I chose not to hunt my own kind. My conscience was hardly clear when I lost it. I don't want to sully it further with murder."

"What noble bullshit."

Raven's fingers closed and opened. Twice. She was pushing him. Willie knew it and gripped the cross tighter.

"I took this from Nekhat, the vampire who attacked me." Raven raised his left hand. A stray beam of light caught the moonstone ring, flashing on the ankh Willie hadn't noticed on its surface. "If I'm forced to use it, to bind my Shade to me until the second night of the full moon, when the Ritual of Rejoining must be performed, Nekhat will know precisely where it is. And he will come for it."

"So?" Willie shrugged, trying to appear nonchalant, though her heart was racing.

Raven never moved, but the Sunday *Boston Globe* levitated from the living room onto the table. It opened in front of her, to the "World News In Brief" column, the same one she'd read in yesterday's *Stonebridge Chronicle*. She still couldn't pronounce the name of the Central American country torn by civil war, but she shivered as she read about it and the cattle mutilations in the Yucatan.

"This is how Nekhat feeds. He could wipe Stonebridge, Massachusetts, off the map in the span of a single night."

"You're lying," Willie said, hoping to God he was.

"What if I'm not?"

"I think you are. I think you're as terrified of Johnny as he is of you. You're petrified he won't want any part of you. That's why you want me to play go-between."

"Don't push me, Willow." Raven made a fist that didn't open. "A bird has an incredibly high metabolism. A raven must eat at least four times its body weight in a day just to stay alive. I'm very hungry and your throat is much closer than the refrigerator."

Scare tactics. Not a good sign. Neither was the faint red gleam in his eyes.

"Let's see how much you remember about being mortal."

Willie picked up her purse, rose and pushed her chair in, mindful of his lightning reflexes. Everything he'd told her could be a lie; maybe he just wanted to get his hands on Johnny, or Beaches, or both. If he was lying he'd kill her now—diary or no diary—unless she could find the blind cord. She inched toward the door, fumbling for the string.

"Let's see how badly you want to be a nice guy and not dirty up your conscience." She found the cord and clutched it in her fingers. "I'll take the diary to Johnny, but I'll leave the decision up to him. I think that's only fair."

One hundred and seventeen years as a vampire, and still the swiftness of what mortals called his temper surprised him.

She never had a chance to pull the cord. In a flash she was pinned against the door, frozen with terror at Raven's red, whirling eyes, her arms crushed in his grip. She wanted to scream with pain, but could hardly breathe.

"Drop the cord."

He growled at her, as Callie had last night when she'd heard the lynx. Willie felt the growl reverberate up her spine, opened her fingers and felt the cord swing free against the glass. Raven threw his head back, flared his nostrils and closed his eyes. Willie could see every tendon, every vein in his throat.

"Don't ever do that again," he snarled, his grip on her arms easing. "I'd kill my own mother if she threatened me with sunlight."

How about a wooden stake, Willie wondered, but didn't dare ask. Raven lowered his head and looked at her. Tiny red pinpoints still leapt in his eyes.

"Or a wooden stake." He let her go, reached over her shoulder and snapped the blind cord.

Willie managed, just barely, to hold herself up. She watched Raven brush his thumb across the moonstone and close his eyes again. They were dark and luminous when he opened them, shoved the diary into her hands and said, "I'll give you until nightfall."

15

AT SIX MINUTES PAST FOUR and forty-seven miles per hour, Willie skidded the Jeep off the beachfront road. Gravel strafed the mailbox and terror drummed in her veins.

The sun would set at three minutes past eight, eastern daylight time. She knew because she'd checked the almanac. That gave her roughly four hours to figure out how much of what Raven had told her was the truth and what she was going to do about it. She hoped the diary would prod Johnny's memory, that she wouldn't have to hop a plane for Alaska, the land of the midnight sun, the safest place she could think of to hide from a vampire.

"Johnny!" Willie shouted as she raced through the house looking for him. "I've been with Raven and he—"

Willie lost her voice as she shot through her office doorway and came to a stunned halt. The room was full of flowers: tiger lilies on the filing cabinets, wild lavender on her desk, Shasta daisies on the bookcases and Queen Anne's lace on Betsy's rocking chair.

Fresh-washed sunshine poured through the windows, filling her nose with the sweet, wild scents of flowers and the sea. Filling her heart, too, as she moved into the room and dropped her purse. This was a lover's gift. She'd received one or two in her time, but she'd never seen anything like this.

Or any man, alive, dead or in between, look at her the way Johnny did when she saw him behind her in the pedestal mirror. She could see her freckles, frizzy hair and not much of a nose in the glass, but not in Johnny's eyes. His dark, strange eyes were so much like Raven's and yet so different.

"Oh, Johnny," she said, her eyes filling. "Thank you."

He touched his fingertips to his lips. Willie didn't realize he'd moved the mirrors until he stepped behind her and she saw their double reflections, one in a wall mirror above the bookcase, the other in the pedestal glass.

"This is beautiful," Willie said on a shaky breath. "But we have to talk. Raven's coming at sunset. He said—"

Johnny shook his head, raised his left wrist above her shoulder and pointed at it as if he were wearing a watch.

"No, there *isn't* time. Raven says you're his mortal half. He wants you back. He says it's possible, that the two of you can be reunited. He gave me one of his diaries, and the Riddle of Rejoining."

Willie dropped to her heels, pulled the cracked red notebook from her purse and felt her head spin. Too much brandy, she thought, shaking it off as she stood. Too quickly, she realized, when the room spun and her knees wobbled.

If Johnny hadn't caught her she would've fallen. If he hadn't swept his arm around her when it hit her that she could *feel* his hand on her shoulder, she would have fainted. She gazed at him, wide-eyed, in the mirror, the diary slipping out of her fingers and bouncing onto the carpet.

"The mirrors. This is how you made love to me."

He nodded and brushed a kiss behind her right ear. A rush of awareness, of his body solid against hers, made her heart flutter. She felt Johnny lift her hair, felt the graze of his lips as he kissed the nape of her neck.

And she felt as fragile as she looked cradled against Johnny, caught in the nimbus of sunlight reflecting off the mirror. She closed her eyes, imagined her turtleneck was a lace collar and savored the feel of Johnny's mouth as he kissed her hair. She felt the chill in his arm as she gripped his wrist, tried to imagine it warm, and swayed against him.

He moved with her, looped his arm around her throat and held her against him at shoulder and hip. She could almost hear lace rustle, the slow tick of a wind-up clock, the whinny of a horse, carriage wheels crunching on gravel.

Oh, it was heaven, but it wasn't real. Johnny wasn't real, except in a mirror. He was trapped in time and she was trapped in his eyes, her heart catching as he raised his head and looked at her.

A lock of his long dark hair curled over his forehead, gleaming in the glass. His eyes gleamed, too, dark and heavy lidded, as he smiled again and dragged his mouth down the curve of her jaw. Her lips parted on a mew of longing and she rolled her head against his chest. She thought he meant to kiss her mouth and strained to meet him, but he kissed the tip of her nose instead, tenderly, keeping one eye on the mirror.

It felt like a tiny electrical tingle. Just as it had all those years ago when he'd kissed her on the beach—when the starfish had stung her, Willie realized, the rest of the memory rushing out of her subconscious: the shimmer she'd seen in the air, the dizzying sweep she'd thought was the poison in the sting.

"It was *you*," she breathed. "You kissed me on the beach. When I was a little girl and a starfish stung me."

He smiled, the bittersweet curve of his mouth making her heart catch.

"The monster in Whit's closet. The pirate on the beach. That was you, too, wasn't it?"

Johnny nodded. Willie's eyes filled again. He'd been here always, the man Raven was and claimed he wanted to be again. Watching out for her, keeping her safe, bringing Granma flowers and sand dollars.

"Oh, Johnny," she said again.

He laid his right hand against the mirror, thumb, index and little fingers raised. "I love you," he said, and all the tears Willie had been too afraid to shed in front of Raven burst out of her in a throat-wrenching sob. She pressed her hand next to Johnny's, thumb, index and little fingers raised. His fingers were strong and brown, sunbaked over a century ago by the Egyptian sun. Her own never tanned, and were splashed with nutmeg freckles.

"I love you. I always have. I thought it was Beaches, but it was you. I was just too dumb to know it."

Johnny mouthed *no, no,* turned her and folded her into his arms. Willie felt the rough weave of his shirt against her cheek, smooth, well-toned muscle beneath the brown skin of his chest, but no warmth, no heartbeat. He felt like marble, beautiful but lifeless marble. She threw her arms around his waist and almost howled with sorrow.

Johnny laid his cheek against her hair, rocked her and let her weep. Willie cried until she'd soaked his vest and shirt, until she tasted salt and rust on her tongue, raised her head and saw the bloodstains she'd smeared with her tears. In the mirror she saw that she'd bitten her lip, and she wasn't sure if the blood she tasted was hers or Johnny's.

"This is wonderful but it isn't real," she said. "It can't ever be real. Not unless—"

Willie's breath caught and her eyes went wide in the mirror. It hadn't dawned on her, not once, while she'd listened to Raven tell her about the Ritual of Rejoining. It did now, and it dawned on Johnny, too. She saw it in the slow, miraculous smile spreading across his face.

It *was* possible—if Raven was telling the truth.

They dove for the diary together. Johnny's hand closed on it first. He snatched it up and opened it, riffling the pages. A piece of illuminated, age-yellowed parchment fluttered out. Willie caught it before it hit the floor.

"Well, this is swell. It's in Arabic or something."

Johnny tapped his finger against a page of the diary and passed it to her. Raven had entered the translation in the same precise copperplate with which Johnny had written the note he'd left on the monitor. Even in English it made no sense. Still, Willie felt gooseflesh rise as she read.

Eternal is the Power of Three,
Father, Son and Holy Spirit,
Sun and Moon and Earth Eternal.
When the Three are One, the One will be Three.
Then the Dark will be Light,
Made One by the Sacred Cedar.
The Dead Shall Live and Stand Unscathed
In the Light of the Sun,
And of the Father, the Son and Holy Spirit.

"I've never been any good with riddles," she said as she gave the diary back to him. "How 'bout you?"

Johnny frowned and shook his head. Willie's heart sank.

"Then we have no choice but to trust Raven."

"I must, yes," Johnny signed, "but you must—"

Something. His fingers moved too fast for Willie to follow. She picked up the dictionary and said, "Sign it again."

He dragged a frustrated hand through his hair, rose and turned on his knees, plucked a pencil and a notepad out of the clutter on her desk, scribbled and gave it to her.

"The Ritual may be dangerous. You must go before Raven comes. You will be safe and the other will not come back."

"Other?" Willie blinked at him. "What other?"

Johnny shrugged, took the pad back and wrote, "I don't know. It came last night in the body of a lynx. I thought it was Raven, but it was a creature far worse. It came for Raven and the stone he wears in his ring."

"Yikes." Willie remembered the column in the *Chronicle* and shivered. So much for hoping Nekhat was just a clever vampire lie. If Johnny had seen him he had to be real. So did the threat to Stonebridge. "Raven said he'd come for the moonstone."

"Who?" Johnny flashed the sign in her face, startling her out of her daze.

"Nekhat," she said, rubbing her arms. "The monster who made Raven a vampire and you a homeless person."

He finger-spelled the name slowly, a frown of concentration drawing his eyebrows together. He spelled it again, shaking his head, and made the swipe across his forehead that meant, "I can't remember."

"Thank God for small favors." Willie sighed and pushed to her feet, steadying herself against the pedestal mirror as her head spun. Too many shocks and not nearly enough brandy, she thought ruefully.

The sun had faded; the shadows beneath the oak tree outside the window were deepening. No wonder. Her desk clock said it was nearly six-thirty. How long had she and Johnny slow-danced in front of the mirror?

Long enough, Willie realized as he straightened beside her, to make her forget all about hopping a plane to Alaska. The open throat of his shirt made her pulse thud; Lord Byron himself would have done murder for the unconsciously artful tangle of Johnny's hair over his forehead. And what a shame it was that breeches that fit like a banana skin had gone out of fashion.

Not that he didn't look good in jeans. Or was that Raven? Willie didn't know. She only knew that she'd no more been sucked by happenstance into Johnny and Raven's struggle than Betsy Boyle had bought Beaches by accident.

It was a heavy concept and cosmic beyond her grasp. She didn't understand it, she only felt the rightness of it in her heart. It wasn't coincidence that she had come to Beaches every summer when Johnny came. She was meant to play a part in this. Willie didn't know the what or how of it, but there was only one way to find out. God help her. God help them all.

"We've met the enemy, Johnny," she told him solemnly. "And he's *you*."

16

IT WAS THEIR FIRST FIGHT, a real doozy. Willie cried and threw things. Nothing worked until she ran upstairs and locked herself in the bathroom. It took Johnny three minutes and four seconds to slide a hastily scrawled note under the door. "You win. I'll let you meet with Raven on the terrace first to make sure of his intentions."

"Yesss!" Willie made a victory fist and opened the bathroom door. Johnny glowered at her in the mirror and handed her another note. "Next time I'll have my body back and I'll break down the door."

"Oh, yeah?" Willie ripped the note in two and tossed it in the air. "Before or after you hit me over the head with your club and drag me off to your cave?"

Johnny grabbed half the fluttering note, scribbled with the blue pencil he'd found on her desk and thrust the note at her. "Gentlemen of my day used a buggy whip."

"Oh, really?" Willie's gaze shot from the note to Johnny's face. "Well, now, hear this, Mr. Edwardian tyrant—"

He grinned and winked, his eyes dancing with amusement. Willie stared, openmouthed. She was looking straight at Johnny, not the mirror, but she didn't feel the least bit dizzy. Yesterday he'd looked fuzzy; now he looked—opaque. The outline of his body was quite distinct.

"Either you're getting stronger," she said, "or I'm getting used to this. I can almost see you without the mirror."

He blinked, held up his hands, turned them over several times, then raised an eyebrow at her. She could also see the first fingers of sunset backlighting his hair and washing his shirt lavender.

"Uh-oh," she said. "It's almost sundown."

Johnny glanced at the window, then at Willie and made a sign with his arms crossed.

"You bet I'm scared. You've had 117 years to get used to the idea that your evil twin is a vampire. I've only had a couple days."

Two days that seemed like a lifetime. How ironic that was, since two lives, hers and Johnny's—three, including Raven's, if you figured it that way—hinged on what would happen when the moon was full three nights from now.

Not only full but eclipsed. Willie had read that in the almanac, too, but Raven hadn't said a word about it. He'd told her only that the Ritual had to be performed on the second night of the full moon. The night of the eclipse, when the earth passed between the sun and the moon.

Maybe that was what the line in the Riddle meant—"When the Three are One." Still, she didn't like the fact that Raven hadn't mentioned it. But if he was up to no good, she intended to find out. Brave talk from the woman who'd almost wet her pants when he'd eaten her clove of garlic.

"Well." Willie smiled and wiped her suddenly clammy palms on her jeans. "Guess I'll light the luminarias."

Johnny nodded absently, a thoughtful frown on his face as he held his hands up to the window and studied them. Willie left him to it, touching the cross around her neck for comfort as she went downstairs. The chain was whole, and had been when Raven gave it back to her. She had no idea how he'd done it, or what she was going to say to him.

Pretend he's alive, she told herself. You didn't have any trouble talking to him when you thought he was a living, breathing, rich young doctor.

What would he be—or better yet, *who*—after the Ritual? Still Raven, cool and remote as the moon, or Johnny, warm and vibrant as the sun? Would Johnny still love her? Would she still love him? Would the Ritual even work?

How on earth was such a thing possible? How could the dead become the living? Was she talking to herself? Yes, but not answering—not yet, anyway—so there was still hope.

Was there hope for Johnny's immortal soul? Or was it Raven's?

Was it even a mortal soul, and was it theirs rather than his? Willie sighed and ruffled a hand through her hair.

"You're right, Frank," she said as she stepped outside through the French doors. "I *am* strung out."

The sky was a pale, washed-out blue from the storm, fading into a tired, mostly mauve-and-orange twilight. The moon was up, a gray, pockmarked ghost. From the almanac Willie knew it was two-thirds full. A hunter's moon, she thought, and shivered. She opened the storage bin, plucked up three luminarias in each hand and looked at Frank's house. The windows were dark, the carport empty, and she was glad.

She'd promised to tell him what was going on, but what could she say? Raven's a vampire and Johnny's his disembodied soul, but don't worry. They're getting back together, and then he and I will. Until death do us part—again.

The thought gave Willie a chill as she went back for the rest of the luminarias and the butane fireplace lighter she kept in the bin. She laid it on the table next to the watering can she'd forgotten to put away last night.

She was exhausted, physically as well as emotionally. Her back and her head ached, her good-as-new-in-the-morning ankle pulsed like a sore tooth. She hadn't had a shower since . . . the night before last. Good grief. No wonder she thought she smelled something dead.

And then she heard the low, snarling growl behind her. She hadn't smelled anything so vile since old Patches had lugged home a cod that had lain rotting on the beach for at least a week.

"Like father, like daughter, eh, Callie?" Willie pinched her nose and turned around.

The cat crouched on the edge of the terrace was a lynx, tawny and spotted. Its tufted ears lay flat against its head, its bobbed tail flicked like a snake's tongue, and red flames flickered in its eyes.

Willie's heart slammed into her ribs, then plummeted to her toes. It came in the body of a lynx, Johnny had told her, for Raven and the stone he wears in his ring.

The lynx growled, causing goose bumps to rise on Willie's flesh. She flung a panicked look at the French doors she'd left open, twenty feet away across the flagstone terrace. Quick as a cat moved, she'd never make it.

Something flickered in the doorway. Hope and her pulse leapt, but it was only the sheers lifting in the evening breeze. *Oh, God! Oh, Johnny, help me!* she screamed silently, but he didn't come. She was on her own, her only weapon the butane lighter on the table a good five feet away.

The lynx crept closer, its growl deepening, reverberating up Willie's bones like the thrum of a big engine in low gear. She thought she saw a flash of red near the top of the driveway behind her Jeep, but didn't dare look at it.

If she survived this, she'd tell Lucy there really were bobcats in Stonebridge. She took a deep breath and a sideways, backward step toward the table. The lynx snarled and she froze, her breath seizing at the gleam of its fangs.

Oh, God, it was big. Forty, maybe fifty pounds of spotted, muscled cat. It turned its head toward the table, the flames in its eyes shrinking. Willie had a heartbeat's glimpse of wary intelligence keen enough to register the lighter as a threat.

When the flames in its eyes leapt again, so did Willie. So did the lynx, like lightning, swiping a paw at her as she grabbed the umbrella pole and pulled herself onto the table. She felt her jeans rip and pain shoot up her left calf, fire and ice so intense it paralyzed her.

The table rocked beneath her on the flagstones, splashing rainwater out of the watering can, rolling the lighter out of her reach. For a second she could only cling to the pole and watch it wobble toward the edge. Until she saw the wavery image of the lynx through the glass top, gathering itself to spring after her.

She threw herself across the table at the lighter, her right knee slipping in spilled water. She hit her chin, hard, and her shoulder, too, as she flung out her arm and her hand. Too late to stop the lighter, but just in time to see Johnny's opaque hand snake out of nowhere and catch it.

Relief shot through Willie, and another stab of pain, as she pushed up on one elbow and watched him, grim faced, wad one of her best yellow bath towels and strike the lighter. She heard gas hiss and held her breath as Johnny set fire to the towel and threw it at the lynx.

The cat snarled and cuffed the fireball aside, bouncing it onto the lawn where it lay smoldering in the wet grass. Willie's heart sank, and her only hope with it, until she heard gravel crunch, lifted her gaze and saw the red Corvette rocket over the crest of the driveway.

The lynx saw it, too, and wheeled, screaming. Its eerie cry raised the hair on the back of Willie's neck. So did Raven's answering snarl as he swerved the Vette around the Jeep, slammed on the brakes and vaulted out of it. The damp grass at his feet burst into smoky flames, and so did his eyes as he turned on the cat.

Willie wanted to scream but couldn't. Horror held her captive; she was unable to look away from the claws sprouting from Raven's fingers. The lynx leapt at him, its fangs bared at his throat. Raven spun on one foot, raking his raised right hand at the cat as it hurtled toward him. It fell with a thump, its throat torn open and bleeding, its paws twitching.

Willie's throat clenched with terror at the silvery shimmer rising from the body. It shifted and wavered into the shape of a man, tall and broad shouldered with long braided hair. His skin glowed bronze; the gold kilt slung low around his hips gleamed in the flames leaping around him.

"Nekhat," Willie breathed.

He spun toward her, bands of color streaming like tracer bullets from the beads woven into his braided wig. His burning gaze raked over her, almost stopping her heart. She saw a flash of bared fangs, the wink of gold in the amulet around his neck, the hole gaping in its center like a dead, empty eye. Then Nekhat whirled and swung a powerful arm at Raven.

Willie screamed, but his claws, thick and shiny as steel spikes, passed harmlessly through Raven's body. Nekhat threw back his head. The muscles in his arms and throat bunched. He bellowed like a storm tide crashing on the beach—and vanished in a swirl of iridescent sparks glittering on the wind billowing the fire toward the house.

Raven swept his right arm over the flames, snuffing them as abruptly as a pinched candle flame. Red flames still flickered in his eyes, though. There was nothing at all sexy about his mouth now, pulling back into shape over his receding incisors, nothing gentle about his fingers straightening out of gnarled hooks.

Oh, God. Retractable fangs and claws. Willie felt her gorge rise, her head spin and a slow, icy numbness seep up her leg. She let her head fall on her outstretched arm long enough to draw a shaky breath, inhaling the acrid, burned-toast smell of scorched grass and the rusty stench of blood.

She snapped her head up in time to see Johnny duck out of the house with a dish towel in his hands. He tore it in two and flipped half over his shoulder. Willie glanced at her shredded pant leg and swallowed hard at the sight of blood pooling on the tabletop. Dizziness washed through her and she shut her eyes, until Johnny wrapped half of the towel around her leg and wrenched it tight just below her knee. She gasped then rolled over and leaned back on her hands.

Johnny was glaring at Raven. Willie had flipped through the dictionary enough to recognize the swift, curt sign he made, right fist on his left palm as he raised both hands—"Help me."

Raven wanted to help, all right, help himself to the blood pulsing out of Willow Evans's leg. The scent of it, hot and pungent as raw chocolate, sent his senses screaming. He was ravenous, his system stuck in overdrive from the day spent in avian form. It was easy to gorge, so he'd fed lightly. He hadn't anticipated this, or the brush with Nekhat. Even in essence he was staggeringly powerful. Raven felt weak and shaky, his hunger a raw, gutting pain.

He forced his hunger back, and his fangs into their sheaths, and then he approached the table, slowly, where his Shade hovered protectively over Willow Evans. It didn't shrink away, yet Raven wished it would. It was agony to see his face after so long a time, to taste the emotions radiating from his Shade: cold tart fear, hazy brown confusion, hot red anger. The feelings tugged on his senses, yet repelled him. He felt sick and wanted to gag.

Willow Evans nearly did when he cupped her badly clawed calf in his hand. The shiver of revulsion that ran through her made his fangs slide forward reflexively. They pricked his lips and filled his mouth with saliva.

"So, are you going to sew me up?" she asked breathlessly. "Or am I dinner?"

17

HER VOICE WAS AS THIN as the pulse Raven could feel skipping erratically behind her knee. Her brown eyes were glassy, the irises huge, her pupils dilated. Sure signs of hysteria and the beginning of shock from blood loss.

Even in the smoky dark he could see the torn gastrocnemius muscle and shredded anterior tibial vein. There was still some seepage from the three-inch slash crawling with staph bacteria from the cat's claws. He was the only doctor on the planet who could see the bacteria without a microscope—and the only physician with a screaming need to drink his patient's blood.

He closed his eyes and his nostrils until the heady scent of blood faded. He felt his Shade edge closer, wary and warning; felt, too, the cool clamminess of Willow Evans's skin through her ripped jeans. It would be flaming by the time he got her to Stonebridge General. There were antibiotics there, plasma to replace the blood she'd lost, and questions he couldn't avoid.

And there was Nekhat. Long before the first Norseman sailed into Stonebridge harbor, Nekhat had learned how to master the elements. Already the wind had shifted, gusting out of the south. Nekhat would be here within hours to reclaim the moonstone and wreak vengeance for its theft.

"I can't sew you up here," Raven said. "You need surgery to repair the vein and physical therapy to rebuild the muscle. Neither of which we have time for."

"I was afraid you were going to say that. How long before Nekhat comes for the moonstone?"

"Soon." Sooner than she could imagine, but there was no point frightening her. "If we aren't here, most likely he'll by-pass Stonebridge in favor of pursuing the moonstone."

"How likely?"

He rubbed a hand over his mouth, but it didn't help. His fangs still throbbed. "I don't know," he admitted.

Willie blinked, surprised. She'd expected lies and false assurances. "I can't go anyplace with this leg. You're the doctor. Short of surgery, what do you suggest?"

He was a vampire, too. A very hungry one. Willie saw it in the faint red gleam in his eyes and the tremble she'd noticed in the hand he'd wiped across his face.

"A vampire rarely kills its victims," he told her. "A corpse drained of blood with punctures in the neck points rather obviously at the cause of death. My saliva actually contains an ingenious coagulant and several fearsome antibodies. I can close your wound within minutes and kill any infection."

"And have dinner on me while you're at it?"

"By morning you won't even have a scar."

"You could make a killing in plastic surgery."

Willie knew she sounded as goofy and giddy as she felt. She knew, too, that something had to be done about her light-headedness. And fast.

"You needn't be aware," Raven said. "I can make you think of something else."

"Like what'll happen if we don't leave before Nekhat comes back? No, thanks. I prefer to keep an eye on you."

She had no choice. Raven felt her horror at the realization, and the terror and the fury blazing from his Shade. He swung his head away as his Shade flew around the table signing frantically to Willow Evans.

"If you don't like it, then *you* sew me up," Willie snapped. "You're a doctor, too!"

Johnny's hands flashed pale and opaque in the darkness. She recognized the sign he made, the brush of his right index finger across his left for "I can't," figured the cupped palm he held up to his face and rotated from the wrist signified mirror. He meant he couldn't do it without the mirrors, which Willie had already surmised.

"You said you had no choice but to trust Raven," she reminded him. "Clearly, I don't, either."

It wasn't exactly what he'd said, but it was close enough. So was Raven, so close that Willie could see dark spatters of blood on his white shirt. Her head spun sickeningly; Raven's fingers pressed the pulse point in her right wrist.

"Your blood pressure is dropping. It's now or never."

Some choice. But life was slipping away from her. She could feel it in the dull ring in her ears, the spots swirling at the corners of her vision.

"Tell me first where we're going," Willie said, sliding weakly down on her elbows.

"To Italy." Raven felt her pressure drop another notch, tightened his grip on her wrist and gave it a boost. "To collect the last item I need for the Ritual."

Tending to her took strength he didn't have and sent his hunger soaring. He closed his eyes until it eased, opened them and saw his Shade offering him the spare towel. Raven glanced at his blood-smeared hands. He wanted to lick them clean but resisted the urge, taking the towel, dipping it in the watering can and wiping them, instead.

"Obviously Johnny has to go with you, but why do I?"

"Because now you are known to Nekhat."

He didn't say that made her number one on his hit list, but he didn't have to. Willie figured as much.

"If we go with you, if the three of us aren't here when Nekhat comes back, he'll leave Stonebridge alone, right?"

Raven didn't answer. Willie pushed up on her hands, but her arms were too weak to hold her. Johnny leapt to catch her as her elbows buckled, but he couldn't, for there were no mirrors. There was only Raven to slide his arm beneath Willie and ease her back down on the table.

Raven's arm, too, should have passed through him like smoke, but it didn't. His wrist bumped Johnny's elbow as he did so, hard enough to shoot pins and needles all the way up to Johnny's shoulder. It was impossible. He had no body, no nerves, yet he felt it. Physical sensation, for the first time outside of a mirror in 117 years.

Raven felt it, too. Johnny saw it in the startled leap of his gaze, felt the same jolt that laced up his arm shoot through Raven. He felt his yearning and his loathing at the touch of human flesh—and he felt his hunger. It roared through Johnny, white-hot and ravening, a surge of raw power that sent his senses reeling. He wanted to sink his teeth into Willie's throat, throw back his head and howl at the moon.

Johnny gripped Raven's wrist, felt his own flesh, cold and lifeless as the grave. Awareness washed through him, and recognition. It flickered in Raven's dark eyes, too, beneath the flame of his hunger—for only a moment, hardly more than a heartbeat before he dropped his gaze—along with a gleam of remorse so deep and wrenching it nearly staggered Johnny.

So did the realization that he was no different than Raven. He was a thing neither dead nor alive, a horror trapped in between, an abomination never meant to have existence. He knew it as surely as he knew that if the Ritual didn't work he would die, and so would Raven. As they should have, as perhaps they were meant to, in Egypt over a century ago.

The certainty of it clutched him, as icy and inexorable as the void waiting to reclaim him on the full moon. He felt only sadness, a deep, grinding sorrow that he'd evaded Raven for so long, so very long, when he was and always had been his only hope of salvation.

The cloying stench of pity rolling off his Shade almost gagged Raven. It singed his senses and burned his nostrils. He beat back the hunger clawing at him. If his Shade hadn't tightened its grip on his wrist, hadn't forced his gaze from the pulse throbbing in Willow Evans's throat, he would have taken her.

For the first time since he lay dying on the floor of Nekhat's tomb, Raven looked directly into his own eyes. They were dark as midnight. No pupil, no iris. He remembered they'd once been gray, like his father's. He grasped the memory and clung to it, twisted his grip and grasped his Shade's wrist. His hunger screamed, recoiled from the contact and curled into a tight, whimpering ball.

His Shade felt it. Raven saw it in the shudder that rippled through him, the tears that welled in his eyes. He felt the ducts swell and overflow, saw his dark fringe of lashes shimmer like the stars winking behind the racing clouds.

A single tear slid from his Shade's left eye and splashed the back of Raven's left hand. He felt his skin sizzle, and pain—real, nerve-generated pain—flash up his arm. He jerked his hand free and almost fell, but caught himself on the table, palms spread on either side of Willow Evans.

There was a burn on the back of his hand, about the size of a glowing cigarette tip. It throbbed a raw, angry red, the edges boiling as if he'd spilled acid on his hand. Only a second passed—barely more than a flutter of Willow Evans's pulse—before the surrounding tissue reacted.

The burn vanished but the pain lingered for another few seconds. It hurt abominably, throbbed all the way up to his shoulder, and filled him with such joy he almost laughed.

It was possible. The Ritual could work.

His Shade realized it, too. Raven saw it in the wondrous smile that spread across his face as he wiped the tears from his lashes and rubbed them into his fingertips.

Ten, Willie counted, and opened her eyes.

"Decide quickly, Willow," Raven said, "or I will."

"Promise me Nekhat will bypass Stonebridge."

"I can't. He's an aberration, a horror even among vampires. The sooner we go, the better the odds."

Raven wasn't asking her to decide the fate of the entire world, just her little corner of it. Still, Willie felt frozen with panic, her hands icy with indecision. But how could she choose wrongly when there was only one choice? She looked at Johnny for reassurance, could see his face and his do-it nod in the flickering moonlight.

"I won't turn into a vampire, will I?"

"No. I'd have to kill you to turn you."

"All right." Willie sighed shakily. "Go ahead."

"Bring a pillow," Raven said to Johnny.

Needlessly, for he'd already slid a padded vinyl seat cushion from the nearest chair under Willie's head. Air whooshed out of it as she lay back and tilted her head to keep an eye on Raven. She stiffened when he raised his right hand and a long, thin claw, razor sharp and silver in the moonlight, slid out from the tip of his index finger.

"I'm going to cut away your pant leg," he said, and did. Willie felt the denim split, smooth and whispery as silk. Her skin crawled and gooseflesh sprang from every pore.

"You'll feel this, but I don't think it will hurt."

"What do you mean, *think?*" she demanded, her head spinning as she sprang up on her elbows.

"There's a certain amount of sensation in any exchange of body fluids. If it hurts, tell me."

"You bet your ass I will."

Willie lay down, flung out her arms and gripped the edges of the table. Gently Raven lifted her leg, sat on the table and loosened the tourniquet. Willie sucked air between her teeth as icy-hot needles of feeling came prickling back. She drew a breath and tried to relax—until the implication of what he'd said hit her. She shot up on her elbows again, in time to see Raven bend his head over her slashed calf.

Moonlight glinted on his fangs, three inches long, curved and needle sharp. Pain knifed through Willie as she jerked her leg away and Raven whipped his head toward her. Red flames leapt in his eyes and a growl rumbled in his throat.

"You *have* passed an AIDS test?"

"Don't be idiotic," he snarled. "I'm dead."

"Yeah, but I'm not, and I don't wanna be."

"Suffice it to say that several HIV positive patients in my care have experienced miraculous cures."

"Oh." Willie lay down again, the pain in her calf easing but her heart slamming against her rib cage. "In that case, you oughta bottle that stuff."

"Lie still." Raven removed the tourniquet and raised her leg from his lap.

"How do you handle being around blood all the time?"

"I feed well before my shift."

"What's a good meal for a vampire? Two pints? Three?"

"Willow." The growl in Raven's voice deepened. "Shut up."

"Sorry! I'm nervous, okay?"

Johnny leaned over her and smiled, not exactly blocking but at least blurring her view of Raven. He held up his right hand and signed, "I love you."

"Oh, Johnny." Willie sighed shakily. "I love you, too."

He leaned closer and traced the curve of her jaw with his curled knuckles. She could almost feel it, as she'd almost felt the kiss he'd given her when the starfish stung her. She knew Johnny was deliberately distracting her from whatever Raven was doing, and that was peachy keen with her.

The moon glowed faintly through him, and two stars drifting beside the moon seemed to be flickering in his eyes: tiny points of light winking like the gems flanking the moonstone. Of course, they weren't winking. It was only a trick of the light, caused by the clouds scudding across the moon, maybe, or the madly thrashing trees.

Such things weren't possible. Neither were vampires, but there was one sucking on her leg. She could feel the tug on her flesh, the blood being syphoned from her body. Terror shot her heart up her throat and snatched her breath.

She couldn't breathe, she couldn't move. Her heart beat more and more slowly. She imagined an EKG printout: spikes rolling into waves, the waves evening out into a flat, dead line.

Oh, God, she was dying. Raven had lied to her. He was killing her, as Nekhat had killed him, and she couldn't stop him. Her muscles were frozen, her vision was fading. A scream she couldn't voice rang in her head. She couldn't see Johnny's face anymore, only the stars in his eyes—cold, fiery suns blazing millions of light-years away, yet so close she could reach out and touch them. If only she could move.

Raise your hand, Willow, Raven snarled in her mind. His voice vibrated with annoyance, in her bones and every cell in her body. *You are not paralyzed. Nor are you dying.*

Her right wrist jerked involuntarily. Relief flooded Willie, and a surge of something that felt like adrenaline. Only ten times better, ten times stronger than the hypo she'd taken for a killer case of hives from a penicillin allergy.

It sent her senses spiraling out of her body. She felt as if she was floating above the terrace. The stars in Johnny's eyes spun closer in slow motion: blinding and glorious, pinwheeling colors she'd never seen before in her head. Oh, wow, Willie thought dazedly. Oh, wow, what a light show.

His Shade shot Raven a worried frown as Raven raised his head. His fangs retracted, sated and dulled. His hunger quieted and began to purr. So did the small calico cat that came slinking out of the shadows and jumped onto the table. She sniffed at him and Willow Evans, sensed his Shade and hissed, her gold eyes narrowing. Raven soothed her with an outstretched palm and glanced at Willow.

Her pupils were huge, her lips parted in a lopsided grin. Raven brushed her mind, caught a glimpse of the fireworks streaking behind her eyelids and adjusted her blood pressure to ease the intercranial pressure causing it. Medically speaking, she was higher than a kite. An interesting effect to have on a woman, Raven reflected wryly. One he'd never even imagined, let alone possessed, when he was mortal.

"She'll be fine in a moment," he told his Shade, shifting his attention to her leg cradled in his lap.

The vicious slash was now nothing more than a puckered pink seam. Raven raised her leg again and ran his tongue slowly along the ridge of newly healed flesh. He felt the chill of gooseflesh that crawled through her, the shudder of revulsion from his Shade. When he raised his head the seam had faded to a thin white line, and Willow Evans was blinking at him, bleary-eyed.

"Thank you," she said, swallowing hard, "but if you ever touch me again, I'll put a stake through your heart."

"Don't worry." Raven pressed his fingertips gently between her eyebrows. "You'll get your chance."

When her lashes fluttered shut, he picked her up and carried her into the house. His Shade followed, hovering anxiously, covering Willow with a crocheted afghan as Raven laid her on a rose-colored couch. He said nothing when his Shade sat beside her and smoothed her tangled hair off her brow, merely shivered and went back to the terrace.

He lapped up the blood spilled on the table, growling in the back of his throat when the calico cat crept too near. She fled, her tail bristling, when he set fire to the carcass of the lynx with a flick of one finger, but came back once he'd scattered the pile of ash over the burned lawn and regenerated the grass with what passed in his body for urine.

The cat sat on the table watching him. When the new seed sprouted, hissing softly above the rustle of the wind in the trees as it sprang up and swallowed the scorched spots, her ears pricked forward and her eyes narrowed. When he came back to the table she arched her back beneath his outstretched palm.

You must go. Raven purred to Callie, fixing in her mind a place he remembered from his boyhood with trees and water and fat rabbits—a place he'd fought to hold in his memory when so much else of his mortal life had slipped away from him. *You will know when it's safe to return.*

Callie blinked up at him and meowed, jumped off the table and disappeared into the darkness.

18

TWELVE HOURS AFTER RAVEN sank his fangs into her leg, Willie was in Italy. On the island of Sardinia off the Mediterranean coast, driving a green Fiat convertible through the Gennargentu Mountains where she was supposed to meet Raven at sunset, in the provincial town of Nuoro.

She didn't need a road map. Before she'd boarded the flight to Rome in Boston, Raven had put into her head the directions and all the Italian she'd need to negotiate the car rental, find bathrooms and buy food. He'd done it with a two-fingered touch between her eyebrows. Sort of a Vulcan mind-meld.

She wished Johnny was with her. He'd signed to her before they'd left Beaches that he would be, every step of the way; she just wouldn't be able to see him. And she hadn't since he'd blown her a kiss and faded away into the garish lights of the parking garage in Boston.

"Don't worry how I'll get there," Raven had told her curtly when she'd asked. "The moonstone will see to it."

She'd puzzled over that until the pink haze of dawn overtook the jumbo jet halfway across the Atlantic and she remembered Raven telling her the ancients called the moonstone the traveler's stone because it protected those who traveled by night—particularly on the water when the moon was full. Then she'd closed the shade and decided what she didn't know couldn't scare her any more than she was scared already.

She wondered if Frank had found her note, if Whit had played the message she'd left on his voice mail. She wondered how her father had taken the news that she'd run away with a handsome, rich young doctor. Probably turned cart-wheels.

The elopement was Johnny's idea. Not that Willie thought Whit or Frank would believe it. She was worried sick they'd come after her, wondered how she'd explain coming home alone if the Ritual didn't work. Mostly she was just plain scared.

The awful mountain roads, narrow and twisting through heavily wooded highlands and stretches of heath, didn't help. As the sun sank lower toward the craggy peaks squeezing the road between them, long shadows began to slant across the hood of the Fiat. The dashboard clock said it was almost five. She didn't feel as though she'd been driving for two hours. She felt as though she'd been driving forever.

She leaned forward and peered up at the sky. It was still clear as a bell, the hot, milky blue of the lowlands deepening to a vivid cobalt just tinged with sunset as the road wound higher. It was not comforting. It meant Nekhat had yet to sense the moonstone's direction. She yearned to see angry dark clouds boiling over the jagged slopes, as they had swept furiously out of the south across the freeway when Raven had driven the Corvette hell bent for leather toward Boston. Only because it would mean Nekhat had bypassed Stonebridge.

The sun dipped out of sight below the bulk of the mountain, sifting gauzy mauve twilight over the road and turning the Fiat's hood purple. Willie saw a turnaround ahead and pulled in to it. Raven had told her there were still *banditos* in the mountains and had warned her not to stop, but Raven wasn't here; neither was Johnny, and she needed a break.

The turnaround overlooked a gorge funneling away to the southwest into a gorse-dotted valley thick with purple shadows in the fading daylight. Looks like *bandito* country, Willie thought, chafing her arms as she got out of the car and leaned on the trunk. It was much cooler up here, even cooler than it had been in the car with the air on. Time to put on the black turtleneck Raven had insisted she bring.

Willie turned to open the trunk and saw the raven perched on the guardrail edging the turnaround, the moonstone ring flashing dully in its beak. The keys slipped out of her fingers and landed at her feet with a jingling clunk. She snatched them up and glared at the bird.

"You made good time," she said. "Catch a tail wind?"

The raven swooped onto the Fiat's black vinyl top and dropped the ring. It cawed at her, wings spread and neck feathers ruffled.

"Oh, calm down. I haven't seen a single bandit." Willie took Raven's grip out of the trunk, tossed it onto the driver's seat and opened the passenger door. "If it's all the same to you, I'd rather not watch this. Once was enough."

The raven picked up the ring in its beak, hopped from the top of the car to the ground, then onto the passenger seat. Willie went back to the trunk and shut it and leaned against it, her heart thudding in her throat.

What was she doing here? How could she be in love with Johnny? She'd only known him three days, and he didn't even have a body, for God's sake. If the Ritual didn't work, what would happen to him? What would happen to her? How in hell would she ever be able to put her life back together?

Willie closed her eyes, prayed Nekhat had bypassed Stonebridge and that Frank was all right. A stiff gust of wind skittered grit across the toes of her Reeboks and blew her hair in her face again. She reached up to tug it away, felt something brush her cheek and almost wrenched her arm out of the socket flinging it away.

Her eyes sprang open and her heart leapt up her throat when she saw Johnny standing in front of her, his hair and the sleeves of his shirt fluttering in the wind. She didn't know where he'd come from or how, and she didn't care.

"Oh, Johnny." Willie pressed her hand to the base of her throat and sighed. "Thank God you're here."

He gave her a wry, where-else-would-I-be smile with a lifted eyebrow, swept the hair out of her face and tucked it behind her ear. Willie strained her senses to feel his touch, almost could and savored the feathery brush of his knuckles against her cheek.

"Willow," Raven said behind her.

Willie glanced at him over her shoulder. He stood beside the car shrugging into a dark long-sleeved shirt. He caught her eye and nodded toward the gorge. Willie looked and shot off the Fiat, gooseflesh rising on her arms.

Moments ago the sky had been clear, now there was a bank of dark clouds soaring above the far horizon. No natural storm could move so fast. It was Nekhat. It had to be.

"Don't even *think* his name." Raven came quickly around the car, shut his grip in the trunk and plucked the key from the lock. "Thought is a magnet. It will only draw him."

"Oh, wonderful." Willie felt Johnny edge nearer and her knees start to tremble. "How close is he?"

Raven looked down the gorge, then lifted his head into the wind. His eyes narrowed and his nostrils flared.

"Just making landfall," he said. "Near Oristano."

Roughly a hundred miles, Willie knew from the map in the guidebook she'd bought and read on the plane. Nowhere near as close as it looked from this vantage point. Still, panic jolted through her. All she could think of was Nekhat, all she could see in her head was the slow, horrifying replay of his rise from the lynx.

The wind gusted, sending Johnny's hair streaming behind him as he came up beside her and looked down the gorge. Willie shivered at his grim, tight-jawed expression, the eerie flash of distant lightning flickering across his face.

"Willow." Raven caught her chin and turned her face toward him, trapping her gaze in his dark, strange eyes.

The last time Raven had felt such numbing terror he'd felt it in himself, as he lay dying on the floor of Nekhat's tomb. He could see it now and taste it, could sense its paler shadow in his Shade: stark, blanched-white fear, reeking of ozone. He felt Willow Evans's heart pound wildly, her blood pressure rocket and her pulse skip erratically.

He traced his way backward through her veins and arteries, calming her, slowing her heartbeat. When she blinked he eased his grip, dipped into her mind, found her terror there and eliminated that, too.

His hunger stirred and his Shade whirled toward him, its fear and alarm vivid as a laser. Raven flicked the beam aside with a thought, caught Willow as she swooned and lifted her back onto the Fiat. She wobbled dizzily but flung out her hands and steadied herself, leaning forward with her head bowed over her knees.

His Shade swooped closer, wary, warning—and jealous. Raven almost laughed, amazed, for its aura truly was green— and electric, sizzling with musky cinnamon pheromones that burned in his nostrils until he took his hands off Willow. Then his Shade relaxed, his jealousy fading to sea-foam envy and longing as salty as tears.

Raven's hunger howled at the sting of it on his senses. He looked down the gorge, saw the dark stain of the storm thinning as it spread across the horizon. Nekhat was still seeking, but was confused and thrown off the scent.

"Thank you, I think," Willow said, raising her chin bravely when he faced her. "But if you ever touch me again, so help me God I *will* put a stake through your heart."

"Hold that thought, Willow. You'll get your chance."

"I'm sure you'd hold still for that." She snorted ruefully.

"Hopefully I'll be able to."

She tipped her head to one side and asked warily, "What do you mean?"

"Think, Willow," Raven snapped, a faint snarl in his voice. His senses crawled with hunger and Nekhat's nearness. "The Sacred Cedar. What do you suppose it is?"

"Well, it's wood, I guess." She shrugged, then froze, her spine snapping straight, her eyes leaping wide with disbelief. "Oh, my God. It's a *stake*."

Of course it was. It had to be. Raven's smile confirmed it, and explained his comment that hopefully he'd be able to hold still for it. The question was, could Willie?

"Wait a minute," she breathed shakily, and slid off the Fiat. "Now you are known to you-know-who, my foot. You brought me along to put a stake through your heart."

"If I could I'd do it myself," Raven replied matter-of-factly, "but a vampire's primary instinct is to survive. I can't kill myself. Believe me, I've tried."

"Not very hard, I'll bet," Willie retorted. "You don't look the least damn bit miserable to me."

"I'm not. He is." Raven nodded at Johnny, who was frowning worriedly between them. "My body is dead, Willow, but my brain is every bit as alive as yours. My Shade took my emotions with him, but I can read yours as easily as I read a book. I know what I am through you, and I loathe myself."

"That doesn't tell me why I have to put a stake through your heart."

"It's the only way to kill a vampire, and the monster must die for the man to live. It's as simple as that."

"Simple?" Willie heard the shrill in her voice, felt her heart thumping in her ears. "How can you call killing someone— even a vampire—simple?"

"There's no other way."

"There must be!"

"I've spent the last 117 years looking, Willow." Raven's smile twisted wryly. "Believe me, if there was, I would have found it."

"Well, you better keep looking, 'cause I won't do it."

"Then go. You aren't indispensable, merely expeditious. I'll take some other mortal in Thrall to do it."

Raven tossed her the car keys. She caught them, her eyes widened with surprise, then narrowed as she wheeled away with a curt, "Let's go, Johnny."

Willie slid behind the wheel and started the engine before she realized Johnny wasn't with her. She looked up and saw him in the rearview mirror, still standing behind the car with Raven, his hair and his sleeves fluttering, his gaze locking with hers in the mirror through the back window. She knew what it meant, switched off the engine, got out of the car and bit her lip to keep from crying. Or screaming.

"I can't do this, Johnny," she told him shakily. "I can't kill anyone. Not even a vampire."

"You must," he signed, and more, but too rapidly for her to follow. She looked at Raven and asked, "What did he say?"

"He says the Ritual is his only chance for happiness. Yours, too. He wants to be with you, alive and whole, or he wants to be dead. Either way, his torment will end."

Johnny added a sign Willie knew, a clockwise, open-palm circle over his chest. "Please." She clapped her hands over her face and sobbed.

Raven tasted the black, tannic wash of her heartbreak and horror on his senses, the musty orange tang of indecision from his Shade. But a surge of warm, rosy relief washed through his Shade as Willow lowered her hands and raised her face. Tears hung on her lashes; they shimmered in the artificial twilight.

"All right, I'll do it," she said, her resolve as shaky as her quavering mouth, "I *think* I love you enough to kill you."

19

"WHEN THE THREE ARE ONE, the One will be Three, Then the Dark will be Light, Made One by the Sacred Cedar...."

A fierce gust of wind snapped the Fiat's vinyl top. The little car rocked on its springs, wobbling the flashlight in Willie's hand, lifting her gaze from Raven's diary.

The car was parked out of sight between two huge boulders on the edge of the road and the sheer precipice beyond the guardrail. Behind Willie reared the colossal bulk of Monte Corrasi; below, the lights of the provincial town of Oliena twinkled like diamonds on a bed of black velvet.

Raven had left her here about half an hour ago and gone up the mountain with Johnny to reconnoiter. Her skin still crawled from the grave-deep chill that had gripped her when she'd clamped a panicked hand on Raven's arm. He'd shrugged her off, shuddering, too distracted and preoccupied to maintain the projection of body heat.

"You'll be fine here, so long as you stay in the car," he'd told her. "I'll make sure no one can see it."

The finger waggle she'd watched him do in the rearview mirror didn't look like much of a magic spell. She wasn't even sure that was what it was. She wasn't sure of anything—except that Raven was dead. Unequivocally, but, please God, not irretrievably.

He'd told her he was dead. As a doornail or a mackerel. She hadn't believed him, but she did now. Unequivocally. But she still had her doubts about how the monster had to die so the man could live.

She couldn't feature Raven saying it unless he believed it was true. He might, but she didn't know if she did, and was desperately searching the Riddle for a way to reunite him with

Johnny without putting a stake through his heart. So far, she hadn't found one, and didn't think she was going to.

As much as she loved Johnny, she wasn't sure she could kill Raven. If the Ritual worked, great, but what if it didn't? The monster would die, and so would Johnny. Then she wouldn't have him at all. If things continued the way they were now, at least she could have him part of the time. She'd still have Raven, too—a vampire hanging around trying to steal the man she loved.

Only he wasn't a man, just a shadow of one, able to touch her and make love to her only in a mirror. How long would that satisfy either one of them? That wasn't living.

It wasn't fair, but the Ritual was Johnny's only hope. Hers, too. Willie knew it; still, it terrified her. So did the possibility that the Ritual was never meant to work, that it was nothing more than a cosmic lure. If Nekhat hadn't turned Raven into a vampire, Johnny would have died long before she was born. Maybe he was supposed to, and maybe that was the Ritual's purpose.

But Willie didn't think so. The God she believed in wouldn't give Johnny to her just to take him away. He'd give Johnny a chance to redeem himself and Raven. He'd give him a chance to live the life Nekhat had taken from him. She hoped, she prayed with all her heart as she peeked up at the night sky, still clear and black and dusted with stars above Oliena, that Johnny and Raven would come back.

There was still no sign of you-know-who, thank God. Willie tucked the diary and flashlight into the backpack between her feet, next to the leftover bread and cheese and apples Raven had bought her in Nuoro but she'd had no stomach for.

The knapsack was black now, like her sweater, her jeans and her Reeboks, though it had been a bright, shiny red nylon when she'd found it in the back of her closet. Raven hadn't liked the color, so he'd changed it. Willie didn't know if it was permanent or a projection, but she guessed from her Johnny Cash color scheme that she was going to be climbing Monte Corrasi. She hoped not all the way. She didn't know how high it was, but it looked like Everest looming over the roadway and the little green Fiat.

The thin, rocky trail leading up the flank of the mountain looked no wider than a goat track, but Raven and Johnny came down it walking abreast. Willie's heart leapt with relief at the sight of them in the rearview mirror.

"Let's go," Raven said curtly, taking the backpack from her as she swung out of the car. "It isn't far."

"What isn't far?" Willie asked, but he'd already crossed the road and started up the trail. She shot Johnny—a pale, silvery silhouette against the dark—an exasperated look. "Do you know where we're going?"

He gave her a brusque, you'll-see nod and reached for her elbow. She couldn't feel his hand on her arm, but she could sense his urgency, and muttered, "All right, I'm coming," as he led her across the road and up the trail behind Raven.

He didn't wait for them; Willie assumed because Johnny knew the way. The wind cut through her sweater and the knit pullover she'd kept on underneath. Her hair kept blowing in her eyes. She kept pushing it back, teeth clenched to keep them from chattering, and followed Johnny.

Where the trail was steepest there were steps chiseled into the rock. Goats didn't need footholds, but people did, which gave Willie comfort. Raven's expression, however, when they caught up with him at the top of a sharp rise, did not.

In the bright wash of the moon his face looked as cold as stone and every bit as bleak. So did Johnny's as he moved past her and stood beside Raven gazing at something beyond the edge of the trail. Their destination, Willie hoped.

"I should've brought a rope and pitons," she grumbled, stopping to catch her breath and rest her shuddering legs before tackling the last few feet of almost straight-up trail.

Raven glanced back at her and offered his hand. Johnny did the same, taking a step down to help her. Where the moonlight touched his face now it was softened and diffused. A faint silvery nimbus shimmered around him like a halo.

Willie reached instinctively for Johnny's hand and gazed up at Raven. The moon glittered like ice on the moonstone on his finger; its reflection slanted hard and sharp across his features. So like Johnny's and yet so different; separate, but the same. The same face, the same man.

The Dark will be Light, the Riddle said, *Made One by the Sacred Cedar.* Willie hoped so, with all her heart. She took a breath and Raven's hand, too, in her free one. She couldn't feel Johnny's fingers close over hers, but Raven's were solid and strong. And warm, thank God, though lifeless as the rock surrounding them, Willie reminded herself as he tugged her up beside him and she saw what they'd been looking at.

A nuraghe, one of the cone-shaped hill forts named for the Nuraghesi, the tribe who'd built them all over Sardinia during the Bronze Age. Willie had read about them in the guidebook, had seen a couple along the road from Olbia. This one was tucked into a fold of the mountain across a stretch of heath dotted with dew-jeweled gorse. Another set of rude steps led toward it around a right-hand curve in the trail.

"What is this place?"

"A monastery, of sorts," Raven replied. Hallowed ground, Willie thought, even before he added, "Since I cannot, you must fetch the Sacred Cedar."

She could handle that, if only she didn't have to drive it through his chest. Why had she said she'd do it? Why? A shiver swept through Willie, a shiver of her own doubt and uncertainty she thought, until she felt the shadow slide across the face of the moon.

The wind fell in a hush, a quicksilver flicker of cold and dread. A shudder rippled through Willie and turned her toward the nuraghe. A shadow blacker than the night hovered above the heath, beating like a giant black wing.

"Oh, no," she moaned, terror plummeting her heart to her toes. "Nekhat."

The wind lifted, tangling her hair, filling her nose with the stench of blood and sun-bleached sand. The low growl Raven made shot her with gooseflesh and spun her around. His eyes were red and glowing, his fangs and claws sprouting.

Willie thought she couldn't possibly be more frightened, until the moonstone on his finger went suddenly dark and began to smoke like a snuffed candle flame. Johnny moved beside her, his hands hovering above her shoulders.

"Get out of here," Raven snarled, shoving the backpack at her. "Run for the nuraghe. You'll be safe there."

"And leave you here?" Willie clutched the bag to her chest to keep her hands from shaking. "No way!"

"It's the only way." Raven wrenched the moonstone off his finger, laying two of his knuckles open with his claws.

Willie saw the skin split, but no blood. She thought she'd faint when his flesh zipped back together almost instantly. She didn't, though, only because she couldn't run if she fainted. She couldn't leave Raven here, either, any more than she could leave Johnny.

"You guys seem to be forgetting something," she said, managing to sound calm in spite of the scream stuck in her throat. "Without you there's no Ritual."

"We'll be there. Make sure you are. Tharros by sunset tomorrow." Raven grasped Johnny's hand, slapped the ring into it and closed his fist around it.

The silvery nimbus shimmering around Johnny flared like a torch. Spears of light shot between his fingers, so blinding Willie flung her gaze away. She blinked and saw the shadow roil and twist above the heath, heard a faint howl above the wind that bristled every hair on her body.

The moonstone burned like fire in Johnny's hand. So did the memories flooding back to him. *He remembered.* Everything that had befallen him—and Raven, too—in the past 117 years. The camp at Thebes, Jolil and his dusty prayer rug, the black Arab mare whose name he still couldn't pronounce.

He remembered the moonstone flashing in the amulet around Nekhat's throat as he'd wheeled and toppled Yusef and Jolil. Johnny knew, somehow, that so long as he held it now, the moonstone would be safe—and that Raven would not.

It was happening again, as it had so long ago in Nekhat's tomb, but he couldn't let it. He tried to break Raven's hold on his wrist, to give the stone back, but couldn't. Weak as he was—and Johnny felt the tremor in his fingers—Raven was still unbearably strong.

So were the other lives and recollections trapped in the moonstone, crying and clawing to be free of the shadow billowing like a dark sail above the heath. There were thousands of them, dark skinned and light, young, old and in between. Now he knew why the stone was so important to Nekhat, why he could not be allowed to reclaim it. At any cost.

The howl on the wind rose to a shriek, ringing in her ears. The shadow wheeled toward them, shriveling the gorse in its path, spinning Willie on one foot toward Raven.

"You can't fight that!" she cried.

"I don't intend to," he said, his red gaze narrowed and fixed on the shadow. "I mean merely to distract it while you run for the nuraghe."

"You're crazy! You're insane! You can't—"

"I'm dead, Willow." Raven gave her a bleak smile, let go of Johnny's wrist and brushed his knuckles across her cheek, his claws carefully tucked against his palm. "He can't kill me twice."

"No!" she shouted furiously, but Raven had already leapt over the edge of the trail, and Johnny had already grasped her arm and yanked her toward the steps.

His hand on her elbow was as solid and unyielding as the mountain. How it was possible she didn't know. She was mindful only of the shadow, booming like thunder behind them. She looked back once, when she tripped on the steps, and saw Raven standing on an outcrop of rock below the trail. She saw the shadow engulf him, Raven close his arms around it and tumble off the mountain into the darkness.

A chorus of screams rang across the heath. Or maybe just one, just hers. Willie thought she'd faint, but she didn't. Johnny's hand on her elbow kept her up and running, stumbling through the gorse tangling around her legs; she sobbed with terror and effort.

A gate in the nuraghe wall opened. A robed figure appeared, faceless in the spill of yellow light through the gap.

Her lungs were on fire, her legs numb. But she was almost there, almost safe. Relief washed through her, guilt hard behind it and then a jolt of panic when the figure moved out of the gate and into the light. It was a man. A rough-woven robe had been thrown over his dark clothes and burly shoulders. He held a rifle with a webbed strap at a meaningful angle across his chest.

He looked squarely at Johnny, who still shimmered in the wash of the moon and pulled Willie to a staggering halt beside him just inside the ring of light. She could see now that the man had a clipped, salt-and-pepper beard and that the crown of his head was bald. It was natural, she thought, not tonsured.

"Oh, it's you. I've been expecting you," he said to Johnny in perfect and Willie thought Irish-accented English. His grip on the rifle relaxed and he glanced at her with a quizzical smile. "However, young lady, *you* are a surprise."

So was the push forward Johnny gave her. Willie should have seen it coming; Raven had wanted Johnny to take her, not stay with her. Still, it caught her off guard and off balance. If the commando-sized monk hadn't slung his rifle over his shoulder and caught her she would have fallen on her face.

It was bad enough that her heart fell when she tried but couldn't twist out of his grasp. All she could do was fling a backward, how-could-you glare at Johnny.

He was already backing away, still shimmering, the moonstone glowing in his hand. He signed something to Brother Brawny, too rapidly for her to follow.

"I understand," he said. "I'll see to it."

Johnny raised his right hand and signed "I love you" to Willie. His tight-jawed expression softened, but only for a moment, then he wheeled abruptly away, out of the light and into the darkness.

20

OH, NO, YOU DON'T. Willie gritted her teeth and stomped on Brother Brawny's foot. "Ow!" he howled, his grip loosening enough for her to wrench free and race after Johnny.

She'd run only a few yards when she realized he was gone. She couldn't believe it. She'd turned her head for just a second. She whirled, one-footed, but there was no sign of him anywhere. He'd vanished, disappeared.

So had Raven and the shadow. The heath was suddenly as empty as Willie felt. She stopped and stared blankly at the hillocked stretch of gorse. The wind—just the wind, no shriek, no howl to it—tugged her hair and stung her eyes.

"I'm afraid you can't follow where he's gone," Brother Brawny said behind her.

Willie drew a shaky breath and turned around. "I don't suppose you know where he is."

"Not exactly, no. Nor do I want to, especially."

"Raven said you have something for me. A stake."

"I have several things for you, beginning with a nice hot cup of tea." He gestured toward the gate, the Irish that had sometimes found its way through Betsy Boyle's starched Yankee vowels lilting in his voice. "Interested?"

She wasn't, but since she had nowhere else to go, she shrugged and walked into the nuraghe. Brother Brawny followed after shutting the gate and dropping a roughly hewn crossbar the size of a felled tree. It boomed into place, the sound echoing down the narrow, circular passageway, along with the rattle of thick chains he had used to secure a lock the size of his fist.

"Crude but effective." He winked at Willie, unlooped the rifle from his shoulder, ejected the bullet from the chamber and pursed his whiskered lips as he held it up to the light.

The lamps hung from the stone walls were electric but not very bright, and they flickered every few seconds. Still, Willie had no trouble seeing that the bullet Brother Brawny held between his thick fingers was silver.

He must have heard the gulp she made, for he looked up at her and smiled as he hung the rifle on two sturdy, well-spaced pegs tapped into the gate wall.

"Can't be too careful on the full moon, you know."

"Do you have many *banditos* who howl at the moon?"

"Not like we once did, praise God." He crossed himself quickly and led Willie away from the gate.

The nuraghe was a lot bigger than it looked from the outside. The stone walls were chinked, the floor mortared, but only in places. Some of the short hallways connecting the circular passages weren't paved. Some adjoining rooms had doors, some floors, some had both and others neither.

In the center of the nuraghe was a courtyard, and in the center of that a tower. Round and built of stone.

"Welcome to my wizard's tower." Brother Brawny opened the door and led the way up a wooden spiral staircase.

Except for two glassed bay windows facing north and south and a telescope resting on a tripod in each, the room at the top looked like a nineteenth-century country squire's study. The only hint that it was a monk's cell was the narrow bed beneath a crucifix. The rest was a jumble of rugs and shelves, tables piled with books, and a big, cluttered desk near a hearth built out from the wall where a peat fire hissed.

"I dig my own peat." Brother Brawny laid his robe over an armchair behind the desk, his broad back to Willie as he moved toward a small gas stove in a squared-off curve in the wall. "There's a lovely bog at the bottom of the heath."

An exquisite crystal ball in a clawed pewter stand took up one corner of the desk. On the shelves tucked among the books were chunks of quartz and amethyst. A Native American dream catcher hung on another wall by the bed, and spears of crystal and gemstones were suspended everywhere with nylon wires.

A wizard's tower was definitely more like it than a monastery. Brother Brawny was the only monk she'd seen. And there was no sanctuary. Not that he'd shown her, anyway.

From this height and the south-facing window the heath was a lumpy, stubbled expanse silvered by the moon. A warm draft from the fire stirred the suspended crystals, bumping one gently against Willie's temple; a deep blue spear shot with green. Lapis, she thought, touching it with a fingertip, watching it flash with moonlight and fireglow.

"It's azurite and malachite," Brother Brawny said. "They often occur together like that in nature. A marvelous stone for promoting vitality and transformation."

Willie looked at Brother Brawny, standing with his back to her still, pouring boiling water from a kettle into a pot. She sat on a folding camp stool next to the telescope and clutched the edges of the cracked leather seat when it rocked on an uneven leg.

"Go ahead and take it. It's one of the things I have for you." He glanced with a grin at Willie over his shoulder. "I'm highly attuned to rocks, especially ones I've lived with for a long time. I was a geologist before I joined the order."

"Really?" Willie's voice squeaked. "Which order?"

"I'd love to tell you, really I would," he said soberly, "but I'd have to kill you."

And then he laughed, a big booming laugh that made the crystals nearest his head shake. Willie stared at him, nonplussed. Brother Brawny frowned and pursed his lips.

"I'm kidding." He put the pot and cups, a sugar bowl and small pitcher on a table that was only half-piled to the ceiling with books and papers. "Do please take the azurite. I've been saving it for your friend."

"Friends," Willie corrected him. "I came with two."

"You came with one in two pieces." He glanced at her over the table, his eyes twinkling. "Humpty *and* Dumpty."

Willie gritted her teeth to keep herself from screaming. Or crying. Her fingers clenched the edges of the stool so tightly the leather groaned.

"Not a laughing matter, eh?" Brother Brawny frowned and plucked a jade green crystal from the closest cluster. "Come along and bring your stool before the tea cools."

He moved toward the desk, unwrapping the crystal from its nylon wire. Willie had two choices. Jump out the window or humor Gandalf the Goofy. She got up and moved the stool.

It put her chest high at the table, even with one foot tucked under her. Brother Brawny seemed not to notice, his attention on fastening the green crystal to a copper chain with a small tool as he came back to the table.

"Here you are, with my blessing." He sat in a lattice-back chair and handed it to her across the table. "It's chrysocolla. Great for eliminating tension and subconscious imbalance." He filled the cups and put the pot down. "Alleviates guilt feelings like that."

He snapped his fingers and Willie, in the midst of fastening the chain around her neck, burst into tears. Brother Brawny drank his tea while she sobbed. When she sniffed and wiped her nose with her sleeve, he put his teacup down, bent his elbow beside it and leveled a blunt index finger at her.

"And that, young lady, is why your mother always told you never to speak to any man with a severe widow's peak."

Willie laughed, a quavery, watery laugh. Brother Brawny smiled and produced a handkerchief from his pocket. She blew her nose until her ears rang.

"I'm Willie Evans," she said, offering her hand.

He took it across the table and inclined his bearded chin. "Father Bertram. Drink your tea while I make you an omelet."

He stood and waggled his fingertips. "Poof," he said, and Willie finished with him, "you're an omelet."

They both laughed. Willie didn't feel guilty, just sad remembering Raven's doornail comment and Johnny's line, *Gentlemen of my day used a buggy whip*. Father Bertram went to the stove and made the best omelet she'd ever eaten, a four-egg wonder sprinkled with chives he grew himself, and thick slices of bread toasted on a fork over the front burner.

He made fresh tea and let her drink two cups before he said, "That's a confirmation cross you're wearing."

"Yes." Willie started as she touched it, at the jolt she felt when her fingers brushed the chrysocolla's chain. Dry air, she thought. "My grandmother gave it to me."

"Didn't help, did it?"

Willie sighed. "Not a bit."

"That's why I'm here. That's why this place is here." Father Bertram leaned back and spread his hands. "We'll have you all fixed up in time for the Ritual tomorrow night."

"You know about the Riddle of Rejoining?"

"Of course. I've got the Sacred Cedar, don't I?"

"*Is* it a stake?"

"Yes, indeed. A very special one. You have to promise you'll bring it back when you're finished with it."

"I promise. What's so special about it?"

"We'll talk about it in the morning. You need sleep, and some things are best not discussed at night. Especially when the moon is full and something as old and evil as a certain entity who shall remain nameless is still more or less in the neighborhood. If you get my drift."

"Raven said thought is a magnet."

"And right he is. Now off to bed."

Willie didn't think she'd sleep, but she did, in a down sleeping bag Father Bertram unrolled near the fire. When she woke up a little after nine, she found the note he'd left.

"I'm in the garden. So's the privy. P.S. Just kidding. It's the door at the foot of the steps next to your suitcase."

The car keys were on the table beside a pot of tea in a cozy. Willie took a cup with her, found the overnight bag she'd brought along, and a remarkably modern bathroom. She took a shower and washed her hair, wondering how Father Bertram had known where to find the Fiat. She asked him about it—and about how he could have a shower in a Bronze

Age hill fort—once she'd put on clean jeans, a white sweat-shirt and found him in the garden behind the tower.

"The nuraghe has its own well. I added the pump. It runs off the same generator that powers the lights." He shrugged as he finished hoeing a row of potatoes. "As for your car, I followed the trail and my nose."

He put his hoe away in a shed beside the tower, swept off the wide-brimmed straw hat that made him look like a Span-ish padre and led her into the nuraghe. Outside one of the rooms with a floor and a door, he gave her his hat.

"You'll need this," he said. "It's still the custom in this part of the world."

He opened the door on the sanctuary, the most beautiful one Willie had ever seen. It was very small. The roof, a stained-glass skylight, depicted the ascension of Christ. It bathed the simply carved white marble altar, the chinked walls and rough-hewn pews in glorious splashes of light.

Willie put on the hat, dipped her fingers in the font, gen-uflected and followed Father Bertram to a shrine built on a side wall. Rows of candles flickered around a statue of Christ on the Cross and gleamed on a plain wooden stake about eighteen inches long lying at the feet of the icon.

"Is that it?" Willie whispered, lowering herself onto the unpadded kneeler before the shrine.

"That's it." Father Bertram knelt beside her. "All that re-mains of the True Cross, hewn from one of the cedars of Le-banon. Hence its name in the Riddle of Rejoining."

"Oh, my God," Willie said and clapped a hand over her mouth. When Father Bertram chuckled, she took it away and said, "You trust me with this?"

"If God trusts you, who am I to object?" He took her hand and clasped it tightly in his. He murmured a prayer in Latin, crossed himself and rose, his knees cracking. "You'll have to sign for it. Your name and the name of the friend you're bor-rowing it for. Over here."

A candle burned in a wrought-iron holder above a large book on a three-legged stand near the shrine. It was bound in leather and looked very old. Father Bertram turned to a fresh page and handed Willie a pen from his robe pocket.

She wrote her name and paused, remembering what he'd said about Humpty *and* Dumpty. She shook her head and, smiling, wrote Jonathan Raven and the date, July 19. A chill shot through her when she realized today was Johnny's birthday. Raven's, too. Happy 152d, she thought, wherever you are.

The ribbed cuff of her sleeve caught the edge of the page as she turned to give Father Bertram his pen. It was just as well that he'd walked away from her to the altar, because the page preceding hers lifted and fell open when she raised her arm, carefully, so she wouldn't tear it.

Her gaze caught on the few lines of hurried copperplate scrawl. The breath in her throat caught, too, as she read. "Borrowed by Samuel Raven of Stonebridge, Massachusetts, this eighteenth day of May in the year of Our Lord Jesus 1884, for my brother, Johnny. God have mercy on his soul."

21

HOW MANY SAMUEL RAVENS from Stonebridge, Massachusetts, could there have been in the world in 1884? Especially in Sardinia? And how many with a brother named Johnny?

Only one, Willie decided, trying to recall what Lucy had said about wolves and the winter of '79, about Samuel running away. Where had he gone for five years, before he came here to fetch the Sacred Cedar?

"Something wrong, Willie?"

Her gaze shot from the book to Father Bertram, frowning at her from the altar. Maybe everything. Maybe nothing. The stake *had* been returned. But if Samuel had borrowed it 111 years ago, why was she borrowing it now?

Father Bertram had been expecting Johnny, though he hadn't said how he'd known he was coming. He hadn't said much of anything, really. How much did she dare tell him? What if there was a one-to-a-customer rule? Johnny and Raven were sunk. And so was she.

"I was just wondering," she said, smoothing the page back into place, "if the Ritual has ever failed."

"You don't really want me to tell you, do you?"

"No." Willie sat down on the closest pew. "I want you to tell me it'll work, that everything will be all right."

"I'd dearly love to, but I'm not a very good liar." He smiled and came to sit beside her. "It'll be better if you go. At least you won't spend your life wondering what would have happened if you hadn't."

"How far is Tharros, anyway?"

"A couple hours' drive. We'll have to take your car, by the way. I don't own one."

"Do you think Johnny will be there?"

"I'm sure he will. Your friend is right. Nekhat can't kill him twice."

"Johnny isn't dead, Father Bertram. Raven is."

"There you go again, trying to make two out of one." He slapped his hands against his knees and rose. "Come along when you're ready. And don't forget the Sacred Cedar."

Willie's courage shrank along with the flames of the candles in the draft of the door closing behind Father Bertram. Was it too late to promise God she'd never skip Mass again if only He'd put Raven and Johnny back together? Probably.

No lightning flashed, no trumpets blared when Willie picked up the Sacred Cedar. It looked and felt like what it was: a wooden stake, wedge shaped, maybe from an ax blow, its edges worn smooth by time.

"I promise I'll bring it back," she told the icon. And hopefully, she prayed with all her heart, Johnny with it.

Father Bertram fed her another omelet, put on his padre hat, picked up her overnight bag and the smaller burlap bag he called his tote sack and led her out of the nuraghe. Willie followed with the backpack and the sleeping bag; Father Bertram thought she might need it.

Dark flashes of her terrified run with Johnny jerked through her head. She looked for the dead swath she'd seen Nekhat's shadow slash across the heath but couldn't find it; not even when she looked back from Monte Corrasi, from the spot where Raven had leapt off the trail. She knew she hadn't imagined the gorse shriveling and dying. Then again, Father Bertram had already passed this way once to retrieve her bag.

She followed him, wondering, until the backpack began to clunk against her shoulders. The stake was inside, along with a thermos of Father Bertram's tea.

"Wait a sec," she said, slinging the pack off. "The Sacred Cedar's getting knocked around."

"Don't fret." He put down her bag and turned around. "It takes care of itself, and the person who's carrying it."

"Is it any good against really nasty vampires?"

"You mean Nekhat." He picked up her bag and started off again. "I don't know. He's not your run-of-the-mill vampire. He was born that way, not made, like your friend."

Willie blinked, stunned, at Father Bertram's retreating back. He wasn't wearing his robe—too hot, he'd said—just a dark shirt and trousers. The sun shimmered on his broad shoulders. Willie felt her head start to spin, shook it off and ran to catch up with him. "You're kidding."

"Not at all. The ancient Egyptians were very gifted in certain sciences. Genetics, unfortunately, wasn't one of them. Their religion got in the way. All that nonsense about the divinity of the pharaoh caused some serious inbreeding. Princes died very young, like Tutankhamen. A few visionaries took a shot at genetic engineering, in the hope of strengthening the royal line. It didn't work."

Willie wasn't sure she wanted to hear the answer, but she asked, anyway. "What d'you mean, it didn't work?"

"Nekhat is one of their experiments that failed."

Willie stopped cold. Father Bertram walked a few feet ahead before he realized it and glanced back at her.

"How do you know all this?"

"A little bird told me." He winked and kept walking.

A little bird, Willie puzzled, then it hit her: Raven. She ran again to catch up with him. "Is that how you knew Johnny was coming?"

"More or less. I've met your friend. Not here, of course, not at the nuraghe. But other places."

"And other times, Father?"

"Perhaps." He gave her a sideways smile, the sun sliding under the brim of his hat. She had thought his eyes were brown; now she saw they were much darker, with no discernible pupil or iris. "You don't want to know any more about vampires than is absolutely necessary. They're a very scary lot."

So was Father Bertram. Another whoa-wait-a-minute rush swept over Willie as she watched him stride ahead. She followed slowly, wondering who—or what—he really was.

The world's worst driver, she discovered when they reached the Fiat and he took the wheel. When they stopped for gas she fished the guidebook out of her bag and buried her nose in it—until she saw on the map that they'd pass through Oristano, where Nekhat had come ashore . . . and that Tunisia lay just across the Mediterranean from Tharros . . . and that only Libya separated Tunisia from Egypt, where this whole horrible mess had started 117 years ago.

Is this why Nekhat had landed in Oristano? Did he know about Tharros? Was he there, waiting for them? Willie raised a hand to her throat, touched the azurite Father Bertram had given her, set in copper like the chrysocolla, felt the tingle in her fingers when the two stones tangled with her little gold cross.

"He's somewhere about, I'm sure," Father Bertram said, as if he'd been reading her mind. And Willie, clutching the armrest as he screeched the Fiat around a curve, the last one out of the mountains, was sure of it.

The western coast shimmered on the far horizon, a blue-white smudge beyond rolling green stretches. The sky was calm and perfectly clear. Willie felt the same way, so long as she kept one hand near the stones.

She forced herself to eat lunch in Oristano, but regretted it when Father Bertram stopped at the Church of San Franceso. The wasted, tortured body of Christ draped on an austere crucifix on the left altar turned her stomach and started the Sacred Cedar throbbing, almost as if it were crying, inside the backpack.

It quieted and so did her stomach when they reached Tharros, the ancient Phoenician port on the very tip of the Sinis Peninsula. Most of the city was underwater; crumbled walls glimmering beneath the very blue Mediterranean. Father Bertram joined the last tour of the day to explore the above-ground Roman temple and Punic shrine.

Willie stayed on the beach, close enough that she could still see the tour party winding through the excavated fortifications, but far enough away that she couldn't hear the guide's voice. With her arms looped around her drawn-up knees and her eyes closed, she could almost be at Beaches.

In Stonebridge the sun would be well up rather than setting, and there would be a dune at her back rather than an almond grove. The sand would be cool and gray, not hot and white.

Willie took off the pack, looped it over her right arm and stretched out on her back, fingers laced over her stomach. The first streaks of bronze were just beginning to swirl and funnel together above the Mediterranean. It would be a while yet before she needed to keep watch for Johnny and Raven. She sighed and closed her eyes.

She didn't mean to fall asleep, but she did, lulled by the surf and the rustle of the almond trees. She didn't wake up until her right wrist thudded heavily onto the sand. Then she jolted upright, her eyes dazzled by the glare of the sun. She remained fuzzy headed until she felt the backpack slide down her arm, heard the straps being dragged through the sand.

Her heart slammed into her throat. She shot up and clutched the bag to her chest. Over the dull ring in her ears she heard someone chuckle. A man. His voice was very deep and very close.

Willie scrambled around and saw him behind her, squatting on his bare heels in the sand, elbows resting on his knees. His shirt and trousers were so white it hurt her eyes. His eyes were very dark, with no discernible pupil or iris. In the shadow of his wide-brimmed panama hat, his face was the color of creamed coffee. His features were so perfect and so beautiful she caught her breath. His hair was glossy black, done up in a long queue that fluttered over one shoulder.

It was Nekhat. She knew it before he smiled, showing her the tips of his very long and pointed incisors, before she tore her terrified gaze away from his face to the heavy gold amulet with the gaping hole in the center at his throat.

"I love your name, Willow. You remind me of my father's palace. We had willows there along the banks of the Nile. I would lie under them while I fished when I was a boy."

Scream and run, Willie told herself, but she couldn't. She could only stare at him, paralyzed with terror.

"I'm not a monster. I'm a prince. I'll be king someday. I can make you a queen. I can make you anything you want, if you give me that bag you have clutched to your heart."

The backpack was on fire, searing her hand. She wanted to throw it at him and run, but she tightened her grip. She felt the jolt when her fingers closed on the hard edges of the Sacred Cedar, saw Nekhat flinch and spring to his feet. The wrenching cry he gave rang across the beach. So did Father Bertram's shout: "Open the bag!"

Willie barely heard him above the sudden boom of surf at her back and the snarl from Nekhat. He was shimmering out of focus in front of her, his fangs and claws sprouting. A plume of spray soaked her and snatched her breath as she jerked her head around and saw Father Bertram running toward her, his hat clenched in one fist.

Foam swirled around her ankles, clawing at the sand and clamping a breaker like a vise around her legs. Half a second before it yanked her knees out from under her, Willie caught the zipper of the backpack and ripped it open.

A million peals of thunder, a thousand flashes of light tore it out of her hands and sent her skipping like a stone across the water, until the breaker curled over her and dragged her under. She'd been caught in surf enough to know to relax and not to fight. When the wave let go, she kicked, twice, toward the flickering patch of light on the surface.

She came up coughing and gasping for air, in the lull between breakers, felt the next one rise and whoosh behind her. She had a glimpse of the beach and Father Bertram, the backpack in one hand, his hat in the other as he ran back and forth along the edge of the water, before she took a breath and tucked herself into the wave. It flung her toward the beach and dumped her there, shivering and shaking, her teeth chattering.

Father Bertram scooped her under one arm and carried her, choking and gagging salt water, up the beach to the almond grove. He put her down on a patch of bristly grass, knelt beside her and took a silver flask out of his tote sack.

"Drink this," he said. "It's brandy."

Willie did and coughed, her lungs burning. "You said," she gasped, "the Sacred Cedar protects whoever carries it."

"You're alive, aren't you? Not ripped to bloody shreds."

Willie shuddered. "Where's Nekhat?"

"Gone." He handed her a small, rough towel from his sack and smiled. "He won't be back. Not as himself, anyway. He was rather badly singed, last I saw of him."

Willie slapped a hand against her chest, felt the chrysocolla, the azurite and her little gold cross horribly tangled in their chains but still miraculously around her throat.

"I don't get it. My crucifix had no effect on Raven. He touched it, he played with it. It didn't faze him."

"Your little cross is but a symbol, Willie. The Sacred Cedar—" he nodded at the backpack lying in the sandy grass at her feet "—is the real thing."

Which was the real Nekhat, Willie wondered, the horror in the gold kilt and braided wig or the handsome prince in white khakis? She hugged her knees to keep from shaking and watched the sun sink slowly into the darkening blue waves of the Mediterranean. The beach and the ruins of Tharros glowed a soft gray mauve in its fading light. Over her right shoulder the crest of the just-risen moon, still pale and pockmarked, rode above the leafy green crowns of the almond trees.

"Well, finally," Father Bertram said, nodding down the beach. "Here comes your friend at last."

Willie turned her head and saw Johnny coming toward them, one arm around Raven's bowed shoulders, the other around his waist. The nimbus she'd seen shimmering around Johnny in the moonlight on Monte Corrasi was still there. Only now it was flickering like a light bulb on the verge of burning out.

Panic shot Willie to her feet. She ran toward them. Johnny saw her, stopped and smiled. So did Raven, lifting his head and blinking at her. He looked gray and gaunt; his strange dark eyes were eerily pale in the deepening twilight.

"Are you all right?" she asked, pelting to a halt and sliding her right shoulder under Raven's left.

"I'm—tired," he said, using a word she'd understand, letting her loop his arm around her. "Is Father Bertram with you?"

"Yes," Willie said just as he came hurrying up to them, his bearded face glowering.

"Cutting it close, as usual, I see," he said, nudging Willie aside and taking her place to support Raven.

"Don't start, Bertie. Did you bring what I asked for?"

"Don't I always? It's synthetic, unfortunately. It's all I had."

"It'll suffice," Raven said wearily.

Willie hadn't a clue what they were talking about until the men swung Raven down on the sand in the shadows beneath the almond trees and Father Bertram took a blue thermal-lined bag out of his tote sack, like the one Willie had carried her lunch in when she'd worked at *Material Girl*. When he opened it and withdrew a bag of blood like the ones she'd seen in Raven's refrigerator she spun away, swallowing hard.

"I hate this stuff," she heard Raven say. "It's like Chinese food. Half an hour later you're hungry again."

"Oh, God," Willie moaned weakly, clapping a hand over her mouth as she rushed away down the beach.

Johnny watched her go, saw her fall to her knees at the edge of the water. He wanted to go with her, as much to escape the soft sucking sound behind him as to comfort her, but he couldn't. Raven still needed the moonstone close.

The moon was fully up above the almond trees: a bloated silver disk. The wind that had risen with it sent sand scurrying across the beach. The moonstone flashed as he raised his hand.

A faraway rumble of thunder brushed a finger of unease up the back of his neck. He didn't like this beach. It reminded him of Egypt. He wanted off it and away from here. He glanced at the water and saw Willie still on her knees at its edge, saw a distant flash of lightning above the dark Mediterranean, leaping in the midst of a soaring bank of clouds sweeping in from the west. From Africa, from Egypt.

"Much better, thank you." Raven sighed behind him.

He heard plastic crumple, burlap rustle, saw Willie rock back on her heels and wipe a hand across her mouth. He longed to touch her again while he could, just in case. But he couldn't, not in front of Raven and the priest.

He felt the tug of the moon and glanced up, then heard thunder rumble and a breaker boom. After watching it foam and hiss like a horned viper, he turned toward Raven, still sitting on the sand, caught his eyes and signed urgently to him, then nodded at the moon.

"It isn't far, but yes, we should be going." Raven glanced down the beach at Willie. Her head was bent as she slogged her way slowly toward them through the sand. He smiled and shook his head. "What an incredible woman she is. I hope one of us remembers her in the morning."

Johnny wasn't even aware he'd moved, let alone leapt on Raven and locked his hands around his throat, until he saw the flicker of surprise in Raven's eyes; he'd forgotten he still had the moonstone. Then he saw nothing but dark sky and stars and he threw back his head, gritted his teeth and did his best to choke the dead life out of Raven.

He knew he couldn't and so did Raven. Johnny supposed that was why Raven let him bang his head up and down on the sandy grass until he wore himself out.

"I meant to tell you," Raven said then. "In fact, I could swear I did."

Johnny relaxed his grip. Since he'd held the moonstone, he'd had trouble discriminating between Raven's thoughts and his, difficulty figuring out where Raven ended and he began. The Ritual of Rejoining, he thought, had already begun.

"Memories don't always carry over," Raven said. "There's every possibility neither of us will know Willow Evans from Adam in the morning."

Forgetting terrified Johnny even more than Nekhat. He loved Willie, he always had, but he knew better than anyone how easy it was to forget and how difficult to remember.

The moon tugged at him again, rolling him off Raven and to his feet. Please God, not this time, he prayed. I'll forget anything else, everything else, just please let me remember Willie.

"The vials are in the backpack," Father Bertram said, helping Raven to his feet.

"Yes. I'll tell Willow. Thank you, Bertie."

"I wouldn't be here for anyone else and well you know it." Father Bertram gave Raven a clap on the arm that nearly knocked him over. "I pray to God you'll be here when I come back in the morning."

"If I could pray, Bertie," Raven replied with a rueful smile, "so would I."

22

WILLIE WISHED THE WIND hadn't carried Raven's comment to her, that he'd at least warned her before they'd left Beaches, though she knew why he hadn't. She might not have come. And then who would have put the stake through his heart?

The Sacred Cedar and the thermos clunked in her backpack as she struggled up the hill above the beach between Johnny and Raven. She'd found the holy water after she'd ducked into the almond grove to change into the clean jeans and ribbed green henley pullover Johnny had fetched from the Fiat. When she'd opened the backpack to put away her wet things, she had seen the vials.

"Dare I ask," she'd said to Raven as she'd shrugged into the pack, "what I'm supposed to do with holy water?"

"Cleanse the Sacred Cedar once you've used it."

What an interesting euphemism, Willie had thought, for *after you kill me.* "What about the second vial?"

"You'll need it if the Ritual doesn't work," he'd replied as he led the way off the beach. "To clean up the mess."

He hadn't told her where they were going, and after the holy water business, she was afraid to ask. She wasn't sure Raven would hear her, anyway, over the wind pushing her up the hill behind him. Johnny wasn't much of a windbreak, but she was glad to have his loving presence at her back.

She could have done, however, without Nekhat howling in her ears, whipping her clothes and snatching her breath. How he was pushing such a fierce wind inland without advancing the ugly black storm looming offshore she didn't know. Nor did she want to. She had a nasty hunch what he planned to do with it, and that was scary enough.

So was the ruin she saw when she stopped behind Raven to catch her breath: all crumbled arches and broken stones glowing in the moonlight. By the time she realized what it was, he'd stridden a good ten yards ahead of her.

"Yo, Vlad!" she shouted, hands cupped around her mouth.

In midstride, one foot raised on a rock, Raven swung around and arched an eyebrow at her. "Vlad?"

"It got your attention. Isn't that a church?"

"It's a temple. Pagan, not Christian."

It was Roman, Willie thought when they reached it and she sat down to rest. Or maybe Punic. Maybe both. Whatever it was, it wasn't much larger than the sanctuary at the nuraghe and was shaped like a bowl scooped out of the side of the hill.

Arches that once supported a ceiling had been snapped off like broken teeth. A dais, crowned by a shattered marble altar, sat in the middle of a faded mosaic floor below the flight of broken steps where she sat.

Johnny stood, feet spread and arms folded, watching Raven sweep debris with one foot off the dais—debris that would have given a large crane trouble: shattered tops of columns, the head of a god with a curled Grecian beard and eyes with no pupils. Eyes just like Raven's.

When he looked at the sky, so did Johnny, and Willie, too, her breath catching. Directly above the altar the moon shimmered in a silver nimbus, its lower curve already erased by the shadow of the earth. The eclipse had begun.

"Come here, Willow," Raven said, turning toward her.

He looked so calm she was suddenly a wreck. Her heart pounded, her hands went clammy and her knees shook as she made her way across the mosaic and stopped next to Johnny. The altar was a lot bigger up close, the dais a lot higher. Raven looked ten feet tall standing on top of it.

"Up here, Willow." He offered his hand, the moon riding above his right shoulder, his dark hair fluttering across its cratered face. The moonstone ring he'd taken back from Johnny on the beach flashed on his hand. "It's all right," he said, almost gently. "It's warm."

Willie took a breath and let him help her up the three giant-size steps to the dais. The temple was pitched at an uphill angle, which gave her a dizzying view of the beach rimming Tharros, a pale gleam of surf-washed sand in the failing moonlight. The black mass of clouds hanging over the water flashed with dull, brooding lightning.

"Doesn't he ever quit?" Willie said exasperatedly.

Raven laughed, the azurite Father Bertram had told her to give him gleaming in the hollow of his throat. His eyes, dark and fathomless again, glimmered as he smiled at her.

"You're a rare mortal, Willow."

"Rare, hell," she snapped. "I'm scared to death."

"Do you think I'm not?" Raven nodded at Johnny. "Do you think he isn't?"

He winked as Willie glanced over her shoulder. Johnny looked so handsome and so composed, she felt even more afraid. Oh, God, she wailed silently. What will I do if he forgets me?

"Take heart, Willow. I might remember you."

"Oh, big comfort," she retorted. "You don't love me."

"But I might." Raven smiled. "In the morning."

"Will the Ritual take all night?"

"Your part, no." He glanced up at the moon and shrugged. "If the Rejoining works, it could."

"How will you know?"

"We won't. You will." Raven kicked a last chunk of marble off the dais and looked at her. "If we haven't risen by dawn, rejoined in this body, we aren't going to rise, ever again, either one of us. If you love Johnny, use the second vial. Don't let the sun have us."

Willie dreaded the answer but asked, "What do I do?"

"Sprinkle the body and leave. Immediately. Don't linger." He said it curtly and then smiled. Or tried to. "And if you would, say a prayer."

Dear God. Willie sat down on the altar, too shattered to think, too stricken to cry, until she looked at Johnny. He raised his right hand, signed "I love you" with shaky fingers, then made a clockwise circle over his heart. "Please."

"I promise I will," Willie said, her voice thick with tears, "but you have to promise you'll remember me. And, believe me—" she shot Raven a quavery glare "—I'll *know* who's doing the remembering."

The wind shrieked suddenly through the temple with such ferocity it almost blew her off the altar. Raven caught and shielded her against him. Willie raked her hair back and looked at the moon. Three-quarters had vanished behind the shadow of the earth; what little remained flickered in and out of the black clouds streaking across the sky.

"The timing of the Ritual is critical," Raven said calmly in her ear. "When the three are one, when the shadow covers the moon completely, then the Sacred Cedar must be driven. He thinks he can stop me by hiding the moon."

"How will we know anything if we can't see it?"

Raven pointed at the megabuck chronometer on his left wrist, doing his best, Willie thought, not to laugh at her.

"By the time, Willow."

"Oh," she said stupidly. "Of course."

"His prehistoric mind-set has always been his downfall."

What downfall? Did I miss it? Willie turned her face into Raven's chest as another tearing gust nearly ripped her out of his hands. It would have torn the pack off her back if Raven hadn't grabbed it. She felt a flash of heat against her shoulders and heard Raven cry out above Nekhat's howl.

Clutching the marble edges of the altar, Willie crawled off the dais and down the steps where Johnny crouched on the floor out of the wind. Raven came after her, dropping onto the bottom step, gripping his right hand in his left, his palm pulsing a vicious, angry red.

"Now you know," he said between gritted teeth, "why I can't just fall on the stake." Then he threw back his head and roared at the streaming black sky, "Damn you to hell!"

The wind laughed, a horrible, rumbling echo that groaned through the stones of the temple. Gooseflesh shot through Willie. She shivered and moved closer to Johnny.

"It's almost time!" Raven checked his chronometer. Even he had to shout now to be heard. "Stay here—" he pointed at Willie, then at the floor "—until I tell you!"

She nodded and bit her lip. Johnny raised his thumb, index and little fingers, touched them to her cheek and followed Raven up the steps to the dais. She watched him go, heart thumping, wondering if she'd ever see him again. Then she turned her back to the wind, took out the stake and tucked it into the waistband of her jeans under her sweater.

"Willow!" Raven shouted. He was naked, bending on one knee and stretching his bare arm down to her. Behind him she could see Johnny undressing.

When her hand met Raven's, the wind gave an ear-shattering bellow. It took Willie two shallow gasps to realize she was on the dais with Johnny and Raven, that she could breathe without hyperventilating, that the wind had died as suddenly as it had risen. She saw why when she looked up. The sky was utterly black, without so much as a tiny sliver of light to show where the moon was.

"Where's the Cedar?" Raven asked.

"Here." She pulled it out of her jeans, keeping her eyes on his face. He led her to the altar, where Johnny already stood, only his nearly transparent chest visible above the stone.

"Position the stake here." Raven pointed at his chest, a wry smile on his face. "Where my heart would be if I had one."

Willie wiped her palms on the thighs of her jeans and raised the stake to his chest, being careful not to touch him with it. "Oh, God, I hope I can do this."

"You must. The monster must die so the man can live."

And the monster was back, its red gleam beginning to flicker in Raven's eyes. Willie swallowed. Hard.

"You said you'd hold still for this."

"I'm trying, Willow. Your waffling doesn't help."

Neither did the low, eerie howls and short, echoing barks that rang over the hillside. Willie didn't think it was possible, but Johnny turned even paler.

"It's a projection," Raven snarled at him, his fangs half distended. "There are no jackals on Sardinia."

Something moved beyond the far wall of the temple. A flash of red, a gleam of white. Willie thought her heart would stop when she heard a growl, the scrape of claws on stone. Raven was wrong; there *were* jackals on Sardinia. Three of them were scrabbling over the shattered temple wall.

Moonlight flashed on their fangs and snapping jaws. Willie lifted her head and saw the clouds drifting away from the moon. Its face was completely covered by shadow. Only the nimbus remained, a vibrant silver corona shimmering like a halo.

The jackals were nearly over the wall. Johnny was frozen and almost invisible behind the altar. She knew then that she couldn't kill Raven, and she knew why. Because she loved him. She loved Johnny, too. She loved both of them.

It stunned and amazed her, and Raven, too, when she cried, her voice shaking, "I can't! I can't kill you. I love you!"

She saw his amazement in his eyes, in the brief flicker of the red flame. I can do this, she thought, I can save him without the stake, until Raven snarled and his fangs flashed.

"Then I'll kill you," he growled, and dived at her throat.

Willie screamed and wrenched free, saw Johnny wheeling toward her. But she didn't need his help. Her arms were already drawn over her head, the Sacred Cedar gripped in her hands.

It was all deliberate. Willie realized it when Raven shifted, not to evade the blow but to take it. She tried to pull back, but he caught her and embraced her. She felt the stake pierce his chest, the bone-deep shudder that racked his body, saw the jackals melt into the darkness and disappear.

"*You tricked me!*" Willie cried, her heart breaking in her voice as Raven sagged against her shoulder.

Johnny froze and clutched his chest. He looked down and then at Willie, a startled, bewildered smile on his face.

"I'm sorry," Raven panted, his voice raw with pain. "Don't touch the stake. Just—help me—onto the stone."

Oh, God, help me, Willie screamed inside, tucking her left shoulder under Raven's right. His legs buckled, but he flung out his hand and caught himself on the altar. He threw his head back and gritted his teeth. "Great gods, this hurts!"

Johnny sagged on one elbow against the altar as Willie helped Raven onto it. When she looked again, he'd sunk to his knees and pressed his forehead against the stone. He raised his head as Willie wheeled toward him, lifted his right hand and vanished in a shimmer of silvery sparks.

"Oh, no," she sobbed. "Oh, Johnny."

He was gone. So was Raven, Willie saw when she turned toward him. He'd pulled the stake from his chest and dropped it on the stone beside him, near the half-curled fingers of his left hand.

His eyes were closed and there was a smile on his face.

23

THE SMILE STAYED on Raven's face until the eclipse ended. As the shadow receded, so did the curve in his mouth, in small stages and tiny flickers. By the time the moon was full and bright again in the sky, his smile had vanished.

So had the two stars riding next to the moon, like the diamonds flanking the moonstone. Willie sat on the sleeping bag watching them. One second they were there; when she blinked, they were gone. She didn't even think it was weird.

The moonstone had lost most of its fire. So had Willie. The stone flashed now and then on Raven's hand, less often as the night dragged on. The second vial of holy water and the Sacred Cedar lay in her lap. She felt as dead as Raven looked, except for a tiny fear that Nekhat would show up.

If he came for the moonstone, she'd kill him. She'd killed once, she could do it again. Maybe this time without throwing up, which she'd done after she'd cleansed the stake and spread Raven's shirt over his chest.

She'd found it on the dais, along with his trousers and his shoes. Johnny's boots stood beside her, his prickly wool socks tucked inside. Willie wondered if Rachel had knitted them, how Johnny had stood them in the Egyptian desert. One had a hole in the heel. He'd worn it on his left foot, where the boot heel showed the most wear. She'd cried over the bloodstains on his leather vest and dried her tears with his shirt. It was yards too big, but she put it on anyway over her pullover, rolled up the sleeves and felt better.

The left sleeve was slashed; so was the yoke near the collar. If she ended up going home alone, she'd wash it and mend the ripped buttonholes and rents made by Nekhat's claws and fangs. She'd sleep in it every night for the rest of her life and make Whit promise to bury her in it. Willie didn't plan to bring any heirs into the world. Not without Johnny.

The last cup of tea from the thermos was cooling rapidly. Better drink it, Willie thought, and did, then bent her elbows on her knees, bowed her head and closed her eyes.

A trill of bird song jolted her awake, snapped her chin off her chest. She couldn't believe she'd fallen asleep. The shock pushed her to her feet; the Sacred Cedar rolled out of her lap. She caught it before it hit the step and smiled bleakly. Pretty good reflexes for a zombie.

A few stars still winked in the smudge of light rimming the dark crest of the hill. It was almost dawn. Either Johnny's first in 117 years, or his last.

I love you, he'd said. *Please.*

Don't linger, Raven had warned, so Willie rolled up the sleeping bag and put everything but the Sacred Cedar and the holy water in the pack. The stake she tucked through a belt loop; the vial went in her pocket. She climbed the dais and inched up to the altar with her heart pounding in her ears.

Raven hadn't moved. One corner of his black shirt collar was still flipped across his jaw. The right sleeve draped his groin. The rest of the shirt covered his chest and abdomen. His chin had dipped toward his collarbone; his left knee was slightly raised and bent, and his fingers were half-curled.

"Wake up," Willie murmured. "Oh, please, wake up."

The sky lightened slowly. The temple columns flushed pink and still he didn't stir. Willie glanced at the sun rising and beaming like klieg lights behind the hill. *Don't let the sun have us.* How long should she wait? She fished the vial out of her pocket, worried the stopper with her thumb and her lip between her teeth.

"Come on, Johnny," Willie begged, her voice quavering. "Please wake up."

He didn't. She glanced at the sun again, its fiery rim about to break the horizon. *I love you. Please.* Willie's heart raced in her throat. She pushed the stopper with her thumb, then snapped it shut. No. Not yet.

The tears in her eyes blurred the first ray of sun that slanted over the hill. She watched the golden swath of light spread downhill toward the temple. When it broke over the wall, she yanked the stopper out and threw it away—savagely, almost blind with tears.

Sobbing so hard the holy water in the vial trembled, Willie raised her arm over Raven and peeled his shirt collar away from his jaw and his throat. The azurite lay on its pooled copper chain in the hollow of his collarbone; there was no pulse, no breath to move it. *Say a prayer for us.*

"Our Father who art in heaven, hallowed be Thy name. Thy kingdom come, Thy will be done—" Willie's voice broke on a wrenching sob. She shut her eyes, her throat aching. "I love you, Johnny. And God help me, Raven, I love you, too."

She dragged the sleeve of Johnny's shirt across her face, took a deep, shuddery breath of sun-bleached sand and bloody death, lowered her arm, opened her eyes and tipped the vial. Just as the sun washed up on the altar, just as Raven's nostrils flared, his chest heaved and his lungs drew breath.

His eyes sprang open and locked on her face. The vial slipped out of Willie's hand and shattered on the dais. His eyes were gray; only the pupils were black, tiny pinpoints dilating as he blinked. Did he know her? Did he remember?

"I made it," he said, his voice soft and filled with wonder. He blinked at the sky, a soft pastel swirl of blue and mauve. A smile more breathtaking than any sunrise Willie had ever seen spread across his face.

"I made it," he repeated, his breath catching as he shot up, his shirt clutched to his throat. His pulse beat there wildly. He peeled the shirt away slowly, almost cringing.

The ragged puncture wound that had sent Willie gagging and running for the temple wall was gone. He pressed a hand to his chest and looked at her, his eyes filling with tears.

"Oh, God. Dear God." He threw back his head, flung out his arms and shouted, "I made it!"

His voice rang through the temple. And in Willie's heart when he swept her onto the altar, wrapped her in his arms and buried his face in the curve of her neck. Just long enough to take a shuddery breath; then he lifted his head and his hands to the buttoned front of her pullover.

"Let me, please." He ripped the placket open, fumbled with his hand inside, pressed his hand to her breast and sighed, his head tipped back and his eyes closed. "At last. Oh, God, at last. Flesh warmed by a beating heart."

The sun flushed up his throat, shimmered on the azurite and the tears in his lashes as he looked down at her, his mouth quivering. He touched her face with trembling fingers, traced her eyebrows and the curve of her cheek.

"Willie. My beautiful Willow. Oh, God, how I love you." His fingertips brushed the corner of her mouth, parting her lips and catching his breath. "I've made love to you but I've never kissed you. I haven't kissed any woman in 117 years."

Willie couldn't even speak around the tears clogging her throat. But she didn't have to.

He pressed a kiss between her brows, a chuckle thrumming in his chest, where Willie could feel his heart beating. His mouth settled over hers, breathless and tentative, causing a deep, sweet ache to well up inside her. His lips were warm, oh, so warm and trembling against hers.

"I love you so much. I want you so much." Tears jeweled his dark lashes when he raised his head. "But not here, not in this place."

A shiver ran through him, and Willie, recalling the long, awful night she'd spent here. She couldn't begin to imagine what it had been like for him, wasn't sure she wanted to know, or would ever have the courage to ask.

"I'll get your clothes." She slipped away, hugging the chill she felt after the warmth of his arms, down the steps to his folded clothes. Both sets. "Which ones?"

When she turned around he was sitting on the side of the altar, the shirt draped modestly over his lap. He was wincing and clutching his abdomen. Dread seized Willie. She flew in a panic up the steps, afraid to touch him, afraid not to, her hands fluttering around his face.

"What's wrong? Are you sick? Do you need a doctor? Oh, God. You *are* a doctor. Are you all right?"

"Willie, hush." He caught her hands and held them tightly, reassuringly. "I'm fine. I'm just hungry."

His stomach growled. Willie didn't mean to cry, she meant to laugh, but she burst into tears as she wheeled off the dais, snatched up her pack and dashed back, digging out one of the apples he'd bought her in Nuoro.

It was bruised and battered, but so was he. And so moved by the joy and relief glistening through her wet lashes that his throat ached. He took the apple, then captured her mouth with his, tasted the salt in her tears and wondered what he'd ever done to deserve such a woman.

"Dearest Willie. My darling Willow." He took her hands again, pressed and held them to his chest. "Will you be my wife? Will you marry me?"

He felt the pulse in her wrist leap; she felt his heart pound. Yes, she wanted to shout, yes, *yes!* He saw it in her eyes and felt his heart begin to swell, then freeze when her smile curved downward.

"Are you sure? I mean, really? This isn't some postvampire hormone rush?"

"Oh, yes. Most definitely." Her face fell and he laughed, folding her against him, pressing his cheek against her hair. How he loved her hair, every wind-snarled, salt-frizzled curl of it. "It's also a proposal. I'd go down on one knee, but I'm not dressed for it."

"Then yes. Oh, *yes.*" She raised her face and her index finger, her eyes glistening with mischief. "Change your mind and I'll put another stake through your heart."

"I won't change my mind between here and the beach." He kissed her nose. "That's where Father Bertram is waiting to perform the ceremony."

"Here?" Her eyes widened with dismay. Her fingers plucked at her dirty jeans and his ruined shirt. "Now?"

"Why do you think I asked him to come?"

"I thought—" Willie stopped, swamped with tears and confusion. She thought he'd asked Father Bertram to come to help her clean up the mess, but she couldn't say it.

She didn't have to; he read it in her face. "You thought Raven asked him to come, didn't you?" She nodded, blinking and biting her lip. He said as gently as he could, "I did."

"But I thought Raven—I mean, I didn't think he—" She stammered to a halt, her pulse thudding visibly, uncertainty flickering in her gaze. "Who *are* you?"

"Who do you think I am?"

"I thought you were Johnny."

"I am, Willie."

"Where's Raven?"

"Right here, Willow." He tapped his chest.

Panic leapt in her eyes. He thought she meant to bolt. He didn't blame her, but he wouldn't have let her. Instead she grabbed the stake out of her belt loop, gripped it like a knife and blinked at it. She looked—stunned.

He didn't know why. It was just a sliver of old wood to him now, worn smooth and dulled by time, the tip rounded and so blunt he couldn't think how she'd managed to drive it through his chest. Nor did he want to.

"I get it now. I think." She let the stake fall and tipped her head at him. "Father Bertram was right. I did come here with Humpty and Dumpty, didn't I?"

"Humpty and Dumpty?" His eyebrows shot up and his shoulders went stiff with indignation.

He looked so insulted Willie laughed. She laughed until she cried, until her knees buckled and dumped her, hard, on her tailbone on the floor of the dais. He shot off the altar to catch her, one-handed; the other hand still clutched the shirt to his loins.

His knees were no steadier than hers. He fell on them in front of her, felt a slice of pain in the left one and cried, "Ow!" He rocked back and saw blood. A sharp-edged sliver of marble stuck to his knee.

"You're bleeding." She sprang up and flung her arms around his neck. "Oh, Johnny, you're bleeding!"

And flaming suddenly with lust as sweet and lush as the soft curves of her breasts. He swept her against him, under him and rolled over her, thrusting against her hard, twice, before he realized what he was doing and managed, somehow, to stop himself.

"No. Not like this." He pushed up on his elbows and sucked a breath before he dared look at her. "I won't take you like an animal in this heathen place."

"You aren't an animal. Or a monster. Not anymore." She smiled, her face flushed, mischief flirting in the curve of her smile and love—love for him, God, what a miracle—glowing in her eyes. "I don't mind. I love you."

"Willie, *think*." He needed her to, because he couldn't think beyond the need throbbing between them. "If I take you to my bed without vows, your father will never receive me."

"Oh, Johnny." Willie laughed. She couldn't help it.

"You dear, darling, wonderful, sweet man." She cupped his face and kissed his chin, felt the scrape of his whiskers and grinned. "Just wait'll you meet my father."

He sat up, pulled her closer to him and said, "Close your eyes." She did, and opened them when he said, "All right. Toss me my pants," and saw him standing behind the altar.

His modesty was a total one-eighty from the shamelessness of the brazenly naked man who'd laughed at her in his living room in Stonebridge. She went down the steps for the black trousers and pitched them to him. He caught them and asked, "Do you think your father will approve of me?"

"He'll adore you."

"Why?" She heard him zip up and watched him shrug into his shirt, his smile as smoky as his gray eyes. "Because you do?"

"Hell, no." Willie laughed. "He'll love you because you're rich and you're a doctor. He'll want to see your medical degree, though."

"All eight of them?" he asked, buttoning his shirt as he came around the altar.

"You've got eight medical degrees?"

"Not all in my name, but yes." He tucked in his shirt and sat down to put on his shoes. "I had to appear to die every so often, if you'll recall."

Willie doubted she'd ever forget, but it didn't matter. Not when he stood, held out his hand to her and asked, "Ready?"

"I've been ready my whole life." She slipped her fingers into his, felt them close warm and solid around hers. "Since the starfish stung me and you kissed my nose."

A startled flicker lit his eyes. "You remember?"

"Yes, I told you. In my office." A tiny frown puckered his mouth. "In the mirror," she prodded and he said, "Oh, yes. I remember now."

He didn't, but it didn't matter. She remembered and she knew—though she hadn't a clue how—that she was meant for this, meant for him. And it was enough.

He helped her tuck his boots and breeches in the pack, swung it on his back and carried the sleeping bag in his left hand, where the moonstone still flashed on his finger. With his right hand he held her hand and led her out of the temple.

Neither one of them saw the black shadow that slipped out of a dark corner the sun had yet to reach. Neither of them sensed it slithering in their wake, slow and sinuous as a snake.

24

THEY WERE MARRIED on the beach, the sand dazzling and already hot, the sun bouncing off the glassy blue Mediterranean. The ceremony was in Latin, by Father Bertram, which took a while. Long enough to sunburn Johnny's nose.

Willie noticed the burn midway through their wedding breakfast, a picnic provided by Father Bertram. She waited until Johnny washed down a mouthful of chicken with a swallow of champagne, then kissed him, lightly, on the very tip.

"Ouch!" He jerked away and rubbed his nose. "Ow!" He winced, then grinned at her. "I'm sunburned, aren't I?"

"Yep." Willie kissed him again, gently. "Right there."

"Let me see." Father Bertram leaned toward him, lifting one hand and peering through the spectacles he'd needed to read the marriage lines. "You have to be careful."

"Oh, Bertie, don't fuss!" Johnny brushed him away, sprang off the blanket spread in the shade of the almond grove and ran barefoot down the beach.

He'd taken off his shoes and rolled up his pants after the wedding. Willie watched him splash into the surf and lean forward to admire the reflection of his red nose. He was her husband, Jonathan William Edward Raven, and he'd promised to love, honor and cherish her, Willow Elizabeth Christine Evans.

"How careful does he have to be?"

"He should always use sunblock and wear a hat."

Father Bertram was watching Johnny and frowning, the brim of his padre hat fluttering in the salty offshore breeze.

"Why does he call you Bertie?"

"That was my name before I was Enthralled. That's what vampires call their human slaves. I was Raven's Thrall until he released me." He pursed his lips and filled the plastic champagne cup in Willie's hand. "That was back in—1906."

Willie emptied her glass in one quick, heady swallow that left her gasping. "How old are you?"

"A hundred and sixty-seven, but I'm not immortal. I'll die eventually. I've aged a bit since Raven let me go, since he stopped feeding." He showed her the scars on both wrists, the faint white nicks left unmistakably by fangs. "I'm the one who brought him the Riddle of Rejoining."

"Then I thank you, Father, with all my heart."

"Thank God it worked, Willie. I was merely doing His work, even then, when I was a Thrall. Raven let me go once he'd deciphered the Riddle, because human beings don't enslave other human beings. He was a rare vampire."

The wind stiffened, rustling the almond trees. One corner of the blanket fluttered. So did Johnny's hair as he turned his face up to the sun.

"Will he be all right now, do you think?"

"If you can keep him out of the sun," Father Bertram said, then gave Willie a grave frown. "And if you can convince him to give the moonstone back to Nekhat. If he remembers he'll want to keep it."

Willie shivered and glanced down the beach at Johnny coming toward them. He smiled and stretched a hand out to her when he reached the blanket, pulled her up and swept an arm around her waist.

"It's time to go," he murmured, nuzzling her throat.

Past time, Willie thought as he pressed himself against her. His eyes, half-lidded and smoky, said the same thing.

"Can we drop you somewhere, Bertie?"

"Don't be ridiculous. This is your honeymoon." He winked at Willie and tapped his white collar. "I'm an easy pickup in this."

On the back seat of the Fiat there was a large box wrapped in white paper. The card attached to the ribbon said, "For the bride, with love from Father Bertram. P.S. Keep in mind I wasn't always a priest." While Johnny drove, Willie opened it, peeled back the tissue paper and shrieked.

He glanced at her sideways. Her cheeks were nearly as red as her hair. "What's in there?"

"Give me twenty minutes in a bathroom—" Willie clapped the lid back on "—and you'll find out."

They soon arrived at their destination. But he didn't want to give her twenty seconds in the bathroom. He wanted her naked and underneath him—or naked and on top of him, whichever she preferred—in the king-size bed overhung with chiffon drapes that stirred in the breeze blowing through French doors. The latter led onto a covered, walled lanai with a hot tub that overlooked a strip of pure white sand murmuring with lazy surf. Willie murmured, too, as she felt the soft down mattress.

"Did you book this room before we left Stonebridge?"

"Yes. Why?"

"You weren't you then. You were Raven. I can't feature him doing anything like this." She looked around the room and shook her head. "Maybe I don't get it, after all."

"I don't understand it all, either, if it makes you feel any better. I remember thinking you'd like it here."

"Oh, I do. It's beautiful. A sitting room, his and her bathrooms. A lanai and a private beach." She smiled at him, her eyes shining. "It's the honeymoon cabana, isn't it?"

"Yes." He shut the French doors and turned the key behind him. "You do realize you're locked in a room with a man who hasn't had a woman in 116 years."

"Seventeen." She picked up Bertie's gift from the bed. "And boy, do I have a birthday present for you."

He dived at her and she ran, laughing, into the closest bathroom and locked the door. He spread his arms across it, leaned his forehead against it, listened to his heart pound and wondered why it didn't burst with happiness.

"Willie?"

"Yes?"

"Please don't take twenty minutes."

"Oh, Johnny! There's a Jacuzzi!"

He groaned. She laughed. Then he grinned and raced into the other bathroom. In the mirror he could see the pulse thudding at the base of his throat. He touched it, marveling at the miracle, then rubbed his jaw with his hand and shivered at the scrape of his whiskers. He was mortal.

He'd shower first, then shave. He'd already left a burn on Willie's chin. He didn't want to skin all the soft, sweet places he planned to kiss until she couldn't breathe. He turned on the shower, stripped, then stood still and shaking, fully erect just thinking about it.

Was she thinking about him? Was she nervous? What if he still frightened her? *She wouldn't be here, fool. She wouldn't have married you.* She was his wife. His bride. The first day of the rest of his life, indeed.

He nicked himself shaving. On the throat, which gave him a nasty turn. He used the dryer the hotel provided on his hair, combed it back with his fingers and shook it around his shoulders. It wouldn't break scissors now; he could cut it.

He slapped a hand against his midriff and smiled at the ring of solid flesh. Then he held his breath and watched his abdominal muscles tighten, smooth as a washboard. Not bad for a 152-year-old man.

His wife was still in the bathroom when he came out with a towel cinched around his waist. He hadn't thought to bring the pajamas he owned but never wore.

He felt the cut on his knee and the itch of his sunburn. He also felt a swell of loss and melancholy from the voices trapped in the moonstone, a flame of anger and a resolve to finish things with Nekhat, but he'd deal with them later. He felt too euphoric at the moment; his system was too shot with adrenaline—and testosterone. He looked down at himself and groaned. He couldn't stand here jutting like a stag in rut. He closed the sheers and the heavier drapes on the French doors. The light fell somewhat but not enough. He would have to get into bed and drape a sheet artfully about his loins.

He'd barely crossed the room when the bathroom door opened. He dropped to the side of the bed, wincing at the twinge in his left knee, stretched his arms across the mattress and laced his fingers. *Fool!* he thought. He looked as if he was praying.

And he was, suddenly, for strength enough not to fling his wife on the floor. He watched her edge past the doorway, blinking and looking for him in the darkened room. She was wrapped in a towel, as she had been the first time he'd seen her, when she'd walked through him in her bedroom. This time, her towel was white rather than yellow. She'd washed her hair and pinned it up. Wet tendrils clung to the sides of her neck.

"Johnny?" Her voice was as thready as the pulse he could see skipping in the shiny hollow of her throat.

"I'm here." He smiled when she turned toward him, her head tipped curiously. "Is that Bertie's gift?"

"I'm saving that for later. What are you doing?"

Wishing he had the decency to shrivel from embarrassment. Instead he ached as his gaze took in her round shoulders, her gleaming thighs, the towel-draped outline of her lithe, lush body. Oh, dear God, she was so small. He'd tear her to shreds if he took her like this.

"I'm, ah, looking for my wallet."

"Oh." She sighed and smiled. "I'll help you."

"No!" He barked it so sharply she flinched. "We'll find it later. Just get into bed."

"It won't take a minute."

It'll take less than that, he groaned, mesmerized by the quiver of her breasts beneath the towel as she darted around the bed. She knelt beside him and groped under the bed, the scent of sweet-smelling soap tantalizing on her skin.

"I think I've got it." She bumped and brushed against him. Her eyes leapt and she gasped softly, "Oh." An instant flush, vivid even in the gloom, washed up her throat.

He propped his elbows on the bed and buried his face in his hands, living proof that a man couldn't die of humiliation. He felt her lips touch his shoulder and jerked his face up.

"I'm not shocked," she murmured gently, then dropped her gaze. "I'm not a virgin, you know."

"Praise God for that," he said, the drawn breath gusting out of him. She looked up and kissed his shoulder again.

"Let me help you." She scrambled onto the bed, peeled back the sheets, lay down and tucked one pillow behind her head, another under her hips.

The upward tilt of her pelvis made him groan. She turned her head and reached for him, her hair a glimmering, dark red tangle on white silk. He laced his fingers in hers and let her tug him onto the bed. He wanted to lie beside her, but she drew him over her and spread her knees.

"Happy birthday, Johnny." She opened her towel and reached for his. He grabbed her hand and held it, his eyes tightly shut, his heart thundering in his chest. "Not yet."

"Yes, Johnny," she said softly, drawing his hand between her legs. "Now."

Her curls were as soft and wet as her shimmering eyes. She wanted him, wanted this as much as he did. A surge of raw, male possessiveness shot through him. He went up on his knees, gripped her hips and drove into her. She wrapped her legs around him, lifting her hips and drawing him deeper. He felt her stretch to enfold him, drew back and drove again, twice, hard.

She made a noise, soft and breathy in her throat. He opened his eyes, saw her head and throat arched on the pillow, the wordless "Ohh," parting her lips. He went still, unsure if she was pained or pleasured, until she looked up at him and smiled, raised her right hand and made a clockwise circle with her palm against her breast. "Please."

What little control he had shattered. He took her, hard and fast. Not only did she let him, she encouraged him, inflamed him with her hands on his chest and his hips until a cataclysmic orgasm ripped through him.

When it faded he realized he was crying, sobbing into the curve of his wife's neck. Her arms were around his, her fingers stroking his hair. He was still inside her, pulsing. Shame and, unbelievably, fresh desire washed through him.

"Johnny?" She whispered his name, her voice shaking.

"Oh, Willie, forgive me." He pressed his face into her throat, praying she wouldn't hate him. "I swear I'll never hurt you again."

"*Hurt* me? Oh, Johnny." She laughed, tightening around him, kissed his temple and rubbed her nose in his hair. "I was just going to ask how soon you thought you might be able to hurt me like that again."

He sprang up and blinked at her. Her face was flushed; her eyes were shining. "You *enjoyed* having me rut like a beast on top of you?"

"Actually—yes." She stretched her mouth up to his and murmured, "Wanna do it again?"

He pushed into her and let her feel how much. Her soft sigh thrummed in his bones. She made him feel like a god, but he was only a man, a man completely besotted with his wife. He cupped her left breast and felt her sigh, so he circled the peak with his thumb, then his tongue, and felt her shiver.

The mirror had been exquisite; this was divine. Such glory in her curves and softness, the fullness of her breast in his hand, the rough pebble of her nipple swelling in his mouth when he suckled.

She whimpered when he withdrew, until he rolled her on top of him and cupped a breast in each hand. She clutched his wrists, scarcely breathing as he kissed one and then the other, suckling the tiny pink peaks until they swelled, full and red and quivering for his touch, the graze of his lips, the fan of his breath.

The tears in her lashes spilled when she bowed her head and pressed her mouth over his. She was quivering when he laid her gently on her back, cupped the satin smoothness of her buttocks in his hands and stroked into her—slowly and tenderly, pausing to savor her liquid heat and sweet mouth. When she sobbed against him, he let her go, let her arch and buck and thrust against him, until she cried out with release.

He caught her in his arms, whispered, "Don't move," and held her still until he could no longer feel himself pumping inside her. Then he raised himself on one elbow and smiled at his wife. "Was that painful enough, my love?"

"Yes. Oh, yes." She took his face in her hands, placed a searing kiss on his mouth, then pressed her forehead against his chin and began to cry. "I love you so much it hurts. But it hurts so *good*."

"Can I kiss it and make it better?"

"Yes," she whimpered, her eyes flooded with tears.

"Where?"

"Here." She pointed to her mouth. He kissed her lips. "Here." The hollow of her throat. "Here." She turned her head and swept her hair out of the way, baring her throat and the curve of her neck.

The jugular vein beat there. He knew it well. He pressed his lips to it, felt it pulse and throb. She smelled like sex and sweat, both his. His nostrils flared, his teeth scraped her skin. Deep inside him a faint echo howled, a pale memory of dark need and terrifying lust. He bit her, gently, and the feeling faded. She moaned and shivered, then he raised his head and asked, his heart racing, "Anywhere else?"

"Yes." She flushed vividly again and whispered, "My breasts. Oh, *please*."

25

WILLIE COULDN'T BELIEVE she'd said it. She couldn't believe she'd said any of the things that made her throat scald remembering. Fortunately, she was neck deep in the hot tub and her eyes were closed, so she couldn't see Johnny's face.

She couldn't remember how many of her body parts she'd listed. He'd kissed every one of them until she couldn't breathe, and winced just a little as he'd slipped inside her again.

"Brute," he'd muttered savagely at himself, and carried her out here into the tub.

The warm, pulsing water eased the soreness in her breasts, the ache between her legs, but he was doing it again, playing with her toes, rubbing them against his chest, letting her curl them into hair that grew there, lush and crisp. She'd be a blithering idiot in a minute if he didn't stop. Why had she told him about her feet? What had she told him?

"You said," Johnny told her, his voice as deep and languid as the water, "that foot rubs turn you on."

Willie groaned and sank lower.

"Don't be shy." He chuckled. "I'm your husband. You're supposed to tell me things like that."

Husband. The word still shot chills through Willie. So did the realization that he'd read her mind.

"I read your face." He smiled when she opened a wary eye. "I know it well. I watched you grow up. It's all coming back to me."

Johnny lowered his head and gave her toes a seductive tug. She melted and arched her neck against the rim of the tub.

"You're a beast," she said breathlessly.

"I know. My poor Willow." He raised his head and smiled, his gray-eyed gaze about ten degrees hotter than the water. "You had no idea you were marrying a satyr."

"I thought I was marrying a pirate." She laughed when his eyebrows shot up. "I used to see you on the beach, when Whit and I played buried treasure. Sometimes when the sun hit the water just right, I'd see this wonderfully tall man with long dark hair and knee-high boots."

"Once or twice," he said, his smile and the stroke of his fingers on her ankles softening, "I thought you did."

"I always felt safe on the beach, 'cause I knew you were there. You were my special friend. Especially when I hit puberty and started wondering about—"

Oh, no. He'd sucked her toes and she was babbling again.

"What did you wonder about?" Johnny asked, running a deliciously slow finger up the sole of her left foot.

"Foul!" She snatched her leg away so suddenly she slipped off the seat. She went under with a yelp and a splash and came up straddling his lap, her breasts pressed against his chest. Her sensitized nipples began to throb, so did the ache between her legs when she felt him harden against her.

"What did you wonder about?" He cupped her bottom. Sunlight slanted through the vine-covered lattice roof and shadows flickered across his face.

"What it was like to be with a man." Willie trembled at the avid gleam in his eyes. "Girls have fantasies, too. I had some very sexy dreams about my long-haired pirate."

"Did I make love to you?"

"All night," she murmured against his mouth, water swirling around her shoulders. "Every night."

"Oh, God." His eyes closed and he leaned his head back, the pulse in his throat wet and gleaming as he gripped her hips and rolled her against him. "Like this?"

"Even better." Willie caught his earlobe in her teeth. The hitch in his breath gave her a rush and a thrill of power. "You loved me on the beach, in the moonlight on the dunes. The sand still warm from the sun. I could feel it on my back. The surf crashed and boomed and you—"

"Enough." He forced his eyes open and took a deep, ragged breath. His gaze locked on her breasts, full and buoyant in the water. He touched them lightly with his tongue, bursting the tiny bubbles that were swirling around her nipples. "Still sore?"

"No." Willie arched her head back, reveling in the feel of him, wet and strong in her arms, in the pull she felt deep in her soul when he drew on her nipple. "Go slow," she murmured.

She thought *she* could, until she slid on top of him. She didn't have breath enough to tell him how much she loved him, so she told him with her body. He watched her, his head against the side of the tub, a soft, wondrous smile on his oh-so-sexy mouth.

When he groaned and gripped her, she wrapped her arms around him and held him to her breast, with her cheek pressed to his hair. His breathing was still quick and shallow against her neck; it sent shivers everywhere. Especially when he tipped his head back, gently cupped her breasts and asked, "Do you want children, Willie?"

She leaned away from him and laced her fingers behind his head. "Do you think we can?"

"You mean, do you think *I* can," he corrected her, but he was smiling. "I don't know. Time will tell." He drew soft circles on her breasts until they peaked and tingled. "I'd give almost anything to watch my son suckle here, to suckle after him, like this—" he drew her left nipple into his mouth, pulled on it tenderly, twice, released it and looked up at her, his face flushed "—and taste your milk on my lips."

The glow in his eyes caused tears to well in Willie's and a misty image to rise up in her head, of her bedroom at Beaches—their bedroom now, hers and Johnny's—and a lace-draped bassinet. She could feel the tiny, soft head cradled against her, the silky dark hair. She couldn't see a face, she could only see the glow in Johnny's eyes as he stretched on the bed beside her, elbow bent to support his head, while he watched her nurse their baby. A little girl, but she didn't think he'd mind.

"Oh, Johnny." Willie held his wrists in her hands, melting inside until she stroked his knuckles and felt the wet, cold scrape of the moonstone ring on her fingertips. "What would you give to have a child?"

"Everything I own," he said, his voice deep with feeling. "Except you, of course."

Willie let that one slide, tightened her grip and looked down at him. "Would you give the moonstone back to Nekhat?"

His eyes went as hard and cold as the stone, his dark lashes sparkling with drops of water in the light dancing through the vines. "Bertie put you up to this, didn't he?"

"He said if you remembered you'd want to keep it."

"I *intend* to keep it."

"You don't need it anymore."

"The stone is Nekhat's trophy case, where he keeps and tortures the Shades of those he's killed. I was barely able to free Johnny—it damn near destroyed both of us—when I took the stone from Nekhat. And now you think I should give the others back to Nekhat and his eternal torment?"

"If you keep the moonstone," Willie said, slipping away from him into the water, "you're no better than Nekhat."

"I intend," he snapped, "to set them free."

"How? You're not a vampire anymore, Johnny. You're a man. A mere mortal. Your powers are gone."

"I will not return it!" he shouted at her. Rather, he roared it at her, his eyes blazing as he shot to his feet, streaming water and fury. "That's the end of it. Now leave me be."

Willie watched him vault one-handed out of the tub and stalk into the room. He gave the right hand door such a shove it cracked against the wall, hard enough to shatter a pane and make Willie jump. She sank lower in the tub, suddenly cold and shivering in the warm water.

He came back almost instantly, sprang into the tub and into her arms, burying his face in the curve of her neck. He was shaking almost as much as she was.

"I'm sorry, Willie. Forgive me." He kissed her collarbone fervently. "I'll never shout at you again, I promise."

"Apology accepted." She kissed his wet, tangled hair and tried not to cry. "I love you."

So much it scared her, even more than it scared her to think what Nekhat might do to get the moonstone back. Especially now that she knew what it was.

She tried twice more to wheedle Johnny into giving it back. She rubbed her toes on the inside of his knee under the table while they ate lunch, but she only made his gray eyes smolder. When they went for a walk on the beach, she backed him against a wet, dark rock in a shallow, shady pool and unbuttoned his shirt. While the surf lapped at their ankles, she teased his nipples with her fingernails and bit them lightly. All that got her was a hard, quick joining and a spectacular climax in wet, warm sand.

It wasn't what she wanted. Neither was the shower he tried to coax her into as the sun started setting, gilding the white sand beyond the lanai.

"Take off the moonstone," she told him, "and I'm yours."

He did and laid it on the vanity. It wasn't what Willie wanted, but it was a step in the right direction. She wanted to spend the rest of her life with her husband. She sighed while he soaped her breasts. When he slid his fingers inside her and nipped her earlobe, she cried out and came in his hands.

He was exhausted after that, every muscle in his body shuddering from the strength it took to pin her against the shower wall with her legs wrapped around him and drive into her until he gritted his teeth to muffle the bull-elephant bellow that rang in her ears. He tumbled, half-dry and yawning, into bed, his face flushed and his eyes overbright as he pulled her after him and pillowed his head on her breast.

"Sweet, blessed sleep at last," he murmured, burrowing into her. "You don't know how I've missed it."

He drifted off with one arm and one leg draped over her. Willie waited until he began to snore, then wormed her way, inch by inch, out from under him. He never budged, not even when she rolled off the bed onto the floor.

She crawled around the nearly dark room, groping for her clothes, her shoes and her backpack. She dressed in the bathroom with the light off, then felt carefully on the vanity for the moonstone, tucked it in her pocket and crept into the sitting room, closing the door noiselessly behind her.

With shaking fingers she switched on the desk light, took paper and pen out of the drawer, scrawled a note and propped it against the lamp. She left it on so he wouldn't miss it. It wouldn't take her any more than an hour, she figured, to drive to Tharros and back, where she planned to leave the moonstone on the altar, right where she was sure Nekhat wouldn't miss it. Hopefully, Johnny wouldn't wake up and miss her while she was gone.

Unfortunately, he did—when a sharp prickle of unease crawled through his senses. His vampire powers were vastly dulled, but still functional. He'd managed to hide that from Willie. There was no point alarming her until he knew whether or not it was permanent, but he knew before he rolled to his feet, instantly awake, that she was gone. He knew where, too, before he snatched up the note and read her hurried, backhand scrawl.

Please don't be angry, but I'm taking the moonstone to Nekhat. Don't worry, I'll be careful. And I'll be safe. I have the Sacred Cedar. If he gives me any crap, I'll just put it through his heart. I love you. Back soon—Willie.

"Oh, dear God." He crushed the note and ran for the bedroom. "She doesn't know the stake won't kill him."

He should have told her he'd spent 117 years looking for a way to kill Nekhat and hadn't found one, that the ancients who'd created him hadn't either, that they'd had to settle for luring him into and sealing him in the tomb.

The void tugged at his heart as he threw on his clothes— not the void that lay in the bottomless, soulless depths of the moonstone, but the void that would fill him, that would be all he had left, if anything happened to Willie.

He didn't realize she'd taken the Fiat until he saw the empty parking space. He closed his eyes and thought *raven*, visualized talons, feathers and a hooked beak just sharp enough to pluck out Nekhat's eyes. Once again he located his vampire powers, but they were as weak and feeble as his frail, mortal flesh.

He stormed like a madman into the hotel lobby, shouting and demanding a car. He terrified the night clerk into giving him his own, slapped down money—millions of lira—and raced outside, hope springing as he slid behind the wheel of a sporty, two-year-old Peugeot.

He spun the tires as he shot the car onto the highway, reaching ahead with his dulled senses searching for Willie. He'd left his mark on her when he'd healed her wound, which made her easier to find. A sigh of relief sagged his shoulders, until he sensed the deadly, telltale, bloodred trace of a fully functioning vampire.

26

IF SHE HADN'T BEEN in such a hurry, Willie might have thought
to check the gas gauge before the Fiat hiccuped, bucked and
died. Luckily, she was within sight of the beach at Tharros.

She had no idea how she'd get back to the hotel, but she'd
worry about that after she got rid of the moonstone. Willie
made sure it was still in her pocket, picked up the Sacred Cedar from the passenger seat and got out of the car.

She could just see the beach, a pale, surf-washed gleam
against the night sky, and the silvery splash of the full moon
on dark water. About where the temple should be on the
hillside there was a dull flicker of something she hoped was
just a weird reflection of moonlight on marble.

She had a bad feeling it wasn't—made suddenly worse by
the high-speed whine of a big engine rapidly approaching
behind her. Willie froze in the bright, white sweep of headlights and whirled at the screech of brakes and the bump of
tires on the rutted shoulder. Just in time to see Johnny stretch
himself out of a low, racy sports job. How he'd gotten his
hands on it she hadn't a clue, but she winced as he slammed
the door hard enough to rock it on its springs and came toward her. Looking as if he wished he had a buggy whip.

"Give me the moonstone." He held out one hand, his voice
as tight as his clenched jaw.

"No." So much for promising to love, honor and obey,
Willie thought, moving away from him. "I'm giving it back
to Nekhat."

"Not alone, you're not." Johnny stopped and nodded at the
temple. "He's sitting up there waiting for you."

Willie looked over her shoulder, at the eerie flicker still
dancing along the gorse-covered hillside.

"That isn't Saint Elmo's fire," Johnny said. "He likes to play with moonlight when he's bored."

Oh, swell. Now what? Willie hadn't expected Nekhat to be here. She'd expected to leave the moonstone on the altar and run like hell. She was no match for a creature who could toss moonlight around like a rubber ball. Neither was Johnny, not anymore. The Sacred Cedar was, and it protected whoever carried it, but they couldn't *both* carry it.

"That's why you're staying here," Johnny said firmly. "I took the stone. I'll give it back."

She knew now that he'd lied to her, that he could still read her mind, but it didn't matter. All that mattered was getting out of here alive.

"And live to tell about it? Not likely, not even with the Sacred Cedar." Willie looked back at Johnny and saw the azurite shimmering against the hollow of his throat, in the gaped front of his ruined white shirt. She wondered why he'd put it on along with his boots and breeches, but didn't ask. "I think it's safe to assume he's still plenty sore at you for taking it."

At Raven, not me. The thought raced through him unbidden, along with another wash of disjointedness. Strong enough to push him forward on the balls of his feet and jerk him—none too gently—toward the temple on the hillside.

"Come see how angry I really am," hissed a soft, snarling voice, "and don't forget the little woman."

Not just in his head, but on the wind fluttering in Willie's hair, a dark tangle gleaming red only where the moon touched it. He realized it in the catch of her breath, in the sudden leap of her lashes. She stared at him, wide-eyed, for an eight count, then she blinked and clenched her jaw.

"You want the stake so damn bad, you can have it!" she shouted at the temple, closing the Sacred Cedar in her left fist and raising it meaningfully. "Right in the heart!"

The wind laughed and swirled around her, tugging at her hair, lifting a funnel-shaped cloud of sand past her ankles. Johnny yanked her out of it and closed his arms around her. She buried her face in his chest until Nekhat's laughter faded and the wind was only the wind again, then she raised just her eyes and looked at him.

"Why is he laughing?" she asked, an uh-oh tremble in her voice.

"He doesn't have a heart," Johnny told her. "Not like you and I do."

"Well, of course not. He's a monster. He's—" Willie's breath caught and her eyes took another oh-my-God leap. "You can't mean it. Everything has a heart. Even a tree."

"What he has is an organ in his groin, on the right side of his body, that's a combination heart and liver." Johnny cupped her face in his hands to still the tremble he could feel seeping through her. "It rejuvenates itself like a human liver, only at an alarmingly rapid rate."

"Oh, God," Willie moaned, thudding her forehead against his chest. "The Sacred Cedar won't kill him, will it?"

"No." He pressed his lips to her hair and savored its green-apple scent. Please God, not for the last time. "It won't kill him, but it should put him out of commission long enough—"

"Shh!" Willie shot her hand over his mouth. "He'll hear you."

"No, he won't. He's gone." Johnny turned her around and felt her quail against him at the flashes of light bouncing like UFOs across the hillside. "If we can immobilize him for a couple of minutes—"

"I've got a better idea," Willie interrupted him shakily. "Let's just hop in the car and get the hell outta here."

"Too late, my love. He'd only come after us."

"I was afraid you were going to say that." She turned in his hands and looked up at him, her cross and the chrysocolla throbbing at her throat along with her pulse. "You *do* have a plan, don't you?"

Plan, hell. He didn't have a clue, but he wasn't about to tell Willie. She was frightened enough. And so was he.

"I've got an idea," Johnny hedged, praying to God he'd think of one. "Just do what I say when I tell you to do it."

"Too bad I didn't," she said, her mouth trembling and her eyes filling, "when you told me to butt out of this."

"No, Willie." He pressed a quick, fervent kiss between her eyebrows. "It's too bad I didn't listen to Bertie."

What he tried not to listen to, as he led her toward the temple, were the voices crying at him from the moonstone. He concentrated instead on the feel of his wife's hand, so small and shaky and yet so trusting in his, and tried desperately to think of a way out of this.

"The only chance we have is the Sacred Cedar," he said to Willie, pulling her to a halt beside him halfway up the hillside. "I don't have a prayer of getting close to him with it, but you might. If I distract him, can you do it?"

"You bet I can." She tucked a fluttering strand of hair behind one ear and notched up her chin. "Just say when."

He said, "I love you," instead and caught her shoulders and her mouth in a quick, hard kiss, his fingers as shaky as hers when he took her hand again and drew her behind him up the thin path winding through the gorse toward the temple.

I've done this once, I can do it again, Willie told herself. No waffling this time, just do it. Don't think about his fangs and his claws. Just think if you don't he'll kill you. And Johnny, too.

The pep talk got her up the hill and over the crumbled stone wall. It failed when she stepped into the temple with Johnny and saw Nekhat, awash in silvery moonlight, sitting on the altar, one leg drawn up on the stone, the other swinging lazily off the side. He wore the white khakis Willie had seen him in on the beach, his hair tied in a queue.

"Be sure you keep the stake where he can see it," Johnny murmured, and led her forward.

Willie did, closed tight in her left hand. She shivered when Nekhat turned his head toward them and she saw the empty gold amulet winking in the open front of his shirt against the smooth bronze wall of his chest.

"Ah, Dr. Raven. You've brought your blushing bride and my moonstone. How thoughtful and how wise of you." He held out one graceful, long-fingered hand. "Put it here, please."

Willie started to reach for the ring in her pocket, but Johnny caught her arm. "Come and get it," he said, his voice ringing in his ears over the crescendo of cries rising from the depths of the moonstone.

"So you can strike me down with your cursed Cedar?" Nekhat laughed softly and shook his head. "I think not."

"Let my wife go," Johnny countered, giving Willie's fingers a trust-me squeeze, "and I'll bring you the stone."

"This is not a negotiation, Dr. Raven." Nekhat's smile vanished. "Don't force me to take the stone."

"Give me the ring and get behind me," Johnny said, and Willie did, keeping the stake ready in her hand, her heart pounding at the faint red gleam beginning in Nekhat's eyes. "Come and get it."

"I'll rip out your hearts and shred them while you die. Then I'll tuck your souls away and wear them here—" Nekhat slid like smoke off the altar, tapping a finger already sprouting a claw against his empty amulet "—where you'll be together forever and yet forever apart."

"I don't think so," Johnny said, and drew back his arm.

He threw the ring toward the sky, the ankh carved into it flashing in the gleam of the full moon riding high above the temple. A thousand screams tore through Willie, or maybe just the terrible roar Nekhat made as he leapt to catch it.

He held it for only a moment, scarcely more than a single terrified beat of her heart, before streams of light so vivid they all but blinded her shot from between Nekhat's claws and he dropped the ring. His bellow of agony knocked Willie off her feet and shattered a nearby column.

She fell on all fours, still gripping the stake, felt Johnny's hand close on her arm and pull her up, staggered to her feet beside him and saw the ring pulsing like a strobe at Nekhat's feet. She winced and looked away from it. Nekhat clutched a ruined, smoking paw to his chest. The vivid, bloodred sheen in his eyes made her want to scream, but she couldn't. Her throat was clenched with terror.

"What did you do to my moonstone?"

Nekhat's voice shook the temple. One column shattered and fell. Another cracked. Fissures raced up its length and across the mosaic floor like the shivers racing through Willie.

"I did nothing," Johnny told him, a puzzled edge in his voice. "Nothing at all."

"Come to me!" Nekhat roared, flinging his good hand at the ring, palm up, claws half-curled.

A laser beam of light shot from the moonstone, caught him in the chest and knocked him back, bellowing and wavering out of focus, shifting from the prince in white khakis to the monster in a gold kilt. Jeweled beads flashed in a braided wig, then his image steadied into four tusklike fangs snarling in the face of an angel.

"Hallelujah!" Johnny shouted, laughing. "Your toys have turned on you. They've had a taste of freedom and they won't go back to being your slaves."

"I'll kill you!" Nekhat roared, first at the moonstone, still pulsing and warning him away at his feet, then at Johnny, his whirling red gaze almost stopping Willie's heart. "I'll kill you all!"

He dived at the moonstone, claws extended, and again it shot a beam of blinding white light, this one strong enough to knock him off his feet. He landed on his back with a roar that broke the altar stone and shattered the dais. Johnny leapt after him, snatching the stake from Willie's hand.

"No!" she screamed, but he was already diving at Nekhat, the Sacred Cedar clenched above his head in both hands, its dull tip razor sharp and flashing in the moonlight.

He brought it down in a single, swift stroke. Willie knew by Nekhat's earsplitting scream and the A-bomb flash that the Sacred Cedar had found its mark.

The temple leapt into the air around her, causing her to tumble backward and scrape her chin on the shattered floor. She managed, somehow, to push herself up on her knees and fling a look over her shoulder.

In time to see Johnny lurch upright, the Sacred Cedar in his hand, Nekhat writhing on the floor at his feet. Nekhat's body was a nightmare of writhing animal shapes and faces.

Willie swung her head away, saw the moonstone ring lying close by, the ankh carved into it winking. She grabbed it just as Johnny took her arm and pulled her up. They ran toward the temple wall. She didn't look back, just clutched the ring in her hand and ran for her life, slipping and nearly falling down the hill, only Johnny's hand on her arm keeping her on her feet.

The explosion came when they hit the beach, and set Willie skidding out of his grasp onto her scraped chin in the sand, the shock wave roaring in her ears. She reeled up on her knees, saw the hillside crumbling, rolling tons of earth and rock over the temple.

The tide was booming on the beach, crashing eight-foot breakers on the sand while great chunks of rock rained down the hillside. Johnny fell on his knees beside her, rolled her onto the wet sand and threw himself over her to protect her from the fallout.

When it stopped, he pulled her up beside him. Both were breathing hard and shaking, his face streaked with sand and dirt. Willie gasped for air and blinked at the raw, still-rolling hillside. Johnny got up on his knees and cupped her face.

"Are you all right?"

"Y-yes," Willie stammered shakily.

"Thank God." He wrapped her in his arms and held her until they'd both caught their breath, then rocked back on his heels and said, "Give me the chrysocolla."

"You can have this, too," Willie said and opened her fist. Johnny smiled at the moonstone glowing on her palm, kissed her and slipped it into his pocket. "We'll give it to Bertie on our way home."

With shaking fingers Willie unfastened the chain around her neck and gave Johnny the chrysocolla. He took off the azurite and winked at her. "Behold. This is real vampire magic."

When he touched the terminals of the two stones they began to glow. When he drew them apart, Willie blinked, surprised, at the sky lightening toward dawn, at the hillside above the beach, and caught her breath.

It was healed and whole, dotted with dewy gorse. There was no sign of the temple, no trace that it had ever existed. It was simply gone, as if it had never been.

"I buried it deep enough so no one will ever find it," Johnny said. "And I made sure none of the tour guides will ever remember it was there."

"A tidy night's work," Willie said around a yawn. "How did you do it?"

Johnny blinked at her, his eyebrows drawing together. He glanced in a puzzled way at the stones in his hands and then at Willie. A slow, joyful smile spread across his face.

"I don't know," he said softly. "I can't remember."

Epilogue

Stonebridge, Massachusetts
One Year Later

HE FOUND HIMSELF on the beach again. Since it was his birthday, it seemed only fitting.

He sat on the flank of a dune, arms looped around his drawn-up knees, his face tipped up to the hot July sun. The baseball cap his wife wouldn't let him out of the house without sat on the sand next to him. He'd catch hell if he went back without it. He smiled and rubbed his thumb across the gold band she'd slipped on the third finger of his left hand on their sixth-month anniversary.

Tomorrow they'd be married a year. He'd hidden in his sock drawer the zircon-and-moonstone-studded band he'd had made for her. "You have my heart," the inside engraving said, "now here's my soul."

His father-in-law wouldn't be impressed, but he'd given up trying to woo Whit Senior when he'd raised a dubious eyebrow at the four-carat diamond he'd given Willie at Christmas when they'd visited her parents in Manhattan. His mother-in-law would love it and that made him smile. He could almost see Amelia Boyle Evans's brown eyes, so much like her daughter's, pooling with tears.

He opened his eyes long enough to glance at his watch, a plain, no-nonsense model on a leather strap. The chronometer he'd worn a year ago had been smashed beyond redemption on Sardinia. He didn't miss it, or the knack he'd always had for knowing the time. It was five-thirty. His in-laws weren't due until six, but he had a feeling they were already here.

Sometimes he still knew things, but not often enough to bother him. That sensitivity was fading, as so much of what he'd been and done was already gone, just simply erased from his memory. He still had his diaries—rather, his wife did, put away in a glassed bookcase in her office—but he felt no desire to even open them.

He'd caught Willie reading them once, avidly. She'd been sitting cross-legged on the floor, a whole stack of them around her. She'd jumped, almost guiltily, her heart pounding visibly in her throat, when he'd come into the room.

"I was just curious," she'd said quickly.

"What about?"

"Oh—nothing in particular," she'd said and shrugged.

He'd known she was lying, but he'd let it pass. He'd made love to her instead, on the floor in front of the pedestal mirror she still kept in her office.

He felt the sun fade against his closed lids, opened his eyes and saw the swells behind the foam-headed breakers beginning to darken toward sunset. He rose and picked up his hat, brushed sand off it and the seat of his jeans, put it on and squinted up at the long silver beams of sunlight shooting through the purple-and-gray twilight gathering on the horizon.

It was time he got himself up to the house. He knew it when he saw Frank striding toward him through the knee-high beach grass, an aluminum can swinging in each hand, their silver labels catching and flashing the last of the sun.

"The warden sent me." Frank grinned and tossed him one of the cans. "She was afraid you'd get lost again. On purpose."

"I only got lost twice." He made a face and held up the beer Frank had thrown him. "What's this for?"

"Fortification." He popped the top on his and took a swallow. "If we play our cards right, we'll both get lost."

He laughed. "How long've they been here?"

"Couple hours." Frank shrugged and took another swallow.

"It's her father, you know," he said, falling into step beside him. "He still thinks he's going to catch me beating Willie, or something."

"Or something," Frank said, his eyes laughing over the top of the can.

"Stuff it, Chou," he growled and tried not to laugh.

The last time Willie's parents had come to Beaches they'd arrived four hours early, just in time to catch him swaggering down the stairs in nothing but his ruined white shirt, lovingly mended by his adoring wife. Just as Willie's mother had come through the front door, with Frank on her heels, of course, he'd shouted, "Ahoy, my love! Let's play pirate!"

The can of beer was still cold in his hand. It made his mouth water, but thirsty as he was, he didn't dare. He had even less tolerance for alcohol than he did for sunlight, though he was working on that. On days like today, when his wife wasn't around.

"Better not," he said wistfully, handing the can back to Frank. "I might tell you something I shouldn't."

"You mean like last time?" Devilment gleamed in Frank's dark eyes. "So, tell me, Doc. Do you still cry in bed?"

He groaned, his face flaming, and Frank laughed.

"I won't tell Will, honest." Frank sighed and flung a companionable arm around his shoulders, though he had to reach up to do it. "You're a lucky man, Johnny. She must be some hot mama."

Wisely he kept his mouth shut. Not yet, he thought sadly, though not for lack of trying.

Unlike most evenings with his father-in-law, this one passed almost pleasantly. The man actually smiled twice, once when he shook his hand and wished him happy birthday. Sometimes he wondered if Whit Senior sensed something, if he knew, inside someplace, what he was—or what he'd been—if he remembered on some deep subliminal level the Christmas Johnny had followed him around in spirit form and made him jump.

"Thank God they're gone." Willie sighed, snuggling into his arms as they stood on the porch and watched the tail-lights of her father's Cadillac wink away into the darkness toward the road. "Thank God I talked Mother out of staying over for our anniversary tomorrow."

"Indeed," he murmured, nuzzling her hair, his nose filling with its wondrous green-apple scent.

"Tonight's the night," Willie said in a singsong voice as she raised her face to his, her eyes dancing. "Tonight you get to see Bertie's wedding present."

"At last," he said and grinned, lacing his fingers together in the small of her back, feeling himself harden as the soft curve of her belly pressed against him.

"Wait right here," she murmured against his mouth.

"I won't go anywhere," he said and smiled.

Never again, he thought, leaning his shoulder against the roof post at the top of the stairs when the screen door slapped shut behind her. The swing creaked in a soft breath of wind and he smiled, remembering sitting here with Betsy in the warm summer dark listening to the whales sing.

A trill of song broke through the still night, springing gooseflesh on the back of his neck and tears in his eyes. If he thought about it hard enough, he could almost see his grandfather's face, could almost feel the rough scrape of the old sailor's hand around his. He rubbed the hook-shaped scar on his index finger, closed his eyes and felt tears slide past his lashes.

Oh, God, it was good to be alive.

"Happy birthday, Johnny," Willie said softly behind him.

He wiped his eyes hastily and turned around. She stood in the half-open door, the spill of light from the living-room lamps outlining her slim body in the voluminous folds of a plain white nightgown with a lace hem and beribboned neck.

"It's, ah—lovely," he said haltingly. "But isn't it a little on the big side?"

"For now, maybe." Willie plucked the front of it between her fingers and gave it a tug away from her stomach, her eyes shining. "But not for long."

He cocked his head at her in puzzlement. "You plan to put on weight?"

"Oh, Johnny." Willie laughed, flapping her arms and making the scooped neck slide off her shoulders. "It's a maternity nightie. I'm pregnant, you darling dunce. Two months and counting."

"Oh, my God," he breathed shakily. "Oh, Bertie, you wise old devil."

It had been a year, almost to the day, Willie thought, since she'd watched such a glorious smile spread across Johnny's face. He laughed, leapt across the porch and swept her into his arms.

"I love you, oh, how I love you," he said fiercely, then held her at arm's length and said, with tears in his voice as well as his eyes, "Wanna play pirate?"

Take 4 bestselling love stories FREE

Plus get a FREE surprise gift!

Special Limited-time Offer

Mail to Harlequin Reader Service®

3010 Walden Avenue
P.O. Box 1867
Buffalo, N.Y. 14269-1867

YES! Please send me 4 free Harlequin Temptation® novels and my free surprise gift. Then send me 4 brand-new novels every month, which I will receive before they appear in bookstores. Bill me at the low price of $2.44 each plus 25¢ delivery and applicable sales tax, if any.* That's the complete price and a savings of over 10% off the cover prices—quite a bargain! I understand that accepting the books and gift places me under no obligation ever to buy any books. I can always return a shipment and cancel at any time. Even if I never buy another book from Harlequin, the 4 free books and the surprise gift are mine to keep forever.

142 BPA AJHR

Name _____ (PLEASE PRINT)

Address _____ Apt. No. _____

City _____ State _____ Zip _____

This offer is limited to one order per household and not valid to present Harlequin Temptation® subscribers. *Terms and prices are subject to change without notice. Sales tax applicable in N.Y.

HARLEQUIN®

Temptation

THREE GROOMS:
Case, Carter and Mike

TWO WORDS:
"We Don't!"

ONE MINISERIES:

GROOMS ON THE RUN

Starting in May 1995, Harlequin Temptation
brings you an exciting miniseries called

GROOMS ON THE RUN

Each book (and there'll be one a month for three
months!) features a sexy hero who's ready to say,
"I do!" but ends up saying, "I don't!"

Watch for these special Temptations:

In May, **I WON'T!** by Gina Wilkins #539
In June, **JILT TRIP** by Heather MacAllister #543
In July, **NOT THIS GUY!** by Glenda Sanders #547

Available wherever Harlequin books are sold.

MOVE OVER, MELROSE PLACE!

In June, get ready for thrilling romances and FREE BOOKS—Western-style— with...

WESTERN *Lovers*

You can receive the first 2 Western Lovers titles FREE!

June 1995 brings Harlequin and Silhouette's WESTERN LOVERS series, which combines larger-than-life love stories set in the American West! And WESTERN LOVERS brings you stories with your favorite themes... "Ranch Rogues," "Hitched In Haste," "Ranchin' Dads," "Reunited Hearts" the packaging on each book highlights the popular theme found in each WESTERN LOVERS story!

And in June, when you buy either of the Men Made In America titles, you will receive a WESTERN LOVERS title absolutely FREE! Look for these fabulous combinations:

♦ Buy ALL IN THE FAMILY
by Heather Graham Pozzessere (Men Made In America) and receive a FREE copy of BETRAYED BY LOVE by Diana Palmer (Western Lovers)

♦ Buy THE WAITING GAME
by Jayne Ann Krentz (Men Made In America) and receive a FREE copy of IN A CLASS BY HIMSELF by JoAnn Ross (Western Lovers)

Look for the special, extra-value shrink-wrapped packages at your favorite retail outlet!

HARLEQUIN®   *Silhouette*®

Announcing
the New Pages & Privileges™ Program
from Harlequin® and Silhouette®

Get All This FREE
With Just One Proof-of-Purchase!

- **FREE Hotel Discounts** of up to 60% off at leading hotels in the U.S., Canada and Europe

- **FREE Travel Service** with the guaranteed lowest available airfares plus 5% cash back on every ticket

- **FREE $25 Travel Voucher** to use on any ticket on any airline booked through our Travel Service

- **FREE Petite Parfumerie** collection (a $50 Retail value)

- **FREE Insider Tips Letter** full of fascinating information and hot sneak previews of upcoming books

- **FREE Mystery Gift** (if you enroll before June 15/95)

And there are more great gifts and benefits to come!
Enroll today and become Privileged!

(see insert for details)

 PROOF-OF-PURCHASE

Offer expires October 31, 1996   HT-PP2